Relic of His Heart

Relic of His Heart

by

Jane Lebak

Philangelus Press
Boston, MA USA

epub version ISBN: 978-1-942133-27-8
Print ISBN: 978-1-942133-26-1
ASIN: B07G5L16Y9
Library of Congress Control Number: 2018957151

Cover art by Charlotte Volnek

Also by Jane Lebak:
  Pickup Notes
  Half Missing
  Honest and for True
  Forever and for Keeps
  An Arrow in Flight
  Sacred Cups
  Shattered Walls
  The Wrong Enemy
  Seven Archangels: Annihilation
  Bulletproof Vestments
  The Boys Upstairs
  A Different Heroism

*Sometimes someone has so much influence on a book
that it must be dedicated to that person.*

*Evan, this one's for you. Thank you for patience,
guidance, advice, and advocacy.
Thank you for everything.*

ONE

Come on, come on, come on... A mother's push, a baby's cry...and Tessa caught a brand-new person.

She laughed as the newborn let out an offended wail. Even before the junior midwife could get the baby wrapped in a receiving blanket, the mother was reaching for him, so Tessa laid him in her arms with the cord still pulsing.

The father choked out, "He's beautiful! You did it!"

"Time to meet your mommy and daddy," Tessa murmured, helping the mother and baby get settled on the full sized bed. The mother stared into her baby's eyes, breath heaving as she took in that intoxicating newborn scent. Tessa checked over the baby in her arms, saying, "And there's your little love. Good breathing. Good muscle tone. All good."

Tessa glanced at the clock to check the time, transcribing the notes in her mind for the midwifery center's birth sheet: 2:35 in the morning. Vertex presentation. Mild shoulder dystocia. Mom and baby doing great.

While Sarah performed the one-minute APGAR tests, Tessa took a moment just to breathe. Breathe and bask in the birth of a new person. There would be time for notes later. Time to clamp and cut the cord. Time to process the momentary fear that had shot through her with those deceptively soft words, "mild shoulder dystocia."

Notes were clinical, but dystocias were a nightmare. The baby's shoulders had gotten stuck in the mother's hips so that his head emerged while the rest remained trapped, a situation that could result in death if not resolved within seven minutes.

Fortunately for everyone, Tessa was trained for handling nightmares. First she'd grabbed the woman's ankles and shoved her knees back to her ears while the mom pushed (McRoberts maneuver). When that hadn't worked, Tessa had ordered the woman to flip onto her hands and knees and push that way (Gaskin maneuver).

Gaskin had worked. Gaskin almost always did, but it only worked because the mother wasn't drugged and was fully able to move. Which, again fortunately, was what Tessa's freestanding birth center specialized in. Unmedicated mothers. Unmedicated babies. Women empowered to help themselves.

In effect, something that could have been a death sentence was now a funny story for this mom to tell at the preschool pickup line. *"She made me give birth on all fours, like a giraffe!"*

It was something Tessa had come to understand, but never to accept: some people have a harder time entering the world than others. That was why her hands came into play. (Or the hands of an obstetrician, when Tessa referred out those moms before the birth.)

Now Tessa's hands had more prosaic work to do, so she started cleaning up around the new parents while the junior midwife Sarah helped get the baby breastfeeding. Then her hands would have to write the medical records, check the phones, and restock the supplies in the birth suite.

By three a.m., with the mom and baby cleaned, the records recorded and the files filed, the supplies in the sterilizer and Sarah with the new parents for the next five hours, Tessa was finally able to take those hands and go home.

This had been the fifty-second baby born at the birth center. The third birth Sarah had attended and the hundred-somethingth baby Tessa had "caught." Overall, a wonderful delivery, even considering the shoulder dystocia. Tessa would touch base with the mom tomorrow, but she'd be surprised if the mom thought of her birth as anything other than excellent.

She ran a hand through her graying black hair, then straightened her sweatshirt and rubbed her hands over her jeans. If only it were professional to attend births in her pajamas so she could just tumble into bed.

As Tessa reached behind the door for her battered coat, an angel appeared.

She closed her eyes. Not again.

"Teresa Testerman," intoned the angel, "you have been charged with the duty of locating and returning a relic of Saint Peter of Verona that was stolen from the Church of the Holy Cross in Barlassina, Italy. This relic—"

"No," Tessa said. "Absolutely, no."

The angel went silent.

She took a stride toward him. The angel resembled a generic Christmas tree ornament, with a white robe, a gold sash, and angular features, although he wasn't blond. He had trim black hair and black eyes so focused they looked fierce.

She tilted up her chin to glare at him. "You can leave me alone. I'm not retrieving this relic. We're done."

He remained expressionless. "This is the second time you've refused."

"Then that makes both of us who can count to two." Tessa folded her arms. "I said no the first time, and I meant it."

"How can you refuse?" the angel said, an uptick in his voice.

"Because I'm not about to head out on crusade in response to a hallucination." She tried to sound breezy. "You're not real, and you know it. Now vanish, or whatever it is hallucinations do."

For that matter, why was she holding an argument with a mirage? But Tessa had never studied hallucinations or lucid dreams, so she wasn't sure what you had to do to dispel them.

"With all due respect," said the angel, "I'm hardly a hallucination."

Tessa turned, hands on her hips. "You've shown up twice, both times after long births, both times at three o'clock in the morning. You didn't turn up at an hour when I'm not exhausted and high on someone else's birth endorphins. If that's not a hallucination, then what is?"

The angel faded a bit. "Your guard is lower under these conditions. You're more willing to accept the impossible.

Plus, you feel confident after a birth. During daylight hours, you aren't open to the idea."

"And that's how I know you're a hallucination. Now if you don't mind, I need to drive home without trees dancing alongside the road. Excuse me, please."

The angel didn't move from the doorway. "How should I prove I'm real?"

She huffed. "If you're really an angel, tell me the time of the next birth I'll attend, plus the gender of the baby."

"Easy!" The angel brightened enough that Tessa squinted. "The next baby will be the Alderman baby. It'll be a boy, six pounds, four and a half ounces. He'll be born at 11:09 a.m. on the fifteenth— What are you doing?"

"I'm writing it down." Tessa pulled a birth information sheet from her desk and filled in the blanks as if an actual baby had just been born. "Alderman. Male. Six pounds, four and a half ounces. You're going to lose this bet. Janice Alderman is only thirty-seven weeks, and her other two babies went post-dates. Michelle Zakaros is at term, and she went early last time."

"We'll see. Nineteen inches." The angel disappeared from the doorway and reappeared leaning over her shoulder to watch her write. "Onset of labor at ten p.m. the evening before, one hour after SROM. Mom will have a first-degree laceration. The baby's name will be Noah Michael, and they'll be disappointed that you know how to spell it."

"N-O-A-H," Tessa muttered. "Very difficult."

"They're spelling it N-O-E. To be unique," added the angel, sounding as if he were fighting a chuckle.

Tessa muttered, "Oh, for goodness' sake."

The angel gave in to laughter. "It's not as if the Biblical Noah's mom printed his name on the birth certificate in English."

"So if the Aldermans travel back in time three thousand years to fantasy-land, their kid will fit right in?" She shook her head. "Whatever. It's not my kid, and I have no right to name him. Is that all, Mr. Hallucination?"

"Almost. There will be a water stain right here because you put the paper on the counter and didn't realize it was still wet."

"Now you're just showing off." Tessa dated the sheet, then capped her pen. "That's four days from now, and I'm not going to be seeing you again. You set the bar pretty high."

"If I don't, you're going to keep insisting I'm a figment of your imagination, and I want that relic." The angel folded his arms. "I'll return in four days."

The room dimmed as the angel vanished. Tessa sighed as she hid the sheet in her desk. In three hours, she had her own five children to get ready for school.

Two

Four days later, cleaning up after the birth of Janice Alderman's third child—a boy, born at 38 weeks on the dot—Tessa dutifully recorded numbers she wished she weren't seeing. Six pounds, four and a half ounces. Nineteen inches.

"What's his name?" she asked, a numb distance between her voice and her ears.

"Noah Michael," said the father.

Tessa dutifully wrote "Noe" and the father, peering over her shoulder, said, "Oh—how did you know we were going to spell it that way? Is that common?"

Tessa sighed. "Sometimes a midwife just knows these things."

In the supply room half an hour later, she dropped the paper onto the counter and was dismayed as a damp spot spread through the lower right corner.

Something warned her to brace herself, and on cue, the angel appeared. "Do you believe me now?" He glowed. "Go get your other paper. It's identical to the one you just wrote, other than the date beside your signature. You might want to remove that from the office though, in case Sarah wants to know why you have a pre-dated birth sheet."

Tessa only shook her head.

"Well, then." With his chin tilted up and eyes shining like obsidian, he smirked. "Now that we've settled matters, we can get down to business. You need to locate a relic of Saint Peter of Verona that was looted from the Church of the Holy Cross in Barlassina, Italy, at the end of World War II."

"No, I don't." Tessa turned her back on the angel and marched to the cabinet, where she filed the Alderman birth sheet with the other records. "I do not have to find anything. You can go now."

The room grew hotter. "You still think I'm a hallucination?"

"You've proven you're an angel." She slammed the drawer. Once again, he was wearing a white robe and had silver wings tucked high at his back. "But that doesn't mean this is some sort of holy crusade where I have to drop everything and go find one of God's toys that He can't keep track of on His own."

The angel's eyes picked up a hue like coals in the fire. "Are you aware of what you're saying?"

"Of course I am. This isn't a holy mission, and I know that because you didn't show up proclaiming, *Thus says the Lord* or *God commands you to find this relic thing*. I may not go to church, but I know the difference between a commandment and a suggestion." She swept the hair back from her eyes. "You want me to go on a wild goose chase, and frankly, I have enough geese right here. This isn't

God's mission. You can go find the relic on your own. Have a nice day."

The angel focused on her. Tessa wondered whether it were only imagination, or did she really feel as if she were staring into a stiff breeze?

When he said nothing else, she continued straightening the supply room.

Finally, the angel said, "That's it? You're going to refuse?"

She didn't reply. Some things should be obvious.

The pitch of his voice went up. "You have an angel appearing before you with an assignment, and you're going to refuse?"

"You have no right to give me an assignment. You may be an angel, but you're hardly my boss. You certainly aren't paying my rent or issuing my W-2s. Thank you for proving you can predict the future. You should also have predicted I'd want nothing to do with your adventure."

The angel sounded dark. "Even I didn't think you'd be quite this stubborn."

"Excuse me." She waited until the angel moved aside, then replaced some folded towels in a cabinet. "Thanks. I have patients to take care of, five children at home, and not enough time. If you want someone to look for your relic, in twenty-five years I'll be retired and my kids will be out of school. If the thing's been lost since World War II, it can stay lost a little longer."

"It needs to be returned now." An urgent note entered the angel's voice, and he moved between her and the cabinet door. She stepped back to maintain her personal space. "If the relic goes home to Barlassina, the people there will rebuild the Church of the Holy Cross. If the church is rebuilt, the monastery will thrive again, and so will the school run by the Dominicans. If the school and the church are thriving, the town will survive. But if the church isn't rebuilt, there won't be a town any longer. The Dominicans will leave. The young people will go to other areas where they can get jobs."

Tessa sighed. "Do I look like the savior of a town?"

"I figured you'd at least help."

"Sorry."

She left the supply room. This time, the angel followed. "The church was destroyed by American soldiers."

"I'm not guilty of everything any American anywhere ever did."

His voice grew even more strident. "But your family comes from Barlassina."

"I'm also not guilty of everything any Italian ever did. And trust me, they do a lot."

The angel huffed, and she detected some amusement. "You're telling me."

"So no, no relic. You can go. Leave me alone."

As she walked the hall, she felt his presence at her back. Into her office. Back into the waiting area. Out to visit the new family again.

The angel's voice came again behind her: "Please? Terry?"

"No."

The presence vanished. Her mouth twitched as she opened the birth suite door to check on the new baby.

At home, Tessa found Gary at the stove simmering lentils in a cast-iron skillet. After hanging her coat on a hook by the door, she kissed him, then dropped her canvas bag and purse on a kitchen chair.

"How'd it go?"

"Six-pound four-ounce boy, Noe Michael, badly spelled." She started unpacking the canvas bag.

"Rough labor?"

"No, pretty standard." She looked up to find Gary studying her. "What?"

"I'd have guessed from the look on your face that you'd had to resuscitate the baby."

Instead of answering, she checked the stove: lentils, rice, chopped vegetables on a cutting board alongside, so she went to the cabinets to take down seven plates for the table. Those set, she looked at the table for a moment before shaking her head and getting down seven cups, one smaller than the rest.

As she passed Gary to get the silverware from the center island, he rested a hand on her shoulder. "Terry? It's me. What's wrong?"

"I can't— You wouldn't believe me." She paused, then hugged him. His arms around her were strong, his scent warm. "Actually, you might believe me. I'm not sure I believe me."

"Give me a shot, then. Have I ever steered you wrong?"

He let her go, and Tessa slid open the silverware drawer. "Not exactly, no. But you don't always think things through."

He laughed. "And when I told you to quit teaching third grade to go ahead and become a midwife...?"

She stretched up and kissed him. "You didn't think that through either. I mean, you were right, but we had a few hard years."

"You would never have been happy if you hadn't." Gary returned to the stove and added the vegetables to the lentils. "I wanted you to be happy. So lay it on me. What's making you unhappy?"

Tessa glanced into the living room where she could see the two oldest playing a video game. None of the other children were visible. Taking a step toward Gary, she lowered her voice. "I saw an angel."

His eyes widened. "Really? Where? Was he with one of the babies?"

"No, he wanted to talk to me. He appears after births because he says that's the only time I'm open to listening to him, when I'm tired and have all those endorphins. I made him prove he's an angel, and he is. At least, I asked him to predict the stats of the next baby, and he nailed them on every count."

Gary beamed. "That's wonderful!"

Tessa chuckled. "See, I knew you'd jump right into this."

"And I could have told the angel you wouldn't. So go on." Gary stirred the vegetables, then set the lid on the pan so they could simmer. "What is he like?"

"He's...he's tall, black hair, silver wings. He shines." Tessa frowned. "But he wants me to find a relic or something that was stolen from a church in Italy about seventy years ago, and I can't do that."

Gary drew back. "Why not?"

"Think about it! I've got babies to deliver and five kids to haul around. And then this angel expects me to don a fedora and coil a whip at my side to go tracking down this thing that even God doesn't know where it is?"

Gary laughed out loud. "Did you ask the angel where it was?"

Tessa rolled her eyes.

"What's the relic of?"

"How should I know? I didn't ask." She sighed. "Peter of Verona. And it came from Barlassina."

Gary rubbed his chin. "That's your mother's town, right? Is that why the angel asked you?"

"I don't care why he asked me. He picked the wrong person." Tessa finished counting out silverware. "The thing's been missing seventy years. It can stay missing a little longer."

Turing to the center island, Gary opened his laptop. "Peter of Verona, huh?" By the time Tessa had gotten the napkins, he said, "Okay, so he lived in the twelve hundreds. Patron saint of inquisitors."

"Inquisitors?"

"That's what it says, but that's much earlier than the Spanish Inquisition. Let's see—martyred near Barlassina. Apparently was a really nice guy, too."

Tessa smirked. "I hear that's a plus if you're trying to become a saint."

"Not as much as you might think." Gary chuckled. "Did the angel say how the relic got lost?"

"I didn't ask. I wanted him to leave me alone." Tessa stopped in her tracks. "You don't seriously think I should drop everything and go look for it, do you?"

"An angel showed up and asked you to do something, and that strikes me as unusual enough that yeah, I'd consider." Gary met Tessa's eyes across the kitchen.

"Sweetie, I'm just gathering information. I'm not saying what you should do. You're right that you're very busy. I just can't imagine an angel appearing to me with a quest and then not doing it."

Tessa said, "I don't even know what a relic is. We could have it in our towel closet for all I know."

"Well, that would be the easiest quest in history. Let's see." He frowned as he searched, then, "Catholic relic. 'Some object, usually part of the body, clothes, or sacramental, remaining as a memorial of a saint.' So I guess it's a worship aid."

"Don't go looking up 'sacramental.' I get the picture." Tessa shrugged. "Still doesn't seem like something I need to be involved in."

"Looks like a lot of people think the same way. Protestants and other groups who don't believe in saints think it's just superstition."

Tessa said, "And generic American atheists? What do we think?"

Gary smirked at her. "Evidence says those folks don't think about relics at all until an angel shows up and asks."

She flashed him a thumbs-up. "Touché, my love!"

He beamed. "I do my best to keep up with you."

Gary kept pecking at his computer while she checked the lentil stew, then the rice. When the table was ready with the milk, the water pitcher, the bread, and the butter, she called the children to wash their hands while she ladled the stew into a serving dish and brought out the rice.

Through dinner, the kids chattered while Tessa and Gary managed the chaos, making sure the younger ones got enough to eat and then actually ate it. Joe told them about junior varsity soccer practice. Alex and Mark talked about how a kid fell down the stairs at middle school and an ambulance took the kid to Boston MetroWest hospital. Brian remained quiet, but Tessa convinced him to talk a little about beginner band. And as for Eric, she had more trouble getting her youngest to stop talking about anything and everything, from begging for playdates with the other kindergarteners to retelling things he'd seen on TV.

Following dinner was the massive kitchen clean-up, an operation Tessa often compared to the logistics surrounding the D-Day invasion. Children went into action clearing the table, sweeping, loading the dishwasher, scrubbing pots, drying dishes, putting dishes away, and she armed Eric with a sponge to clear crumbs off the table. Cloth napkins went into the washing machine. Leftovers were labeled, dated, and tucked into the fridge. Meanwhile Tessa prepared tomorrow's school lunches and checked all the kids for completion of homework.

When Gary vanished into his office to finish an article, Tessa cuddled up on the couch with Eric and Brian to read. It would only be a little longer until Brian no longer wanted her to read to him, a milestone that left her wistful. The older boys sprawled around the family room reading their own thick novels, all dragons or magic that left Tessa shaking her head. But at least they were reading.

It was eight p.m. when Tessa's cell phone rang, and she took the call wondering if it would be a mom in labor: it wasn't the new moon yet, was it? But no, it was her partner midwife's phone number.

"Hey, Karen. What's up?"

"I was just talking to Doctor Cravey." He was their backup obstetrician. "He says the House introduced a little sneaky bill that would make it just about impossible to operate a birth center in Massachusetts."

Tessa's heart hammered. "What?"

She went into her bedroom and closed the door while Karen explained. "The state legislature is considering a bill that would change the way insurance pays for childbirth. It's not a big deal overall, at least not to us, because the things it covers aren't things we offer anyhow, like epidurals."

"So how can it affect us?"

"Because they've inserted legal language that prevents an insurance company from paying any claim we make because we don't offer those services."

Tessa sat on the edge of the bed. "What on earth...?"

"Hospital lobbyists got that language inserted because they're losing patients to us. On the surface, they're not trying to outlaw midwifery, but that's obviously the intent. They're saying instead that it's a matter of public safety and that women need to have immediate access to c-sections and epidurals and so on."

"Of course," Tessa muttered. "Our hundred deliveries a year are bankrupting the hospital system."

"It's a hundred deliveries a year the hospital doesn't get, and when they're getting fifteen to thirty thousand dollars per delivery, the bean counters start sniffing in the corners for more beans." Karen sighed. "I'm contacting a couple of midwifery groups to mobilize. We'll see how they've fought similar measures in other states, or really any measures. Every so often you get the bills forcing every midwife to up their certifications in order to keep practicing, and that's in the name of safety too."

It was laughable to think of Karen as unconcerned with safety. The Milliston Common Birth Center had the best safety record in the state, better even than the local hospitals.

Tessa was thinking out loud. "Maybe Gary can do some digging too." There was probably a conflict of interest in asking Gary to report on a situation that directly affected his wife's vocation, but on the other hand, it was good to have a freelance writer around: he knew people who knew people. Sometimes knowing the key person was all it took to work miracles.

Karen gave a quick rundown of the folks she'd be contacting, then got off the phone. Distracted, Tessa returned to get the boys ready for bed.

At ten o'clock, with all the kids asleep and Gary still typing away in the office, Tessa settled into bed with an issue of *Midwifery Today*. Before she'd gotten further than three paragraphs though, Gary came to sit on the edge of the bed.

"I've done some research." He waited for her to shut the magazine and lay it to the side. "You look upset. Are you okay?"

The words caught in Tessa's throat: the birth center closing because of a law she didn't understand yet, Karen organizing—someone needed to go to the papers. Maybe they'd have to move. It was no problem for Gary if they moved. They could uproot the boys and she could practice elsewhere. But— But—

Instead she swallowed it all down. There was nothing to be done until the morning. In the morning she could touch base with Karen and strategize a plan of attack. Right now, she needed her head clear. "What's up?

Gary took a long breath. "This missing relic actually exists, although it took a little digging to uncover the information."

Tessa sat up. She'd forgotten about the angel. "What did you do?"

"I looked through some news archives and used Google Translate. Apparently the church was destroyed and the relic disappeared, but no one's sure whether it was stolen or just burned with the church. I have enough information to write some editors and pitch them an article."

Tessa frowned. "Wait, you're going to write an article saying an angel appeared to your wife?"

"You think that would be bad for business?" Gary chuckled. "No, of course not. I'll pitch an article about unhealed war wounds. Veterans Day is coming up, and this makes a nice human interest feature. A looted church and a gutted town and a missing relic." He shrugged. "At the very least, I get a byline. But we may turn up some information that can help your angel recruit someone else to help return the relic."

Tessa lifted up her magazine. "Fine. Go ahead."

"I'll send a few emails tonight. We may have a response by morning. I know Ted answers all his queries between midnight and two a.m." Gary got to his feet. "I'll offer a sidebar about what the Catholic Church thinks relics are, and I bet he'll bite."

As Gary stood, Tessa said, "Why do you care?"

"Because you cared, and because someone else cares about that relic." Gary squeezed her hand. "Why should it stay in junk shop or a basement when it belongs in its home?"

Half an hour and one unread magazine later, Tessa went to the laundry room. If she wasn't going to do anything productive, and if she couldn't sleep fretting about whether she'd have a birth center in six months, she might as well do housework.

Five children necessitated one to two loads of laundry per day, and that didn't include incidentals such as sheets and towels. Running fourteen loads per week (even with the high-capacity washer Gary had delighted her with last Christmas), she counted on laundry as a perennial. Were the kids bored? Time to fold laundry. Half an hour to kill while dinner simmered? Enough time to fold a load of laundry. Insomnia? A son out past curfew? A nerve-wracking wait while a primip might or might not be in early labor? Might as well hit the laundry room and start folding.

The clothes emerged from the heap to form eight piles: one for each son, one for Gary, one for her, one for general household use. Socks were the worst. She'd learned long ago never to buy anything but white, but even at that, they had sixteen different kinds of white socks for seven people, plus the confusion when one son outgrew his particular size and moved to the next.

She hummed as she sorted, but her mind flew from one thought to the next the same way her fingers moved from one garment to the next. In the morning, each boy knew to come downstairs to bring his pile to his room. By then the clothes would be cold. Now they retained the dryer's artificial warmth, its unnatural softness. Behind her, another load tumbled in endless circles.

Afterward, in the living room, she opened her laptop and typed "midwifery laws" and "Massachusetts" into Google, coming up with nothing she didn't already know. On one of the midwifery forums, Karen had posted a request for help but hadn't as yet had any responses.

Jittery now, she wrote to a midwife activist she knew, asking her to call Karen.

Then, full of nervous energy from trying to fight a legal hydra with forty heads and its body located in Boston, she surfed to eBay, typed in "relic," and came up with fifty hits. She typed "Peter of Verona" and found an icon, a book, and a wooden rosary with a medal.

This was a bit early, but perhaps the good guys had an advantage in this legal battle. Most likely, the hospital didn't have an angel on their side. She, however, might. Relic or bargaining chip: you decide.

"Okay, angel," she said, swiveling her chair to face the empty room. "Are you still hanging around?"

A sensation like being watched crept over her, starting at her shoulders and spreading to her jaw. In the next moment, she saw the angel standing before her, still wearing white but this time without the sash. The black of his eyes glittered, and he kept his face expressionless.

"I checked for your relic, and it's not on eBay." She let off a long breath. "I don't suppose that fulfills any obligation to look for this thing."

The angel didn't reply. Just what she needed—a humorless celestial inhabiting her living room.

"Gary is going to do some investigating. That's his decision. I still think this is insane." She swiveled her chair back to the computer screen. "I hope you're satisfied with that."

The stared-at feeling intensified.

She turned back to him. "If you have something to say, say it."

"I'm beyond astonished at you." The angel folded his arms. "If it were that easy to find the relic, why wouldn't it already have been found?"

"And if it's that hard to find," Tessa shot back, "I'm not going to be able to track it down either."

The angel glowered. "I'll be helping."

"Which brings up another matter: if even you don't know where it is, what am I supposed to do? You're an angel. Do angel things and make it turn up." She opened her hands. "I can't imagine why you need a human in the first place, but if you were going to appear to anyone, you should have picked Gary."

The angel frowned. "I admit, you're making me wonder why I attempted this at all."

"I'm not hauling my family around the world on an excellent adventure on your say-so." She crossed her legs and leaned back in the desk chair. "I don't even know who you are. What's your name?"

The angel's eyes narrowed. "I'm not allowed to tell you that."

"Not allowed?"

"We're not usually allowed." He shook his head as if the gesture were an afterthought. "You can give me a placeholder name, and I'll respond to that."

Tessa drummed her fingers on the armrest. "Nope. If you expect me to do anything on your behalf, I need to know who you are and why you want it done. And I'll figure out the best way to get it done too." She tilted her head. "So, name?"

The angel looked annoyed. "I'll ask for permission."

The world imploded.

Either the angel or the world around him stretched. He became big enough to fill the whole thing, or else the universe became small and clung to Tessa like wet cellophane. In that thousandth of a thousandth of a second, the angel's eyes turned clear and his clothes flashed like the heart of a nuclear blast. She had no time to flinch or she'd have knocked over her own chair in an attempt to escape, but it was over before her nerves could get a signal to her brain. Suddenly he was normal again (normal? An angel, normal?) but Tessa's every hair had bristled and her heartbeat thrashed a panicked staccato. Her chest was too tight to breathe. She couldn't remember where she was.

Sounding pleased, the angel said, "God says I can tell you my name. I'm Maritenael."

Throat burning, eyes watering, Tessa shook too badly to reply.

The angel's expression flashed to concern. "I'm sorry—don't be afraid! I didn't mean to scare you."

With a gasp, Tessa finally managed to breathe again. The angel crouched close, gazing into her eyes with a steadiness that still couldn't erase what she'd seen. "I didn't think that would affect you."

Tessa hissed, "Get away."

The angel recoiled.

With her hands pressed over her eyes, she counted out deep breaths as if she were a laboring mom.

What on earth had she been thinking, trying to leverage the relic to make the angel keep the birth center open? She couldn't bargain with that! She should find the relic as quickly as possible so the angel would leave her alone. Get Gary to track it down, then hand over the thing so they'd be done with each other. This creature could blast off back to Heaven, and she could return to delivering babies for as long as the law allowed.

That made sense. Give it what it wanted. Get rid of it.

Tessa's voice was hoarse. "Will I be able to see you during the day?"

The angel's voice had returned to its previous authority. "Now that you believe I exist, yes."

"I'll talk to you again tomorrow. But for now—just leave me alone."

When she looked up, the room was empty and the clock hands were together, straight up.

THREE

Again, Gary proved correct. By the time Tessa was walking their youngest to the school bus, he'd gotten a response from the editor of *US News*: they wanted the article.

At the end of the email, the editor added, curiously, "I wasn't going to log on last night to read queries, but for some reason I did. I have an odd feeling that I really need this article."

Immediately after arriving at the office, Tessa did an internet search on the angel's name. To her chagrin, she wasn't sure how to spell it. "And he had the gall to make fun of Noe," she muttered. "At least that's only two syllables."

Walking by with a sheaf of papers, Karen peeked over her shoulder. "Now that's a name. Or is it a country?"

Tessa shivered. "Name."

"I thought I'd seen them all." Karen chuckled. "Martin-ale? Maritime-in-ell? How would you pronounce it?"

Oh, that terrifying angel in the soft brown of her living room, whose mouth hadn't formed the word as much as his heart had. When he'd said it, the name had vibrated in her like a steeple bell, like something linked to the specifics of his identity. In retrospect, that name clearly had a meaning, but what? Her fear had arisen not entirely from the power of his voice but also from the sense of the way the name fit. How strange that a multifaceted creature could be captured by a single-faceted series of syllables.

No, it had been more than that. Behind the audible set of syllables seemed to lie another, as if he'd spoken with two voices at the same time. She'd never be able to repeat it. In the three a.m. darkness of her bedroom, she'd tried. It didn't sound the same.

"I have no idea how you'd pronounce that," Tessa murmured.

"I bet you're glad you don't teach third grade any longer. You'd be saying all these names on a regular basis, and you'd have to keep a straight face." Karen chuckled as she headed to the coffeemaker in the waiting area. "When you get a chance, let's go over what I discovered last night about our friends in the state house."

Karen had attended a birth after midnight. While mainlining coffee to fortify herself against the morning, she showed Tessa everything she'd printed off, including the text of the bill. Karen said, "By the end of the day, I'll have every midwife in Massachusetts mobilized. We'll beat this thing. Striking that part of the bill won't affect the rest of it. Put up enough fuss and they'll pass it without that."

If signed into law, the measure wouldn't take effect for a year anyhow, so their current patients would be able to deliver at the birth center. That was a relief. At least they wouldn't be scrambling to find VBAC-friendly obstetricians and natural-minded hospital practitioners.

At nine, Tessa was ready to see her first patient, a first-time mom named Amanda. At five months, she had a sweet, rounded belly and a genuine pregnancy glow. "Boring, boring," Tessa murmured to Amanda as she looked over the numbers. "I'm afraid you haven't done the slightest thing to worry me. Now let's get the little guy's heartbeat."

Amanda lay back (they used a regular twin bed for exams) while Tessa first measured her belly, then warmed up the Doppler machine and probed with her hands until she could feel the outline of the baby. Head up, shoulder there—that would put the heart at about...here. She pressed the Doppler into position before turning it on, and as soon as she did, the machine amplified the regular whoosh-whoosh of a heart the size of a dime.

Amanda grinned, that compulsive new-mom grin which always made Tessa grin as well. "Awesome sound," she murmured, taking note of the heart rate before switching off the machine. "You're getting regular kicks now?"

"Every day. Sometimes they're just flutters. My mother-in-law says it's gas."

"Your mother-in-law is full of gas. A mom knows kicks when she feels them." Tessa sat in the rocking chair while Amanda straightened her clothes and sat up on the bed. "Now, do you have any concerns?"

For half an hour, she and Amanda discussed pregnancy, babies, her marriage, and what preparations she needed to make for a new baby. Amanda already had folks volunteering to bring postpartum meals. "Everyone's being so good. They're so excited." She hugged Tessa before she left the appointment. "You guys are so good to me too."

After Amanda had gone, Tessa checked the waiting room (empty) and the clock (five minutes until her next patient) so she returned to her office, then shut the door.

The exam rooms (well, the offices—Gary often joked that she had a bed in her office) were soundproof, so without any fear of being overheard, she said, "Angel? I want to talk to you."

She needn't have finished the second sentence. She felt him as soon as she said "angel" and saw him an instant afterward.

"We need to talk."

"I'm really sorry about frightening you." The angel's eyes glimmered, but he didn't stand as near as he usually did.

"Can you sit?" Tessa said.

"You mean, do my joints bend? This is an immaterial form. I created it so you would have something to focus on." The angel sat on the bed, but not as if he walked toward it and bent his knees and lowered himself to a seated position. Instead he blinked out from a standing position by the wall to a seated one on the mattress, like a badly edited film. "Or did you mean you wanted me in a familiar place as if I'm your patient so you can feel you're in control of the situation?"

Tessa's cheeks burned. "Are you quite through?"

"Through with what?"

"Through with being thoroughly superior?"

The angel's eyes widened.

"I'll take that as a yes. We need to set some guidelines. First, don't ever do that thing again to me, where you transform into a being of light who's bending time and space."

"That was a major misjudgment on my part. I'm not going to override your free will and force my way into your head." The angel made that sound like a given. "I already apologized."

"And I've accepted. Don't do it again."

The angel remained impassive. "Next?"

He hadn't agreed. But rather than press the matter, Tessa said, "Secondly, I'm going to take you up on your offer to give you a substitute name, since I can't pronounce the one you gave me."

"It was tough getting my passport," the angel said.

Mid-breath, Tessa stopped cold. She stared at the angel, but he refused to crack a smile.

Then after a very long pause, he laughed. She rolled her eyes. "I only have about three minutes before my next patient arrives, so do you mind?"

"You've got fifteen because she forgot until nearly one minute from now." The angel's image maintained a rigid posture which, now that she knew to look, really was just him giving her something to look at. She had no idea where he was or what he was doing. "Take your time."

Okay, let's see how this worked out. Tessa dialed the contact number listed in the next folder on her desk. Sure enough, Jennifer Wilson answered on the second ring. "This is Tessa Testerman," Tessa began, and Jennifer let out a yelp. "I'm sorry! I forgot! I'll be right over!" Then, "Wait, how did you know?"

"A midwife just knows these things. See you in ten minutes."

As she set down the phone, a prickly sensation spread over her throat. It was the physical sensation of laughter, but it wasn't her doing the laughing. Her gaze returned to the angel. "You enjoyed that."

He brightened. "What's not to enjoy? She'll have her appointment, and you had fun."

And he'd impressed her. That had to figure into it somewhere.

"Back to our conversation." She traced her finger over her jeans. "I can't say whatever is printed on your passport, so I'm going to give you a placeholder name the way you offered." Her heart thumped. "How about Martin?"

He nodded.

"It's kind of close to whatever it was you said last night."

He nodded again.

There was nothing else, as if he didn't care one whit what she called him but was waiting for more points of order. "And third," she said, but this one she hadn't worked out in advance, "I want to be calling the shots. If you want me to go on a relic-hunt, but my kid needs help with his math, I'm going to help my kid with his math. My patients, my kids, and my husband come before your expedition. That is nonnegotiable."

That same duskiness built up inside her, as if she were a cow in the field longing to lie down ahead of a storm front. That had to be coming from the angel. Martin. She might as well begin thinking of him with his new name. Dark-eyed, Martin said, "You could fill your life with those three. There may be times I need you to act immediately."

"Then there may be times you'll be disappointed." Tessa's gaze narrowed as if she were squaring off against the head of the maternity unit during a hospital transfer. "My kids and my husband and my patients come first."

"I'm not disputing the primacy of your state of life duties," said Martin. "But depending on your definition of their needs as opposed to their wants, you might never get around to anything else."

Primacy of her state of life duties? That sounded like a Sunday school thing. "You'll get your share of my time. But not all of it."

Again, he didn't look happy and didn't assent, but Tessa didn't push.

He said, "Is there anything else?"

"Yes." She steeled herself, and as she did, the angel brightened a shade. "The birth center is in trouble because of a bill in the state house. If I look for this relic, I want you to help me keep the birth center open."

The angel sounded puzzled. "What do you believe I can do?"

"I'm not sure what angels can do. I figured you would know more about that." Tessa folded her arms. "I only know that angels can't GPS old stolen relics. But can you do other things? Can you appear to state senators, for example, and tell them that they need to vote against this legislation?"

Martin's eyes glinted. "You won't believe me, but no, I can't."

Her eyes widened. "You appeared to me!"

"There's a reason I appeared to you." The image of him shimmered, and again that tickle presented in her throat. "Sometimes I can influence someone, but it's subtle. If someone already wants something, I can enhance the desire. If they're tangentially under my authority, they might be able to hear me. I might be able to remind someone of something. But I can't make someone act against his will."

She furrowed her brow. "So you can lean on a magazine editor to contract an article he already kind of wants?"

The angel agreed.

Tessa tilted her head. "Can you log in to a state computer and delete a paragraph from a document?"

Martin's eyes brightened, and that pressure in her throat increased again. She laughed too. "Okay, okay. But you know what I want. If there's a way for you to help keep the birth center open—all the birth centers in Massachusetts—then I'm asking you to help me because I'm helping you."

The angel opened his hands. "If I find a way, I'll do what I can." He lowered his light, and Tessa relaxed. "Do you have any more requests?"

"I believe that will do for now."

Martin disappeared.

Turning back toward her desk, Tessa glanced at the parking lot. Jennifer still hadn't arrived, but if the angel was right, she'd arrive in seven minutes. Tessa wondered momentarily if the angel really had departed, or if he'd only removed the image she could see. If he were watching, what was he thinking? What might he be planning? What could an angel could do in the service of midwifery?

But the worst question of all had no answers: whether he would comply with her boundaries, and what she could do if he didn't.

Two nights later, Tessa prepared dinner while supervising the boys at their homework and listening to trumpet practice in the next room. Math, vocabulary, and John Philip Souza. Behind a closed door, Gary worked in his office. His woodworking column was usually due around this time of the month, and the family calendar had two more close deadlines scrawled in red dry-erase marker.

All these were normal, non-supernatural tasks. No angel had appeared since that conference in her office, and although she detected a distinct impatience, for now she had a plan: let Gary do the work. Gary wanted the article, so Gary could do the research.

As she set the table for dinner, the doorbell rang. "Alex," she called, "get that!"

A moment later, she heard, "Grandma!"

At the edge of the kitchen Tessa met her mother lugging groceries and a large canvas bag. Her mother kissed her on the cheek with wind-chilled lips, then handed over the bag (paper inside plastic, doubling their natural resource consumption) and left her canvas bag by the coat hooks.

Gary's office door opened. "Oh, Terry? I invited your mother for dinner."

Mom chuckled. "No wonder you looked surprised!" She handed Alex her coat and purse, then removed her gloves. "Your father did that to me all the time too. Here, can I help with dinner?"

Tessa intoned, "Actually, Gary was just going to set another place at the table," and Mom laughed out loud.

Fortunately for Tessa, her growing sons always required extra-large portions, with all leftovers consumed the next day as lunches. Feeding an unexpected guest wasn't more difficult than adding noodles and shredding up extra salad for the bowl.

After dinner, Mom had to be shooed out of the kitchen while the boys did their cleanup. Tessa finished supervising homework, then took a client call from a patient having contractions. Although Tessa's gut instinct told her these weren't serious, the patient was only twenty-eight weeks and shouldn't deliver now. She offered to drive to the patient's house to check things out, and that took an hour. She returned to find Mom brewing decaf while Gary herded the boys through their evening chores.

Mom said, "You looked so shocked when I arrived that I forgot to tell you I brought dinner rolls. I knew I should have phoned to make sure Gary told you I'd be coming."

As Tessa hung her coat on the peg, she said, "Why did Gary invite you?"

"Don't you speak to your husband at all?" Mom chuckled. "It's about that article on Barlassina. He's getting stonewalled, and he wanted to pick my brain to see if there's anything in this head of mine."

There, Tessa thought in the general direction of the angel. *You should have gone to my mother in the first place. Not only would she have cared, but she's got time because she's retired.*

Then Tessa dropped her hat as a spotlight flooded her.

Not a visible one, but it was again that stared-at sense, accompanied by the conviction that *she* had been chosen, not her mother, and there were reasons. Not a mistake.

She'd never before felt Martin speak without hearing words or having him appear.

Shaken, she picked up her hat and hung it with her coat, then joined her mother in the kitchen.

"How was the patient?"

Tessa shrugged. "A lot of Braxton-Hicks contractions, but they're not doing anything. I advised her to lie down, drink a lot of water, watch a good movie, and get her mind off them. She'll call again if she starts to feel uncomfortable, but I'm betting she won't." The visit had been for reassurance: a midwife's hands to the belly, the victorious "whoosh-whoosh" of the baby's heartbeat, and then the dreaded internal check where she pronounced the cervix tight and long. "He's not going anywhere," she'd said to her patient, gesturing that she get dressed again. "Your uterus is practicing."

Her own mother took a seat at the table. "I was so surprised when Gary called to ask about Barlassina. I'd have thought you would tell him everything, but he said you didn't know all that much. Fine, fine, I'll hunting. So many things." She smiled. "He'll be pleased with everything I brought. There's more, but my brother has it."

"I've been curious about where we came from anyhow," said Tessa. "The boys have questions, and sometimes I can't answer."

Mom nodded. "Well, you should write this all down, because someday I'll be dead and no one will remember," and Tessa exclaimed "Mom!" even as her mother winked.

Tessa got Eric a bath, then put him to bed. Afterward, Brian went to sleep while Mark and Alex set up a two-player video game for their last hurrah. Tessa returned to the kitchen to find her mother and Joe making piles of photographs and other paperwork. "Fifteen minutes, guys," Tessa called into the living room, and one of the boys acknowledged. She always had to remind them to shut it off, but at least one of them had heard.

Joe was saying, "So how many brothers and sisters did Great-Grandma have?"

"Five," said Mom. "And one more born after they got here, kind of a surprise. Oh, are we ready to start?"

Gary came into the kitchen behind Tessa. "If you don't mind, I'd love to."

Mom shuffled through the stack of photographs, then handed one to Gary. "This is the inside of the church, before it was destroyed."

Tessa looked over Gary's shoulder at the black-and-white print, a glance sufficient to identify her grandparents' wedding photo. But as she looked this time, her throat tightened, and in the next moment, her stomach clenched with longing. Yearning. She half-stepped backward, tears coming to her eyes.

Gary passed her the photo, and Tessa blinked until her vision cleared. This was only a photo she'd seen before, a couple posed before a grand altar, tall candles, a tabernacle visible behind and between them. It was gaudy in a way that screamed "old Catholic church," and far too cluttered with mosaics and statues for her to find it in any way peaceful. So why the gut-punch? Her attention drew itself to the carvings on the legs of the altar and then to a lace altar cloth she suddenly knew had been crocheted by her great-grandmother's mother.

Martin? she thought.

Again the sensation. It pulsed in her throat far stronger than nostalgia: this was heartbreak.

Her hand trembled as she passed the photo to Joe.

Joe asked questions, but Tessa interrupted to say, "Mom, that altar cloth: was that made by your great-grandmother?"

"As if I would know." Mom brought the photo close to her eyes, squinting. "I can barely make it out. She used to make them, so I wouldn't be surprised, but back then everyone could crochet. Our family always did things for the church."

As Mom passed around more photos, Tessa braced for that same distraught, but it didn't repeat. Maybe that was the same emotion she felt when she coming across a photo of her father by surprise. There'd be a sudden grief, but afterward it wasn't so bad. Still—shouldn't an angel be happy? Peaceful? They were supposed to float around with banners and trumpets, bringing joy to men of good will. Grieving didn't fit with what she imagined about Heaven.

Not that she'd given much time to imagining Heaven in the first place. But if you could be sad in Heaven, that kind of changed things.

"Oh, here it is!" Mom brightened. "I knew there was one."

Mom handed her a photo of side alcove in the church, again crammed to bursting with its own altar and artwork and statues. To the side was a niche with a platform, and on the niche was an object. The niche was in the upper corner of the photo, but she couldn't take her eyes off that corner. That. *That.* She needed *that.*

Back off, she thought to Martin.

It took a moment more before she could look at the whole photo. The photo turned out to be a First Communion picture, a gap-toothed girl wearing a crown and a gown more ornate than Tessa's long-ago bridal dress. The girl clasped her hands at her chest, holding a rosary.

"That's the relic, in the corner," said Mom. "The oval jewelry it's housed in is the reliquary. You can't really see it because the picture is dark, but at the center is a little piece of the heart of Peter the Martyr."

Joe looked at the photo in her hands. "Hey, Mom, it's you!"

Tessa chuckled. "Yeah, because I'm at least a hundred years old."

Gary looked at the photo even as Mom said, "I always thought that looked like you, Terry, but no one else agreed with me."

"Whoever that is has definitely got Terry's eyes and the shape of her face." Gary held it closer. "But that's not her smile. Who is it really?"

Mom shrugged. "Some relative. I'm not sure."

Martin prompted her, and Tessa repeated, "Great-grandma's younger sister Alicia."

Mom looked up. "Do you think so? My mother told me a while ago, and that could have been."

Gary sounded amused. "I'd trust Terry on this one." He studied the photo closely. "I'm wondering how much I can blow this up to scan it. Are there any official photos?"

"I found a few more like this. People wanted to be photographed in front of it at weddings or First Communions, and sometimes the relic came out at funerals. I don't know if there's an official picture. You'd have to ask at Barlassina"

Tessa looked at it again. "I thought it would be bigger."

Mom shook her head. "It's more like a piece of jewelry on a stand. You can see it's about the size of a dinner roll, with all that filigree on the front and piping around the edges. At the center was a piece of glass around a cloth that had a piece of Peter the Martyr's heart."

Gary made a note on a pad. "Was it certified?"

Mom said, "Do I look like an auctioneer for Sotheby's?" and Gary laughed out loud.

Mom went through the rest of her material. There were postcards in Italian, one of which showed a map with "Barlassina" added in by hand. She had prayer cards with pictures of the Blessed Mother on one side and familiar last names but unfamiliar first names on the other, printed with birth and death dates beneath Italian prayers. "My mother kept in touch with her relatives from back home," Mom said, "but I haven't been so good. What I learned in college was Central Italian, not our dialect. Whenever I tried to write them, they'd write back with 'What's the matter? You're a politician now?'"

Tessa chuckled, and she felt Martin laughing too.

Gary said, "So tell me what you know about the relic."

Alex and Mark were at the door. She gestured them over to the table.

Mom said, "Toward the end of World War II, American troops came through Barlassina. That was unusual because of the way it's situated with all the valleys and mountains. This wasn't an especially important place, so there was no outpost there. But there were some of our boys in the city, fascist sympathizers, and one of them took a shot at the Americans. After that, the American soldiers went through the city hunting down the Italian soldiers. No one was going to turn over their sons or their brothers, so the Americans got mad. Two of our boys fled into the church, and the Americans followed them inside, looted it, shot the priest, and burned it down."

Gary was biting his lip.

"That was my mother's story. My father said the Americans must have detonated something inside the church because the ceiling caved in. They went to the rectory next door and torched that too. When our people finally got inside, the reliquary had been taken, along with anything gold or expensive. The Americans got into someone's wine cellar too, and after that several civilians were killed, including my great-aunt Alicia. Her son was one of the priests, and when she ran to the church, an American soldier shot her."

Tessa murmured, "How awful."

In her heart she felt the stillness of a city in ruins, a people horrified by a war brought into their own living rooms. The sorrow. The damage. The tears. But over all those feelings lay silence, a silence broken only by the clatter of people clearing debris and trash hauled away in piles. There were fresh graves. And overlooking it all, a devastated church.

Gary said, "Why didn't they rebuild?"

"You say that like it's simple." Mom frowned. "I never got a straight story, but you know how things are. One family in Barlassina has the money to fix the church, but another family won't let them. I guess the fascist boy who took the first shot at the Americans was a cousin of the DiOrios, and he was one of the ones who hid in the church. So the Monterosa family, who always seemed to have a lock on the politics, blamed the DiOrios." Mom waved a hand dismissively. "And the relic is just gone, but was it really one of the Americans who took it? The Monterosas said one of the DiOrio partisans stole it in order to protect it, but then he sold it for liquor money. The DiOrios said the Monterosas never had been properly respectful of the relic in the first place, so they destroyed it to make their donations the highlight of the church."

Tessa said, "And between the two families, they never let the church be rebuilt? For seventy years?"

Mom shrugged. "When my mother was still writing to them, every so often I'd hear about the families, and who had done what to whom, but I couldn't keep track. We're from the DiOrio side, so my mother always said the Monterosas were little better than pigs. And you know how it goes. I'm sure the Monterosas are telling anyone with ears that the DiOrios are a bunch of ignorant brutes, all of them criminals."

Tessa let off a long sigh.

Joe piped up, "Kind of like those two great-aunts who didn't speak to each other for thirty years because of who got their mother's wedding ring after she died?"

Mom slapped a hand flat on the table. "Exactly like that! And then over time, the fight gets larger and larger, and you don't even remember why you're supposed to hate that branch of the family, except you do because everyone tells you to."

Alex volunteered, "Do we hate them?"

Tessa said, "At this point, we don't even know them."

Mom added, "But if my mother were here, she'd say you should."

Gary rubbed his chin.. "Do you know anything about the soldiers?"

Mom shrugged. "Other than that they were American? Nothing."

Gary looked back over the notes Tessa now realized he'd been taking all along. She reached for the picture of her great-grandparents again, the black-and-white image of the church with the pre-Vatican II altar, the delicate altar-cloth, and the tabernacle at the center.

Again, deep inside, she detected that trill of sadness.

Mom said, "I've heard the story explained a few different ways. Sometimes a different relative had a different twist, like the Americans had a tank, or that the Italians trapped the soldiers inside and burned the church themselves. But I think the way I told you is the way it happened. The Americans got mad because some Italian tried to pick off one of their own, and they took it out on the town. They got drunk, and they took the object that looked most valuable in the church, then burned it to hide what they did."

Gary murmured, "Yet it's never turned up." He looked up at Mark and Alex. "Hey, boys, time for bed," and when they both protested, Tessa waved them off. "You heard your father. You've got school in the morning."

While Mom and Gary discussed the details again, Tessa sifted photos. Mom had brought more than just photos. She also had old baptismal certificates with the dates of the various sacraments inscribed on the back in tall loopy signatures from old-world handwriting classes.

As she looked at the names, her throat tightened. She found a passport. There was a ship manifesto courtesy of the Ellis Island website.

"Why was the relic so important?" Tessa murmured.

"I can answer that," Gary said. "Saint Peter of Verona was murdered near Barlassina. As best as I can tell, his body was brought to the monastery there, and from the monastery he was transported somewhere else. But they took some relics first."

Mom said, "Ours came from the lance his murderer used on his heart."

Gary added, "The murderer later converted and became a saint himself."

Tessa snickered. "That's one way to get to Heaven, I guess."

"Any way will do." Mom opened a box to reveal a sheaf of envelopes. "These are all written to my mother by various relatives. It will have bits and pieces of the great DiOrio-Monterosa war over nothing, if you're curious. But it's all in Italian, and I'm not any good at translating."

Tessa reached for a random letter and opened it. Again she found the beautiful handwriting of a student drilled in penmanship. The paper felt thin against her midwife fingers in a way that told her there was danger of tearing. She smiled as she refolded the letter.

Gary said, "Can I keep all this material until I'm done with the article?" and Mom said that would be fine. While he packed it back into boxes and Mom got ready to leave, Tessa turned on the tea kettle. The night was about to get even longer.

FOUR

L ater, with the hum of Gary's scanner in the background, Tessa finished steeping her tea and sat back at the kitchen table.

"Martin?"

The next instant, Martin sat across from her, in Gary's seat.

Tessa leaned forward. "What's going on?"

Martin regarded her with an unchanging stare, but when Tessa paid attention, she detected unease. That more than facial expressions would have to be Martin's barometer. The look he gave her now was apparently the default.

She tried to smile. "You're forgetting something: I'm a midwife, and I have to deal all the time with patients hiding things from me. I recognize a partial story when I hear one. So the same way I don't lambaste a woman who claims she's pregnant with her first, but she had an abortion or released a baby for adoption, trust me that I'm not going to yell at you. I know you're holding back something."

Martin didn't respond. Tessa wondered if he would disappear.

Finally she said, "Why the sadness?"

He said, "The church was destroyed."

The body language was all wrong. That should have been accompanied by him staring down at the tabletop.

"Lots of things get destroyed. You were far too sad about that."

His image flickered. "I was the guardian angel of that church."

The instant before she said, "So?" Tessa caught herself and said nothing. No, wait. That was enormous. She had no idea exactly what this meant, but she recognized it implied more than she understood.

She opted to delay. "Churches have guardian angels?"

Martin nodded. "Just about every institution or organization has a guardian."

"Even the birth center?"

Martin laughed. "Yes, in fact."

Tessa blinked. "Say hi to it for me. And tell it to go lean on our elected officials."

Martin nodded.

If Martin had guarded the church, that explained the sadness, although not quite the degree of sadness. This still didn't feel like the whole story. "You recognized my relatives, then, because you had met all of them?"

Again Martin nodded.

"When were you assigned to the church?"

"Right at the beginning." He'd defaulted to the straightforward expression. "It was built in 1022."

Tessa's eyes widened. "You're a thousand years old?"

"Quite a bit older. Angels have been around longer than humans."

That made some sense: an angel was assigned to guard a church, and for nine hundred years he did. But then it got destroyed, and he missed it afterward. Perhaps that was it.

No, there was still more.

"You must have done a good job," Tessa said, and she felt in her heart how Martin recoiled; his outer form remained the same. "When it was built, there wasn't a printing press or gun powder in Europe. You helped it survive the plagues and probably wars and earthquakes."

When he didn't reply, she added, "I'm impressed."

He still wasn't talking to her. This was the moment. She waited a beat, and then, as if asking a new mom about drug use during pregnancy when she'd already guessed the answer, Tessa said, "Or do you think you didn't do a good job?"

In a monotone, Martin said, "I am not one of your clients, Terry."

"Fair enough." Tessa shrugged. "What my mom was saying about the two families, is that true?"

Now Martin reacted with a simultaneous eye roll and huff. "It wasn't even close to the truth! The truth is, the DiOrios and the Monterosas have found full-time employment in despising one another since at least the 1700s. After the church was destroyed, it was no surprise whatsoever that they each blamed the other. No matter what happened in Barlassina for the past three centuries, you ask a DiOrio and they'll tell you it's a Monterosa's fault, and any Monterosa is going to tell you it happened because God hates the DiOrios."

Tessa snickered. Martin leaned toward her across the table. "No, you really have no idea. The grapes were bad this year? The DiOrios must have done something to the field, or maybe that lazy guy you hired for the harvest has a cousin who's a DiOrio and he cursed your vines. After a while, it was so predictable you didn't have to do more than look at the weather to figure out that yeah, a DiOrio or a Monterosa was at fault...again...and half the time the little old ladies would be standing at the back of the church whispering to one another about what this one did or that one, and what a shame it was, or so-and-so's brutta figura, and on and on and on. Seminarians snarling insults at one another during perpetual adoration." Martin's tone grew harsher, his eyes now in high contrast to his face.

Shocked, Tessa nodded, trying to keep him talking.

There was no need to try anything of the sort, any more than you needed to keep the earth moving during a landslide. Martin opened his hands, and for a moment he was talking like a real Italian himself. "The guardian of Barlassina and I used to brainstorm together to figure out what we could do about the rift. In the 1800s we had a momentary sliver of hope when the unthinkable happened. In the ultimate act of rebellion, a DiOrio-by-name, not even a cousin, married a Monterosa-by-name. They even dared to produce children together, and they lived right there in the city, totally shameless. The families stood by them, although of course everyone had to talk about them continuously for the next thirty years."

Tessa ventured, "It didn't help?"

"Not even a bit." Martin took a deep breath. "When they died, each of the children was summarily 'claimed' by each family. 'Oh, he's such a DiOrio,' or 'She's just like her grandmother, the poor thing,' and within one generation there were no olive branches left to extend, although," Martin added sardonically, "the olive crop failed one year, and that was, I'm told, a Monterosa's fault."

Shoulders shaking, Tessa put her face in her hands and laughed helplessly.

When it became clear he'd stopped the story, Tessa asked through the laughter, "What started it?"

"In 1732, Coralina DiOrio wrote a rude-sounding thank-you note to Arlessina Monterosa, and Arlessina stormed over to her house to tell her not to bother coming to her daughter's wedding the next week. They argued for an hour, and people are still arguing."

Tessa kept her fingers pressed against her forehead. "Holy cow."

"Yeah. That was the crime worth three centuries of feuding. No one remembers that now. Other than me, the guardian of the city, and God Himself."

Finally looking up, Tessa said, "You've got to admire their perseverance."

"You've got to admire something about the situation," Martin muttered. "I'm just not sure what."

She said, "Even the war didn't unite them?"

"You never learned anything about the finer points of politics during World War II. It wasn't really 'Italy' at war. The Italians had a bunch of different factions, and when the war started, naturally the two families ended up on opposite sides." It was true; Tessa hadn't learned much about World War II. "Up in that part of Italy, the people still had contadini and tenant farmers. The families with money owned the land, and everyone else got to farm a piece of it in exchange for living there. Each of the families protected their tenants."

"Oh!" Tessa nodded. "So when you have two landholding families in one location, you get a big fight."

"You've got it. Now factor in that tenant farmers tend to side with their specific family. In the government, the fascists came to power, and so Italy allied with Germany. The DiOrios hated fascism while the Monterosas sided with the fascists, but they both hated the idea of the war. In private, that is. Both families decided to keep their heads down and hope the war would pass them by, which it largely did except for when their young men got drafted, leaving the women to farm and run the town alone."

Martin frowned. "A lot of what I heard about the war was third-hand, because I didn't travel far from my church, but I witnessed plenty of fallout. Neighboring towns got pulverized by Allied forces. The Germans had no qualms about conscripting press gangs of Italians and forcing them into manual labor, giving them a handful of bread and little else." His eyes glinted. "The Italians were never full-hearted about the war in the first place. When Italy changed sides, most of their soldiers deserted with their weapons. But some did join the Germans. And there you have it. The soldiers who came home became partisans, fighting against the Germans from the hills. But we still had some Italians working with the fascists, and at the same time, we had fascist-minded Italians who had deserted anyhow."

Tessa frowned. "That's enough to give anyone a headache."

"Being a deserter meant you could be shot on sight." Martin sighed. "There were two Italian policemen in

Barlassina, contadini. They didn't want to report their fellow townsmen as deserters, of course. So they all looked out for each other. If the Germans came through, the police warned the partisans, who hid in the church basement. If the Allies came through, or other partisans, the partisans would warn the police, who would themselves hide in the church basement."

Tessa laughed. "One hand washing the other?"

"This was Italy. There was lather all over the place." Martin loomed darker than before. "Also consider that starvation was rampant. 1944 was the worst winter anyone could remember. The combination of all these tensions created a powder keg."

Tessa shook her head. "They never covered that in history. We got a timeline but not the heart of the matter."

Martin made no response.

She ventured, "After the church was destroyed, was there no way you could use the tragedy to unite the two families?"

Martin's image faded, and his eyes greyed. Then, softer, "I wasn't there."

Tessa frowned.

"The church was destroyed." Martin looked filmier. "The assignment was over, so I had to return." Suddenly he seemed too small for her kitchen, like a toddler in an adult's chair. "There wasn't a chance to make it right. Just, 'Time to come home, Martin,' and I went."

"That seems cruel," Tessa whispered. "You didn't even get a chance to say goodbye?"

"I did, but— It's complicated." Martin averted his gaze. "I wanted to retrieve the relic. If the relic came home to the church, they'd have a reason to rebuild. The church had suffered damage before, but with the relic to unite Barlassina, people got together to rebuild. This time there was no reason for them to rally, and with the families blaming each other ever since, they've polarized the whole city. It's going to end in Barlassina's destruction."

Tessa wrapped her hands around her mug. "Would even the relic reunite people who get so offended over a thank-you note?"

"It was the cheap gift that led to the bad thank-you note." Martin smirked. "But there was a snub that led to the cheap gift. Of course, she only snubbed her because her sister wasn't invited to a dinner party."

Tessa smiled. "I can imagine the rest."

"How bland is your imagination?"

She clasped her hands and leaned forward on her elbows. Soothingly, she said, "You did all you could."

"No!" Martin slammed a hand into the table with a vehemence that made Tessa jump, even though the table made no sound. "It was my fault! I completely misjudged the threat posed by one platoon of threadbare American soldiers who were underfed and fed up with the entire war. A man with a lot to lose may be dangerous, but a man with nothing to lose is infinitely so."

He'd clearly had this argument with himself a hundred times. A thousand. "But—"

Martin's eyes blazed. "And then I misjudged the stupidity of a couple of Italian fascists with their bravado on the line." He shook his head. "Don't soften it, Terry. I should have been there the night before and urged the monsignor to lock the church doors! He used to leave them open because deserters from both sides—partisans, fascists, Germans, all of them!—would hide in the church, and he'd bring them a meal before they continued on. I could have frightened him. I could have encouraged him to lock the doors just that one night so the men couldn't get into the church."

Martin dropped his head into his hands.

"But—" Tessa's brow furrowed. "You can predict the future. You didn't see this was coming?"

In a whisper: "I can't predict the future."

Tessa did a double take. "Was I mistaken when you predicted everything about Baby Noe, right down to his father's reaction when I spelled it correctly?"

His mouth twisted in a wry grin. "That's a parlor trick. Angels aren't linear in time, not the way you are. I just hopped ahead to the next birth, noted what happened, and narrated it back to you."

Tessa took a long moment to process this. Then, "Can you explain that to me?"

"You're not strictly linear in space. Look, I know this is confusing." He shook his head. "I've seen enough human souls figuring it out when they first enter Heaven. Your species thinks of time as a series of train cars, where you pass through one moment in order to get to the next. But imagine the way you meander through the rooms in your house. You can enter different places, go to different areas, and you don't have to work through all the rooms in order."

Tessa nodded.

"Angels don't have to go through time in linear order either, but an angel's ability to shift around in time is limited to certain pockets. I can't step back to the Industrial Revolution, for example, and I can't pop ahead to the year 2025 to figure out which stocks you ought to invest in.”

Tessa’s eyebrows raised. “Or the winning lottery numbers?”

“That I can do.” He smiled. “I can’t tell you, but I could get them.”

Tessa sighed. “You’re not fun.”

“Each pocket of time is closed by pinch-points where I’m forced into linear time the same way you are, in my experience usually around major turning points. They don’t necessarily line up with other angels’ points, either, so when every angel in a local district finds himself inhabiting linear time simultaneously, you can be sure it’s a big deal.”

Tessa tilted her head. “Do you have to live through every moment in a segment before you can proceed through?”

“We can skip the boring stuff.” He laughed. “It all comes naturally, and it’s easy to manipulate events so they happen simultaneously once we get the hang of it. You can’t find your keys for three minutes, for example, and then you find out they were there in your pocket all along. But that short delay means you’re still at home when an emergency phone call comes. Angels move around in time to make that sort of assistance easier.”

Tessa let off a long breath. “Okay, but now what you’ve said makes even less sense. Even if you were surprised, once you knew the Americans were going to attack the church, why not go back in time and stop it?”

“Because once you’ve been through a moment, it’s fixed.” Martin spread out his hands on the table, and it lit up like a tremendous labor and delivery progress chart.

Tessa recoiled, then extended a hand to touch the lines of light while Martin kept speaking. The light didn't feel any different, and it didn't illuminate her fingertips. "Let's say you admit a mom and she's two centimeters, laboring well." That line filled in on the chart. "But then you get impatient and want to see how it all turns out, so you jump ahead to the birth."

Now another line filled in three quarters of the way down the bottom of the page, the baby's gender and weight, and the time of delivery. Martin continued, "Whatever you do afterward, that line will never change. You can go back in time and increase her comfort level, find better positions for her to labor in, give her a snack, put her in the tub..." One by one, every other line on the chart filled in. "But you can't change the time of the delivery because by jumping ahead, you fixed that moment in time."

The light-chart vanished, and Tessa started. "But what if you're not the one who jumped ahead? What if the mother's guardian did that? Or my guardian? Or the birth center's guardian?"

Martin shrugged. "That wouldn't affect my experience."

"It should."

Martin looked amused. "I told you it was complicated. It's easy to understand once you're actually doing it."

"I'll take your word on it." Tessa bit her lip. "What you're implying is that you jumped too far ahead?"

Martin nodded.

"And then you couldn't stop the destruction of the church?"

He nodded again.

"But you tried?"

"Of course I tried! I went before God and begged for the chance to do it over again!" Martin's eyes shimmered orange over the black. "I combed through the city and got as many people out of harm's way beforehand as I could. All of us did. But after I'd finished with that pocket, with the church in rubble and the relic in the hands of the American soldiers, I felt myself pulled into linear time. I was called home, and my assignment ended."

His voice had dropped to a breath.

"I'm sorry," Tessa whispered.

Head down, Martin sat with his wings clamped to his body. She wanted to hug him, but since he had no body, she probably couldn't touch him. Would he even want her to?

The silence stretched, and again that grief washed up against Tessa's heart. What was it like for an angel to receive an assignment from God? She'd been fired once from a job, but even though that had been her own fault, she hadn't felt what Martin was feeling. She'd just gotten another job and worked harder at doing things the proper way. This gut-twisting sensation felt more like the disemboweling pangs of sudden grief. She'd suffered two miscarriages herself, and that had been only a portion of what washed through Martin decades after the loss of his church. He was feeling not only grief, but also failure.

"Martin?" Tessa softened her tone. "Do the other angels blame you for how it turned out?"

Martin huffed. "No. Not at all."

"Does God?"

After a hesitation, she felt him negate it.

That was curious. "Have you asked Him?"

Martin drew back. "No."

"Why not?"

"Because—" He looked up, frustrated. "Because how do you think it would feel? *Maritenael, I hold nothing against you. Besides, we're all charitable here, and no one will blame you for failing to take care of the one little thing I assigned you to protect.*" He shuddered. "I want that relic back. Once you find that relic, we can return it to Barlassina. With the relic in hand, the Barlassinesi families will agree to restore the church. The church will live again, and then I can present myself to God and report my assignment was successfully completed."

Martin's white-knuckled urgency flooded her. She said, "Can you jump into the future to learn where it's going to turn up again?"

"It's beyond the next pinch-point." For some reason his words made her shiver. "I can't go forward far enough to pinpoint it."

Gary showed in the doorway. "Terry, are you talking to the angel?" When she assented, he said, "I have some questions for him, if he doesn't mind."

Tessa looked at Martin, who said, "Fire away."

Gary said, "What American platoon was it? If you give me their number, I can get the names of the soldiers."

"Fifth Platoon of F Company, 304th Infantry Regiment of the 76th Infantry Division," said Martin, which Tessa repeated, "along with five members of the Eighth Platoon, which had been destroyed during a fight in the hills."

Gary said, "Do you know which soldier took the relic?"

Martin said, "The sergeant carried it out of the church. I didn't see who had it afterward."

Tessa related this.

Gary said, "That may be enough for me to do some tracking. The identities of the soldiers will be on record. Thanks."

Tessa watched Gary leave, then turned back to Martin. No longer glassy-eyed and faint, instead he drilled his gaze into her.

Oh boy. Tessa braced herself.

The air glittered around him. "Did you dig up enough information for your new patient intake form?"

Averting her eyes, Tessa clenched her jaw.

"Then I'll be going," and with that the angel left.

FIVE

"Let me see your little darling!" Tessa crooned as she entered the birth suite.

The mom beamed, shifting up in the queen-sized bed so Tessa could see the swaddled bundle lying between her and the father. Dad, of course, lay snoring on the opposite side.

Tessa adjusted the lights to keep them low, then took the baby into her arms. "He's a big one. Sarah said ten pounds."

The mom laughed. "I did think I was carrying a bit more baby this time."

"Mom's always right. How are you feeling?"

Tessa assessed the baby while asking questions, noting the mother's bleeding, her pain level (practically nothing based on external signs, which the mom affirmed), and then handing the baby back in order to take the mother's blood pressure and temperature. All normal, all good.

"Dad's wiped out," Tessa said. So far their conversation had all been a hush, barely louder than the father's rattling breaths. "Sometimes I wonder if it isn't harder on them."

The mom said, "Probably not!" and they both laughed.

The baby stirred, pivoting his face side-to-side while smacking his lips. Tessa handed him to the mom, who positioned him across her lap and exposed one breast. Tessa adjusted a pillow beneath the baby to support him. The mom flinched as he latched on, so Tessa checked the baby's mouth, then flipped his lower lip so he didn't have it caught between his jaw and the areola. The mom relaxed with a sigh.

"He's taking to it like a champ." Tessa adjusted the mom's arm so the baby's head was better angled.

Sitting at the foot of the bed, Tessa asked if the mom had any questions about her delivery, reviewing the chart and explaining some of the details the mom had missed last night while working hard. Assessing her mood, Tessa decided this mom had a positive view of her delivery, and she made a note of that alongside the blood pressure and temperature.

Since the baby was nursing contentedly, Tessa helped the mom lie down alongside him to keep feeding, then left them alone. She'd complete her evaluation later. She'd scheduled a full day of patients, and she could hear the phone ringing in the front office. Another busy day at the Milliston Common Birth Center.

Ten minutes later, the receptionist came to Tessa with the portable phone. "Amanda Erickson is on the phone. She's got some questions and might want to come in."

Tessa took it into her office. "Amanda! How are you? You're twenty-six weeks now, right?"

Amanda's voice, bright but tense, answered with agreement, and then a description of a weird pain up the side of her leg. "Sounds like your sciatic nerve," said Tessa. "Try stretching it out, and alternate heat and cold on it every ten minutes for about an hour. If that doesn't help," she added, "call me back tomorrow and we'll set you up with a chiropractor who specializes in pregnant women. The one we refer to has worked miracles according to some of his previous patients."

Amanda laughed. "You know, as long as it's nothing wrong with the baby, I'm okay. I was just afraid it might mean labor was starting."

"Not at all. You need to bake that critter another twelve weeks." As Tessa jotted a note to place in Amanda's folder, she caught her phone lighting up in her peripheral vision. "We can fit you in today if you feel nervous, but this sounds to me like a straightforward pregnancy discomfort. Make sure to call back if you get worried, though."

Amanda's voice softened. "I'm sorry to bother you over nothing."

Tessa rejoined, "I love to be bothered over nothing. I love nothing better than something, and you know I'd rather you call."

The early morning rapidly filled with similar callbacks: moms worried about this or that little thing that wasn't worth a visit, two worried about something that was worth a visit in the next couple of days, and then one they absolutely needed to see this morning. For a moment, Tessa debated referring the woman directly to Dr. Cravey, their backup obstetrician, but she also realized a 10 a.m. blood pressure check at the birth center was faster than the woman could get seen at the OB clinic anyhow. She fit her between the nine and ten o'clock appointments.

The nine o'clock patient arrived, and Tessa did a standard assessment. All good, although the mom had a lot of scary questions courtesy of relatives butting in with their childbirth horror stories. *I labored for six days, and then my spleen came out with the baby!* Tessa had heard them all and had prepared answers for them all as well. "See that building?" she often said, pointing to the cement shoebox on the corner two blocks away. "That's where the ambulance is stationed. EMTs can be here in sixty seconds. You can be in the hospital ten minutes after that. That's faster than the doctor can get to the hospital when they page her from her office. You're fine."

At 9:45, Tessa met their fitted-in patient in the waiting area. She asked the woman to pee in a cup, then set her up with the blood pressure cuff and confirmed the reading was sky-high. "I want you to lie down on your left side for ten minutes so I can take it again." Tessa kept any worry from her voice. "Let's see if it goes down."

Karen came through waving a few pieces of paper. "Letters for our state senators."

"Write one for me too."

"Already ahead of you. I'll have letters written for everyone I know by tomorrow."

Tessa laughed.

The ten o'clock patient arrived, and Tessa apologized for the delay as she returned to the woman side-lying in her office.

With two minutes until she'd take the blood pressure again, she checked her phone: Gary had called. His voicemail said, "Terry? If you get a minute today, I found a list of names of the American soldiers. I want to run them by your informant."

Tessa hung up with a grin. Her *informant*. Indeed.

"Okay," she said, "time to check that blood pressure."

One minute later, Tessa was on the phone with the backup obstetrician. "I have a gift for you," she said, and Dr. Cravey replied in his low, amused voice, "I hate when you send patients to me. You know that. Should I see her here, or should I admit her directly?"

Tessa glanced at the patient: that drawn face, the fear in her eyes. High blood pressure, protein in the urine, sparkling headaches, dizziness: that meant preeclampsia, bad for mom and worse for the baby. "I'd like her admitted directly, and I'm going to send Sarah with her. She's worried."

It was two o'clock before Tessa had enough time to call Gary. "What do you want my informant to do?"

"Actually, I went ahead and did it anyhow. Four soldiers from those platoons are still alive, and I tracked down all of them. I asked to interview them about a piece for Veterans Day. One turned me down, but the other three agreed. Two are on this coast, and the third is in California, so I'll interview him over the phone. It's not how I wanted to handle things, but it's better than nothing."

Tessa said, "You're a trained professional. I figured you could manage."

"I've also got an interview lined up with two dealers in relics and a church historian who runs a website." Gary chuckled. "So tell your informant I'm on the case, but thanks for his help."

With a few minutes until she needed to be moving again, Tessa said, "Martin?"

Her voice wavered, surprising her. That final look he'd given her last night disturbed her more than she'd cared to admit.

Martin appeared, bright-eyed, his wings in a smart curve. "What took you so long?"

"What's it to you?" Tessa rocked back on her office chair. "I thought you skip the boring parts."

Martin paused, his feathers fluffing. "Oh, do I tell you about the timestream? I'd been wondering whether I should explain that."

Tessa blinked. "So...you haven't been back to yesterday yet?"

This made things awkward. Someday she would be expecting this cheerful version of Martin because their last encounter had been pleasant, only he'd show up infuriated because she'd maneuvered him into disclosing what he didn't want to. And if she wanted to apologize, how could she apologize until she knew she had met a Martin who remembered the event she was apologizing for...and for whom it had been recent?

"I guess I should head over to yesterday, then?" Martin settled himself on the bed. *I am not one of your clients,* he'd said last night, but here he was, playacting as one. "I hopped over to Gary's, and I don't recognize the names of any of the soldiers. I've taken a quick run by all their guardians, though, and I recognize all four." His eyes narrowed. "They recognized me too, I'll add."

Tessa bristled. "Hold on—if you can talk to these guys' guardians, just ask them what they did with the relic!"

Martin straightened. "Why would they tell me?"

"Because they know? Because they'd want to help?"

Martin cocked his head and frowned, and the puzzled expression disarmed Tessa.

"They don't want to help you?" Tessa ventured.

Martin stiffened. "Why would they not want to help?"

"Because—" But then she hesitated. If she said, "Because you said it's your fault the relic got taken in the first place," he'd realize she had gotten information from him that he hadn't intended to give. So she regrouped. "Look, I obviously don't know how guardian angels think. I can barely comprehend how you think. Why wouldn't they tell you if you asked?"

Martin leaned forward. "Stealing and looting are wrong—most of the time. In this case, you can add in the deaths of at least a few civilians and the destruction of a building. These men are bearing the temporal guilt of those wrongs on their hearts."

Tessa exclaimed, "You can judge someone's soul?"

Martin shook his head. "It's more of a deduction thing. Since the relic is still hidden, that means the one who has it is still carrying his guilt, otherwise his guardian could talk about it freely. But because the condition of a man's heart is a sacred trust between him and God, his guardian would never talk about it with another angel."

"You're kidding me!" Tessa sat forward. "What if you really need that information?"

Martin flinched. "Why would I need to know the details of how someone behaved badly?"

"For one thing, so you can help him set it straight! Maybe the guy who has the relic is looking for a way to make it right. If you knew who had it, you could tell Gary, and Gary could give him a mailing box with the Barlassina church address on it and a whole lot of postage.

'Sometimes I just leave these things lying around by accident,' he could say, 'and oops, I also left a roll of packing tape right here. I'm going to leave the room now for a few minutes, and hey, I'll be stopping by the post office later today, if you want me to mail anything for you.'"

Martin laughed out loud, but Tessa's throat burned. "They're making it harder to find the relic," she added. "That's obstructing justice!"

"Believe me, Terry," Martin said with his voice suddenly soft, "justice isn't obstructed. Delayed, sometimes. But never obstructed."

Before Tessa could retort, she noticed the muted glow in his eyes, the abrupt drop of his gaze. He felt responsible for the loss of the church: what kind of justice was he anticipating?

It felt unfair to be holding this conversation now, with information he didn't know she had. But then again, he seemed to have quite a bit of information about Tessa, Tessa's family, Tessa's history, and Tessa's future. Maybe this evened the score with just a bit of conversational justice.

"How about this, then?" Tessa cocked her head. "If these men aren't guilty, and their guardians say nothing about the relic, then that's guilt by association. It predisposes you to think the men participated in stealing the relic, and therefore these silent angels are destroying the men's reputation."

"And of course," Martin fired back, "angels are stupid and never realized this in the thousands of years before the perceptive and brilliant Teresa Testerman appeared on the scene. That's why we never discuss our charges' shortcomings—specific shortcomings, that is, not generalities—with other angels who are currently deployed."

Tessa said, "So the new-guardian-angel support groups don't have a bunch of angels sitting around griping that no matter what they do, their human keeps lying?"

"We share tactics sometimes," Martin said. "That's different."

"How is it different to ask, 'Hey, how do I get a human to stop stealing?' than to say 'My human is stealing?'"

Martin said, "We're charitable here."

Tessa straightened. He'd said the same last night, only with a different edge. "You wouldn't want them to be charitable to you the same way." Yes, this was very unfair. He was going to be furious when he fit it all together.

On the other hand, maybe he said it later because she'd just said it to him now. Meaning there was no causality: she was quoting what he said last night, and when it came time for him to say it, he'd be quoting what she said today. The timeline thing was starting to give Tessa a headache. Show her a laboring woman any day—that she could understand.

Martin flexed his wings. "Then I'd like you to be charitable to me and believe that I would never ask another guardian to break confidence with his charge. Period."

Tessa opened her hands. "Fine. But now you've visited these men, and none of them seems to be the one who took the relic. Meaning your quest may not be fruitful after all."

Martin still maintained that unnerving spotlight-stare into Tessa's eyes. "No, it's going to emerge back into time. I can sense that much."

Tessa said, "But it's in time now."

"No, it's not. It's hidden, buried." Martin's gaze grew suddenly earnest. "You know how you can sense during a delivery when dilation is almost complete just by the way the mom is behaving? I can sense that the relic's hidden time is almost complete too. We need to be with it when it's born back into the world."

That evening, as Gary passed the polenta to Joe, he said, "Terry, I found out a bit more about your friend."

Tessa tensed. "Which friend?"

"Your friend Peter of Verona." Gary chuckled. "He's an interesting character, to say the least."

Alex said, "Mom's got a boyfriend?"

"You don't think she's out all night delivering babies or something, do you?" Mark shot back. "Of course she's got a boyfriend."

"If you don't mind," Tessa said, "your father was talking."

"I don't mind," Gary said, pouring Eric a glass of milk. "I'm feeling intrigued by this revelation. I too always thought you were off delivering babies."

Tessa took some polenta, then spooned some for Eric.

Gary continued, "Peter of Verona was a thirteenth-century Catholic saint. He was born into a dissenting movement, then got converted by Saint Dominic and became a Dominican himself. He went back to the movement he'd belonged to and began preaching to convert them."

Tessa said, "What movement?"

"Catharists, who I guess believed in a dualist system with two gods, one good and one evil."

Joe said, "Like Zoroastrianism?"

Mark said, "Or maybe like Satan got an upgrade."

Gary said, "Exactly. The Catholic Church didn't like it for a number of reasons, and they declared it a heresy. Peter of Verona was then appointed an inquisitor to ferret out his former pals."

Tessa sighed. "Maybe he's not my friend."

"Maybe he is," Gary said, "because he was only an inquisitor for six months and never convicted anyone. The only thing we know he did was to declare clemency for anyone who believed in the heresy or was sympathetic to it. But that wasn't good enough for his former co-heretics because at some point, the Catharists hired an assassin to kill him."

Mark said, "What happened?"

All the boys were watching their father with wide eyes. Gary said, "Peter and a companion named Domenico were traveling near Barlassina, and an assassin named Carino of Balsamo attacked them. He whacked Peter in the head with an axe, and according to the legend, Pete then dipped his finger in the blood and wrote the beginning of the Nicene Creed, *I believe in one God, the Father Almighty*."

"He did not!" exclaimed Joe, even as Mark and Alex were yelling, "That is so cool!"

Brian looked intimidated. "Really?"

"That's the legend," Gary said. "You know those Italians."

"No," Tessa murmured. "What about *those Italians*?"

Gary laughed.

"Watch it, Dad," said Joe.

"There's another version that he recognized his attacker and started to recite the creed before he was struck," Gary said. "That makes a little more sense than writing with your head cut off."

"Sweetie," Tessa said, "let's not talk about decapitation at the dinner table."

"What happened after they cut off his head?" said Alex.

Gary said, "The assassin stabbed him through the heart."

Tessa slammed her hand on the table, and Gary looked chastened. "Sorry, Terry. That's the end of the grim stuff. Peter's body was laid to rest in Milan. His companion Dominic died as well. The assassin converted, and now there's a cult to him too, although he's not a saint, just venerable. Less than a year later, Peter of Verona, or Peter the Martyr, was canonized. That's the fastest saint-making on record."

Tessa said, "Martyrdom is a good way to do that."

Gary shook his head, swallowed, then set down his fork. "No, they were attributing miracles to him even before he died, mostly healings. Sainthood was pretty much a given. And there are quite a few relics of our friend Pete, although most of them are of one of his fingers."

Alex said, "So not only did he write with his head cut off, but he gave us the finger too!"

Tessa fixed a glare on Alex that elicited a quiet, "Sorry."

"I wonder how Barlassina got part of his heart," Tessa said, reaching for her water glass.

"Those Italians again," Gary said. "Someone must have found the knife. Or pulled it out. Or something like that. Your mom said it was from the weapon, but your informant might be able to tell us more."

Tessa said, "I'll ask if he was there when it happened. Apparently he wasn't much for travel."

The boys started chattering about axes and decapitations, but Gary said, "There's one thing more you need to know," and Tessa looked up. "He's the patron saint of inquisitors."

Joe shouted, "No one expects the Spanish inquisition!"

Alex snorted. "It'd be the Italian inquisition, dorkface."

"Our chief weapon—"

Tessa raised her voice. "Boys, cool it!"

Gary said, "But he's also the patron saint of midwives."

Tessa's eyes widened. As the boys went back into the Monty Python Inquisition sketch, she met Gary's gaze across the table.

Gary said in a voice just loud enough to hear, "So maybe he is your friend."

SIX

Gary had more to say about Peter of Verona, but rather than the theology or the politics, Tessa kept dwelling on him as patron of midwives. Martin said she'd been chosen for a reason. Was this why? Because thus far, she'd done nothing special to forward this quest. At the current moment, in fact, she had no intention of doing so.

"Why do Catholics save body parts?" Joe said.

"Come on," said Mark. "Wouldn't you love to have George Washington's finger in a case? Or maybe Alexander Hamilton's heart with a bullet in it?"

"Yeah, it's cool, but what's the point?" Joe shrugged. "So you go and look, and it's a finger. The leftover body parts don't do anything, right? It's not like you pray with the thing in your hand and God appears and grants you three wishes."

Gary laughed. "Although I wish it did work that way!"

Having wondered that herself, Tessa listened while pouring Eric more milk.

"I had to look this up," said Gary. "Protestants say it's superstition, by the way. Catholics and Orthodox are the ones who keep relics." He paused. "You remember when your grandfather died, how your uncles and I divided up some of his things? I got the picture frames, and Uncle Al took his tools? Not because we don't have picture frames and Al didn't have tools, but because they were your grandfather's picture frames and your grandfather's tools."

Mark said, "And now I've got your finger!"

"Pull my finger," intoned Joe.

"For sentimental reasons," added Alex, and Mark howled with laughter.

Joe added, "You know those Italians," and all three older boys roared. Brian tucked his head and smirked.

Alex added, "Gives a whole different dimension to that got-your-nose game!"

Gary lowered his voice, his perennial "settle down, boys" tone. "It's a way of feeling close to someone you love but who's gone."

Had Martin saved any parts of the church for himself, maybe a bit of crumbled stone or burnt wood? Not being material themselves, did angels not feel the need to be close the material part of a thing they loved? Or was the compulsion to touch the thing-ness of what they loved even stronger, since the material nature was something so incredibly different than themselves?

She blew off a long breath. Great. She was wondering about whether angels kept mementos. Next she should go into the backyard with a rainbow to rope a unicorn.

Then she straightened. "Gary? Am I mistaken, or are American soldiers not supposed to loot and torch the territory they go through?"

"They're not," said Gary. "But there's no court martial on record for any of the soldiers, and in fact they all received an honorable discharge. Which raises another question: why weren't they disciplined?"

Tessa said, "What if they sold the relic? Or left it somewhere?"

"Your mom says they may not have taken it at all, but they're our best lead. It could have been one of the Italian factions, or it could have gotten destroyed when the church caved in." Gary pursed his lips, and Tessa didn't correct him that Martin had confirmed the theft. "I'm not looking forward to interrogating a bunch of nonagenarians about a crime older than I am, but hey, that's what crack investigative reporting is all about."

Tessa pointed at him. "You were never an investigative reporter."

Gary shrugged. "You'd be surprised what you can coax people to talk about if you ask the right way."

Guilt twinged through Tessa. She returned her attention to dinner.

"I plan to call the first one tonight. The second of the four lives in Maine, and I've got a train ticket to talk to him tomorrow. If you want to come, I'd love the company."

Tessa frowned. "I'm not working tomorrow, but we'd have to bring Eric."

Eric looked up. "Go where?"

"Maine. On a train."

Eric brightened. Brian groused, "No fair. I want to go too."

"You have school."

"Eric has school!"

Tessa said. "One half-day of kindergarten is not going to affect whether he gets into college. Finish your dinner."

Brian said, "Neither will one day of second grade."

Eric made a triumphant face at Brian, who shoved him, and then Tessa had to deal with the ever-practical details of raising a family rather than daydreaming about angels, relics, and old soldiers.

Gary made the call from his office, and Tessa sat crocheting while he spoke. She had to admit to a vague curiosity as to how Gary planned to get the information, but she also figured she somehow owed it to Martin to remain.

Gary began the conversation genially, explaining that he was writing an article for *US News* to come out around Veterans Day. He thanked the gentleman not only for his time in granting this interview but also for his selfless service to his country.

Michael O'Mara replied, "It was what you did back then. I got called to serve, and I did."

Was that how Martin had felt, called to serve a church high in the hills of nowhere? Like Tessa getting a midnight call to attend a delivery, was it just that simple? Called to serve, you left to do your duty without considering the sacrifices as extraordinary?

Gary had O'Mara on speaker phone, although he spoke into a headset and typed notes at the same time. He started with general questions about O'Mara's term of service, what he remembered of the war, and the other men in his platoon. "Do you still keep in contact?" Gary asked, and O'Mara said yes, he did.

"Only four of us left alive now. But something like that you don't forget."

Gary said, "I imagine that bonds you. You must have seen a lot of horrors."

"More than I'd care to see again," said O'Mara, "but I'd serve once more if I had to."

Gary said, "So you have no regrets?"

O'Mara sounded taken aback. "What man doesn't have regrets? We all live with the might-have-been questions. The things we wish we'd done differently."

Gary said, "Go on."

O'Mara had a scratchy, deep old-man voice, but it momentarily lost its weariness. "There's nothing else to say. You're a young man and you go to do your duty. Then you get out there and realize there's a big difference between saluting your flag and shooting another man because he saluted his. Oh, you tell yourself he's the devil. You know he wants to kill you. So you shoot at him. But after a while, you're just doing what's necessary to survive."

Gary said, "So you never hated the Germans or the Italians?"

"The Germans, yeah. They did awful things. But not the Italians, no, I don't think I ever did."

Tessa could hear the honesty in the man's voice. Gary changed the topic to the loss of some of O'Mara's comrades in arms, and they chatted about the last year of the war. "By the end," O'Mara said, "we were stripped to the bone. We picked up soldiers from another squad, but all those were dead by the time we met back up with the main brigade. It was just us on our own."

Gary said, "That was in northern Italy?"

O'Mara agreed it was.

Gary said, "Did you happen to pass through the town of Barlassina? At the end of 1944?"

O'Mara said, "I have no idea all the towns we went through. Possibly. I'd have to see it on a map, but even then, a lot of it's a blur. I got a commendation for a battle I don't even remember fighting in because after a while, every hill where you dig in for the night starts to look the same as every other hill."

"But you were in northern Italy?"

"I must have been, because we got over to Montecassino."

That name was familiar, at least. Tessa remembered something about that being a pivotal battle.

Gary said, "Montecassino was an abbey, right? It must have been terrible to attack a church."

O'Mara hesitated. "I tried not to think about those things. We were under orders, and they said it was a strategic position."

"But what if it wasn't?" Gary said, "A church in Barlassina got looted and torched. The Italians say it was by American soldiers, but the Army's got no record of it."

"I never torched anything." O'Mara's voice picked up a quick edge, and Tessa blinked at the shift from soft generalities to urgent specifics.

Gary said, "I wondered if you knew who might have been there. I'm sure sometimes that kind of thing happens, and as someone on the ground, you might have heard rumors."

"I heard a thousand rumors." O'Mara's voice grew sharp like barbed wire. "During a war, you never know what you're hearing is a lie or an accursed lie. You get your orders and you do your thing and you keep your head down. I never torched anything."

Gary said, "Fair enough. Tell me a bit about Montecassino."

Even though Gary backpedaled, O'Mara answered with bridled anger and few words.

While Gary was asking a question about O'Mara's return home, Tessa's cell phone rang. She took it in the hallway. "It's time!" sang out a mom. "Contractions are four minutes apart, and—"

Tessa waited while the mom paused for thirty seconds during a contraction. She made a note of the time, then went into the living room for her "labor and delivery" bag. The medical equipment would be waiting on a hook in the garage, but this was her bag of late-night-labor entertainment: more yarn and another crochet hook.

The mom resumed speaking, "That was a bit stronger. Anyhow, they're about four minutes apart and lasting thirty seconds."

"How's your pain level?"

"Manageable. I'm walking around, doing things. I just put in a load of laundry because I forgot I needed to wash up some baby clothes!"

"Good call. Did your water break?"

Tessa still had the mom on the phone when she stopped talking to make it through another contraction. Again Tessa checked the clock: four and a half minutes. Yep, it was baby time.

She tied on her boots, then got her coat. With a signal to Gary, she was gone.

At close to midnight, Tessa left the laboring mom and her husband in their bedroom to relax until active labor started. She allowed herself no such relief: sitting on their worn grey couch with a mug of coffee on the end table, she crocheted a baby hat.

New moms loved watching her crochet while they were in labor. Quite a few told her later that if the midwife felt free to sit with yarn and a hook, making something for the newborn, then of course everything was fine. Tessa figured she was offering rock-solid proof that she wasn't worried, even when she was. Plus at the end, there would be a hat.

Now, though, she had no worries. This mom wasn't even in active labor yet, and she certainly hadn't yet hit transition, those back-to-back final contractions when she'd need all her energy to cope. Therefore it was better for her to get as relaxed as possible, even if she couldn't sleep. The father might even get a nap. The house had fallen silent, the couple's other children overnighting with a neighbor while awaiting their newest member.

As she crocheted, a prickle came at the back of her mind.

Ignoring it, she chain stitched to begin the next round of the hat.

Another prickle.

Mouth tight, she continued crocheting.

Again it came.

Fine. "What is it, Martin?"

Martin appeared, his wings melting into the darkness of a living room illuminated only by the lamp shining over Tessa's shoulders.

"You need to tread carefully with those soldiers."

"I'm well aware of how to deal with human beings who may not want to be cooperative." Tessa's hook shot into the work, caught the yarn, and looped it back again. "We're doing what you want." Looking up, she said, "Hey, you didn't tell me Peter of Verona was also the patron of midwives."

The angel monotoned, "Then that's two categories you fall under."

Tessa's eyes narrowed. Of course. Peter of Verona was also the patron of inquisitors. "Are you saying you're in time after our Barlassina conversation? I didn't know what to make of it the last time you visited, when you were enjoying yourself."

His eyes glittered.

In a battle of wills, Tessa knew how to proceed. "I have a right to know what's going on."

Still that level stare from the angel.

"You approached *me*, in case you forgot." Tessa continued crocheting. "You're the one who wants my help. I haven't asked you for anything except an explanation why I should want to go hunting for relics that don't matter to me." She raised her eyes. "Oh, my mistake. I asked you to help keep the birth center in business, and you said you can't. But I'm helping you anyhow."

"Just tread carefully," said Martin. "And for your information, there are nine patrons of midwifery."

"Wait." Tessa lowered her crocheting. "Since we're talking about requests, I have one. Two, actually. First, don't call me Terry. The only people in the world who are allowed to call me Terry either gave birth to me or are married to me."

A feeling akin to vertigo swelled up from the angel. Then, "My apologies. I didn't realize that would be a problem, *Tessa*."

She steeled herself. "And secondly, you confuse me when you pop around in time. The last time I saw you, you showed up in a good mood, but this time you're angry—"

"I'm not angry," Martin interrupted.

"Well you're doing an excellent imitation of it." Tessa narrowed her eyes. "Here's the score: you may love the time-hopping game, but it's making my life difficult. It's extra work needing to figure out when you are before I begin talking to you. Until we find this relic, would you mind staying linear in time, or at least mostly linear?"

Tessa didn't sense irritation from him, so she returned to crocheting.

"I've been staying mostly linear." Martin had geared down a bit. "You ought to be warned there are a few times my past has already intersected your future."

"Going forward, can you keep your future and my future parallel, or whatever it is you say when you wander around the calendar like a teenage girl at the mall?" She looked up. "It would make interactions a lot more straightforward, and I'd know better how to deal with you."

Martin's outline sharpened against the dark background. "You don't have to deal with me. You just have to find the relic."

"That requires dealing with you. You give me instructions or I have questions, and that means we interact." She paused. "I'm not talking about managing you. You're hard to read because you're an entirely different species, and it gets tougher if I don't know what you already know or what you haven't gotten to yet."

Martin folded his arms. "My being linear would definitely make it harder for you to quote me back to myself."

Tessa hid her interior flinch, coming to the end of the round and chaining the next stitch to continue.

"I'm not giving up one of the only advantages we have in tracking the relic," Martin said, "but I'll try to limit how it affects you."

That was more concession than he ordinarily gave. Or would give. Whatever. "Thank you."

Martin said, "But I'm warning you that tomorrow's meeting is going to be fragile. I haven't been there, but I can feel it. I followed the events of tomorrow morning right up to the time of the meeting."

Tessa looked up. "Is this mom going to have her baby in time for me to get on the Downeaster with Gary? And don't go hopping ahead in time to fix her birth at ten a.m., because I need at least a cup of coffee before I get on that train."

Martin cracked a smile, and Tessa found herself responding with one of her own.

He put his hand on her head. "She'll have her baby, and you'll be on the train."

He vanished, leaving Tessa with the feeling that he didn't care to check further.

SEVEN

At 10:15, as the Amtrak train pulled out of North Station toward Maine, Tessa set up Eric with his juice box, a snack, and a coloring book.

Gary looked through his laptop bag, then glanced at Tessa. "Any other ideas what Martin meant by treading carefully? Because if he has specific instructions, I'd rather know now."

Tessa shrugged. "That's all he said. Not, 'Don't mention avocados.' I don't believe he was working with any tangible information."

Gary chuckled.

"What?"

He squeezed her hand. "I love you, but I have to admit it does my heart good that you're talking to a time-traveling celestial no one else can see."

"I love you, but don't laugh too hard. Next it will be aliens." She half-closed her eyes, then leaned in and kissed him. "How exactly do you plan to tread carefully?"

"I'll go by feel. Richard Pryce is in the early stages of dementia, according to his daughter. She said he was pleased to be interviewed, but she's concerned we might we stress him too much."

Tessa straightened her sweater, a cream-colored Celtic cable-knit. "And you didn't get anything else from O'Mara?"

"Half the time, when the subject thinks the interview is over, you can make a general comment and they'll suddenly come up with all this information and the best possible quotes. I tried that, but he shut me down. When we know more, I can call again." Gary glanced out the window. "There's a third veteran in Pittsburgh, and the last lives in Atlanta. I'll fly down to interview him on Friday. I think this is shaping up nicely."

Tessa said, "What if they genuinely don't have any information?"

Gary said, "Much as I hate to say this, my assignment isn't to find it. My assignment is to write an article about veterans and the looting of an Italian church. If we walk into this man's home and find a shrine to Saint Peter of Verona, I'll take pictures and try convincing him to hand it over. But beyond that, I'm only doing a human interest feature."

"As opposed to an angelic interest feature." Tessa helped Eric with his crayons, then looked into her canvas bag. She decided against a well-loved copy of Ina May Gaskin's *Spiritual Midwifery* and opted instead for the papers Karen had handed her. They amounted to a primer on How to Stop Bad Laws from Being Passed. "At least we got a day-trip out of it."

The ride to Maine took three and a half hours. Eric spent plenty of the ride palms-to-the-windows, commenting on every single thing on the New England coastline. Tunnels were both exciting and boring because of the dark. And throughout the trip Tessa produced an endless parade of snacks, drinks, and two special toys she had found in the attic for just this occasion.

With Eric properly invested in a coloring book, Tessa put a hand on Gary's knee and leaned close to him. In a low voice, she said, "Can we talk?"

Wide-eyed, Gary looked up. "You're not pregnant, are you?"

Tessa laughed. "I almost wish I was!"

Stunned, he clicked his laptop shut.

"The birth center may have to close." Tessa's voice trembled. "I didn't want to hit you with this before I knew what was going on, but there's legislation going through the state senate right now with language that would prevent insurance companies from paying for out-of-hospital births."

Gary's eyebrows raised. "How did that happen?"

"Hospital lobbyists added some language to a bill that was supposed to guarantee that insurance companies would pay for certain procedures surrounding a birth. It would have been great for women, except that they inserted a clause to the effect that if you don't offer those services, you're not a birth provider. Ergo, no payment."

"That's practically criminal." Gary's eyes narrowed. "When are they voting?"

"In a few weeks. Karen's mobilizing all the midwives in the state, but I'm not sure how likely we are to succeed. I mean, no politician's going to vote against a bill making sure women get their births covered by insurance. So it's a matter of getting the language amended, and we don't have the same kind of lobby that the hospitals have."

Gary said, "I'll help."

When Tessa met his eyes, the steel in his expression was as if she'd been wobbling on a high wire and someone on the platform had grabbed her hand. She took a deep breath, and for the first time in days, her lungs fully filled.

"You could have told me about this sooner," Gary said, hugging her. "How long have you known?"

"I'd only just told you about the relic." Her eyes dropped. "You were already doing so much for me."

"We're a team, Terry. I'm not doing everything as a favor." He took her hand, and Eric looked up from his coloring book. "Don't treat me like we're in contract negotiations. We're partners. I'll write every newspaper editor I know on your say-so. We moved from Delaware so you could practice legally, and we'll move again if we have to. But first, we'll give them a fight in the state house. They won't know what hit them."

Closing her eyes, Tessa squeezed his hand.

"What's Karen already done?"

"She's got names and addresses for every state senator, and we're leaning hard on the Joint Committee on Public Health. Massachusetts only has about five hundred home births a year, so there aren't a lot of us, though." Tessa tried to sort her thoughts. "I'm compiling morbidity statistics for our birth center, and I'll be trying to gather stats for the hospital. We're going to show that we provide cheaper care for low-risk women, and that the option to choose an attended out-of-hospital birth needs to be safeguarded. The system is working just fine if they only leave us alone."

Gary nodded. "You get me those numbers and names of other midwives, and I'll get articles in every Boston paper I can and two in Worcester. Half the local ones too."

He looked up at her, then chuckled. "They'll regret messing with you."

The train passed a cow pasture dotted with car-sized cylinders of straw drying in the sunlight. She met his eyes.

"I love you," Gary said.

"I love you too." She leaned closer, and they kissed.

They took a cab from the Amtrak station to a ranch-style home on a quiet state route, surrounded by trees and cow pastures. It had two chimneys, one in the center of the house and the other on the far end, both of them smoking. Hands linked, Gary and Tessa walked up the cracked cement pavement, lined by flower beds bursting with hardy mums.

A woman in her sixties opened the door. "I'm sorry," she said, "but there's been a bit of a problem. My father no longer wants to speak to you. He doesn't even want to let you into the house."

Behind the woman emerged shouts. "Tell them to get out of here! I'm not going to talk to them!"

Gary shook her hand. "You're Ellen Ashland, correct?" The woman nodded. "What changed your father's mind?"

"I don't know." And then, as Tessa had come to expect from her clients, Mrs. Ashland continued with exactly the reason why. "He got a phone call this morning, and as soon as he hung up, he told me not to let you in when you arrived today."

Tessa's heart stilled. "Was it from one of the other soldiers?"

Gary's eyes widened. And in that moment, Tessa knew this was the right group of men. Colluding.

Gary spoke to Mrs. Ashland calmly even as more shouts resounded from inside. *Martin*, Tessa thought, *are you around?* When she felt an answering prickle, she continued, *Can you search the house?*

She got the distinct impression that it didn't work that way.

Can you convince the man to let us talk to him?

Again, as with the state house, it really didn't work that way.

You'll have to explain that one to me later. She looked at Mrs. Ashland. "Would it be all right if I spoke to your father? I'm not writing an article."

Behind the woman came more shouts. "They're here to take me away! I don't want to go away!"

Mrs. Ashland looked over her shoulder, then back at Tessa. "He's very agitated."

Eric said, "I have to go to the bathroom."

As it turned out, Mrs. Ashland was enough of a humanitarian that she allowed them entrance to the house not because of journalistic integrity or a love of unsolved mysteries, but to let a five-year-old use the toilet.

Mr. Richard Pryce thumped into the kitchen with a wooden cane. "Get out! I'm not talking to you! You're going to take me away!"

"Dad! Their little boy is using the bathroom. Leave them alone."

Gary hadn't taken off his coat, and he stayed near the door. "I promise we won't take you away. Did Michael O'Mara say that last night?"

"Yes, he did, and he told me you're a liar and out to get us! Get out!"

Gary raised his hands. "I'm not going to take anyone anywhere, and you don't have to talk to me. I'm not a police officer. But sir, I'm writing a magazine article about World War II veterans and their experiences. I cannot imagine why he thought I would take you away."

Tessa said, "Excuse me, Mr. Pryce? Your daughter is right here. She isn't going to let us ask any questions that would be embarrassing or intrusive. We want to hear your story." She lowered her voice a notch, as she would with a laboring mother in a state of panic. Low and slow. "It's important for the children growing up now, who have never endured the hardships you have, for them to understand the great sacrifices your generation made for our country and for freedom."

Pryce turned toward Tessa, then paused sharply. For a long time, he squinted at her. "Where do I know you from?"

"I can't imagine you do know me." Tessa chuckled. "I'm a midwife. Perhaps I delivered one of your grandchildren?"

"Great-grandchildren, too," said Ellen Ashland.

"Oh?" Tessa smiled. "Do you have pictures?"

Ellen showed her a row of photos on the wall. "These are my five grandchildren. My sister has two more."

"Wow." Tessa turned to Pryce. "Congratulations on seven great grandchildren!" She forced a cheerful note, same as she had for a patient with sky-high blood pressure and protein in the urine, "Do any of them live in Massachusetts? I used to teach third grade too, in Delaware. Maybe that's how you recognize me."

Ellen guided her father to a seat at the kitchen table. "No, none in Massachusetts. They live in Connecticut, New York, and Maine, but none in Massachusetts."

Pryce chanted in a low voice, "I know you. I know you."

Eric wandered out of the bathroom, then let out a delighted squeal as an old dog padded into the kitchen. "Can I play?"

The dog's tail wagged slowly, and Ellen said, "He's friendly."

Eric dropped to his knees and started patting the dog's head. "Good boy! Good boy!"

Pryce turned back to Tessa, still with concern in his eyes.

Tessa held up the box in her hands. "I brought chocolate-almond croissants."

(She'd asked for Martin's help in that regard. Angels could not share their charge's moral weaknesses, but it turned out they thought it acceptable to share a culinary weakness.)

Five minutes later, with coffee brewing and Mr. Pryce set up with a plate at the kitchen table, Ellen returned from tending the woodstove in the living room so they could start.

"Wood warms you three times," Gary said. "Once when you cut it, once when you stack it, and once when you burn it."

"Isn't that ever the truth?" Ellen chuckled. "Dad likes it warm in the living room too, so I'm constantly adding wood to both stoves."

Eric stayed with the dog, who seemed to want nothing more than to either flop at Eric's side and be adored or to go sit on Pryce's feet while Eric played with action figures.

Ellen started the interview with a caution. "Don't ask anything disturbing. I don't want him to get agitated."

Gary reached into his computer bag to click on his recorder (subtle) and brought his hand back holding a paper and pen. Notes were faster on the computer, but Pryce would clam up for a computer more than a notepad.

Gary said, "Why don't you tell me whatever you want? Maybe start with how you joined."

Pryce had a generic life-changing event at the head of his story: he got drafted.

Gary asked about those left behind at home. Pryce said the usual: mother, father, siblings, girlfriend. An older brother was also drafted.

For half an hour, Pryce talked about the beginning of the war, and Gary got down an outline of what he'd done, where he'd gone. For a long time, Pryce had been in France. There'd been hunger, a frozen winter, continuous exhaustion, constant losses. "You didn't have a choice but to survive or die," he said. During one fight, a hot shell landed on his arm and he'd had no time to quit firing in order to knock it off. When the firefight ended, the shell had smoldered through his sleeve and burnt his arm, but he hadn't even noticed.

One skirmish in southern France that had left another squad all but destroyed. "There were only five men left. We absorbed them into our platoon and kept on going to Italy."

Without sounding as if he'd been handed a Christmas present, Gary said blandly, "Where did you go after that?"

Pryce said, "We were headed to Montecassino."

Gary gave a disinterested, "Mm-hmm."

Tessa shivered. He was working the conversation, circling the snake around until it could bite its own tail and then draw in ever closer.

Gary sounded awed. "You guys must have been battered by then. You'd been overseas for over two years at that point, right?"

Pryce said, "Me, only a year. Most of the guys for longer. Our sergeant had been there since D-Day."

Gary didn't look up from taking notes. "You must have just wanted it to be over."

Pryce shook his head. "We did what we had to do."

Gary finished writing something, then looked up. The lack of sound filled Tessa's world. A snap from the woodstove. The scrape of a plate as Pryce took another croissant, followed by the rustle of Eric turning pages on a book.

Pryce looked again at Tessa, then rocked a little on his chair. "I know you. I know you."

Tessa rubbed his hand. "Sir, I would be honored to have known you. You defended freedom."

That's when she got a sense—not the way she got a sense from Martin, but through her midwife instinct—that Pryce disagreed. For a moment he was negating her the same way Martin had when she said he'd done a good job guarding the church.

We really could use an inquisitor right about now, Tessa thought. And then she remembered that Peter of Verona had only one recorded act as an inquisitor: an act of pardon.

She squeezed Pryce's hand. "Whatever happened in the war, no matter what any American soldier did, it was a long time ago. But America's freedom remains. That's something to be proud of."

Pryce shrank into his chair.

Gary said, "What did you do after the war?"

Pryce looked out the window and didn't answer. Ellen prompted, "You went into your father's business at the lumberyard, right, Dad?"

Pryce looked up, then asked her to repeat it. She did. "Yeah, my father's lumberyard."

Gary said, "And you married your girl, I presume?"

He shook his head. Ellen said, "Dad didn't actually meet Mom until a couple of years later. Right, Dad? You got engaged, but then you broke up?"

Tessa said, "Oh, that's a shame. I bet you spent two years wanting to get home to her, and then that."

Pryce said, "I broke it off. Let her marry someone else. She kept the ring."

Again the silence. The woodstove in the corner gave a few pops, and then it settled down too.

Ellen sounded cheerful. "But it worked out just fine. Mom and Dad were married fifty years."

"How many brothers and sisters did you have?" said Gary.

Pryce seemed to have checked out despite Gary's neutral line of questions, and Tessa watched him slipping away into the caverns of a history he'd just glossed over.

War can't leave you unchanged. Tessa knew that, but this was the first time she'd seen a man reliving the changes. How many wounded had he been forced to leave behind? How many had he killed? When he looked at Tessa, was he remembering a girlfriend the war had changed him too much to marry?

Gary said, "Did you ever interact with civilians in Italy or France?"

Tessa almost asked Gary to stop. But they'd come all this way, and Gary was asking gently. Pryce went back to rocking.

Ellen stood. "I think he may need to rest now. Thank you very much for everything."

"No, I'm the one who should thank you." Gary shook her hand, then shook Pryce's. Tessa gathered Eric and his books, and she patted the dog just to watch his slowly wagging tail swing faster. Gary put away his pad, saying, "I'm interviewing Italian civilians about what they saw during the war. It would be interesting if they'd ever met you. Mr. Pryce," he said abruptly, "were you ever in Barlassina?"

Pryce stiffened.

Ellen said, "No, he never was." She opened the front door. "He really needs to rest now. Thank you for your time. You can call me if you need to follow up on anything."

"The Barlassina citizens told me their church was destroyed by Americans," Gary said. "A relic was stolen, and the Italians want it back. It was the heart of that little town, and it's been missing for seventy years."

Ellen said, "That's terrible. Dad," she said, turning to her father, "you go ahead to bed, and I'll be with you in a minute."

Shaky beside the table, Pryce said in a whisper, "It wasn't my fault."

Gary said, "Go on. What should I tell them about their relic?"

Tessa and Ellen both moved to Pryce's side so he wouldn't fall, but Ellen reached him first. "Mr. Testerman, please!" Ellen exclaimed. "He's an old man! What good does it do talking about this now? These things happened seventy years ago!"

Gary said, "Seventy years didn't bring the relic back to that church. It isn't too late to set things right."

"What are you going to do? Throw him in prison for the last months of his life? For something he might not have done, or that might have been done under conditions you can't even dream of, and that he would never do again? For some piece of ornamented superstition?" Ellen pointed to the door. "Leave. I'll call the police if you don't go."

Tessa took Eric's hand. "My family came from Barlassina. If their relic comes back, it would save the town. That's all they want."

Ellen said, "We can't give you something we know nothing about. Good day."

She guided her father from the kitchen. Tessa and Gary took Eric outside, shutting the door behind them.

EIGHT

On the drive back from North Station, Tessa had Gary stop by MetroWest Hospital so she could check on her transfer patient. She found the mom in the maternity area, lying on her side and reading a book.

Tessa sussed out things to make sure the nurses weren't taking any punitive action toward her for being a midwifery patient (it happened rarely, but it still happened; gentle and sweet Dr. Cravey had brought down high holy hell on their heads in the past). Dr. Cravey was being cautious without assuming disaster could strike at any second. The best barometer was the mom's mood: she was a bit bored, a little stiff from lying in bed, but generally cheerful. Cravey had her blood pressure under control, and she reported the baby moving well.

Tessa slipped her a jar of unsalted macadamias, explaining that sometimes you could prevent eclampsia with a high-protein diet. "You can have the best of both worlds," Tessa added. "The medical care is right here. But the self-care is in your own choices, so you might as well have the protein. You don't need a prescription for nuts."

Dr. Cravey arrived before Tessa left, a solid man with grey hair, only a few inches taller than Tessa herself. He fumbled in his breast pocket for one of three pens he used to jot notes while he talked to the patient, always in a placid tone that put Tessa in mind of pine forests. Just listening to him probably lowered a patient's blood pressure ten points. He acknowledged the nuisance of remaining in the hospital, asked about child care options for her older boy, then did a quickie ultrasound. "Looking good," he crooned. "Very, very good. I'd like to keep him in there until he decides to come out on his own, and you're doing everything possible to keep it that way too."

On the way to the elevator, Dr. Cravey said, "Good catch with her. She was just at the beginning."

"There was something about her voice." Tessa sighed. "I didn't want to let it go."

"Did you sneak her a jar of unsalted macadamias?" he asked, and when Tessa's eyes flew open, he chuckled. "Don't worry. I don't tell the nurses about your fascination with protein."

In the lobby, Gary handed Tessa her phone. "You missed a call."

While Gary continued working on his laptop, and Eric played with plastic farm animals on the waiting area chairs, Tessa took a call from the birth center. A primip was in early labor. "Going to be a long night," she told Gary. "Can you handle dinner?"

At home for ten minutes, she changed clothes, gathered her birth supplies, and headed out in the Jeep to relieve Sarah. Sarah wasn't even supposed to be on call tonight.

Unlike the previous birth, Tessa didn't leave this mom's side for a minute. Some women retreat into themselves during labor, focusing deep inside to shut out the world. Other women needed support, and lots of it. A midwife crocheting in the corner would be useless to this mom; she required someone to hold her hands, take deep breaths in unison through an entire contraction, rub her back, help her into the birth tub, massage her shoulders, and sing.

Some moms, usually the quiet ones, required a nest and darkness and stillness. Others needed to wander. Tessa had followed one mother from the labor tub to the bedroom area to the bathroom where she eventually caught the baby while the mother delivered standing with one leg propped on the toilet. ("Try that in a hospital," she'd later told that mother, whom she'd never have pegged for a wanderer—nor would she have guessed that shy slip of a woman would be a naked-birther, who'd barely tolerated her clothes during the ride to the birth center and had stripped bare in the birth suite doorway.)

The current mother was a wanderer, although not a naked-birther. She sat on the labor ball, wanted heat, wanted the tub, wanted to stretch on all fours, wanted to rock on her knees with her head on her husband's lap while he dozed in a rocking chair. All the while, Tessa estimated progress and dilation based on the mother's behavior. She recorded the baby's heartbeat with the Doppler every fifteen minutes, and she didn't crochet a stitch.

At four in the morning, with a mom and a seven-pound baby tucked into the queen-sized bed, and with Karen brewing coffee so she could take over for the next few hours, Tessa headed to her car. The sky had no moon. The full moon got all the old wives' tales, but in her experience, the new moon made all the births. Hadn't she just caught two babies in two days?

Was driving home right now really such a good idea? Fatigue overwhelmed her, so she took a deep breath. She'd had coffee an hour ago. She would make it home and climb into bed, be warm next to Gary for a couple of hours, see her kids off to school (she hadn't done either of those yesterday), and then head back to the birth center for a full day of appointments. She should just sleep-crash in the second birth suite. It would make more sense. But her heart craved home.

The car engine and the radio roared to life. Bleary-eyed, though, she fought the urge to close her eyes at a red light.

And then she had an idea.

"Oh, angel!" she said, then as if calling a long distance, "An-gel!"

No response. She laughed at the ridiculousness of it all. Shouldn't Martin be most likely to show himself now, with her exhausted, high on endorphins, and asking for him? "Are you hiding? Show yourself, mighty angelic being."

He appeared in the passenger seat.

He looked impassive, but something was different. He wore far more formal clothing than the business casual he'd worn yesterday. This was a white robe, and he kept his wings folded at his back even though they seemed to melt away into the seat. His face bore no expression whatsoever, yet Tessa detected from him a kaleidoscope of feeling.

She smiled at him. "Thanks. I need you to help me get home. Can you keep me awake?"

Sounding stunned, Martin said, "Really?"

"It doesn't benefit your assignment if I die tonight by driving into a tree." The light changed, and Tessa accelerated slowly, making a left onto the main road. No other headlights danced over the pavement. Except for the street lamps, darkness reigned while she remained in the residential area; when she reached the more commercial area, logos and half-lit store interiors would populate the world again.

Martin sounded cautious. "Would you like me to tell you a riddle?"

A riddle? "What am I, five?"

"Angels make complicated riddles. They're fun, but they take a while to solve. I'm not sure if a human could do them." He paused. "I could come up with one for you that isn't too hard."

Terrific, the angelic equivalent of kindergarten.

Before she retorted, Tessa detected that bouquet of angelic emotions again, and this time she identified them.

She'd witnessed these emotions before. She'd felt them herself. Martin's feelings were the look in a new mother's eyes when Tessa lay that baby in her arms for the first time. She observed these feelings when a mother touched her seconds-old infant, wet and wrinkled and gasping its first bird-like cry. Martin projected awe at her, awe and delight. More than that: he projected wonder.

Tessa glanced at him. "Are you okay?"

Stiffly, the figure nodded. It was just a projection. She might as well be sitting beside a Ken doll.

No, wait. *Wait.* It was all about time. This wasn't the current Martin, or rather, not a Martin after the Martin she'd talked to last night. This was an early Martin, a very early Martin who wasn't asking about today's interview because Martin didn't know about it yet. Hadn't he said his past had already intersected her future?

Checking him again, she aligned his appearance now with the first time she'd seen him, before he began relaxing. He'd dressed and acted the way he thought an angel should when appearing to a person.

This might well be his first time. From his perspective, he'd never met her before.

And he was delighted. The feeling flooding her now—the feeling keeping her awake without even a riddle—was joy. He adored the idea of talking to her.

There was a reason he'd chosen her to work with him. Maybe this was it: maybe the reason was that she'd already spoken to him, so he thought she'd be open to the idea of a quest. Except again, this was a causality problem. If he chose her because she'd spoken to him, and she'd spoken to him because he'd chosen her, where had it all started?

Now that was a riddle to keep you going for years. Speaking of riddles...

"Try me out with a riddle." Tessa found herself smiling in response to Martin's joy. She couldn't stop. "Just don't make it too hard."

Martin said, "What's so delicate that it's broken if you say its name?"

Her kids had learned this one in fifth grade, so at least she'd graduated angelic kindergarten. "Silence?"

Martin said, "Good, you remembered that one. Okay, what lives if you feed it, but dies if you give it a drink?"

"Not so easy." She thought as she drove, then paused at the next red light, her mind wandering back to the birth center, to Gary, to Maine, and to woodstoves. Woodstoves with their homey warmth and delicious scent, laboring tirelessly at the room's edge while the smoldering wood glowed red and hot.

"Don't fall asleep, Terry. The idea was to engage your brain."

Terry. He was brand-new to this, but he knew her nickname. "Maybe riddles aren't the best idea." She dialed the temperature down, then turned up the radio. "It's only about ten minutes to home, anyhow."

"If you were wondering, the answer is fire." Martin's image shrugged. It looked mechanical: he definitely hadn't gotten the hang of it yet. "Just keep talking to me. We'll get you home."

He began singing with the radio. It was the Beatles' "Here Comes the Sun," nothing Tessa hadn't heard a thousand times. When Martin sang, though, her nerves danced, as if within her bones there was fire clawing to get out. No, not fire, because fire would mean pain. More like light. A living, growing light, like the plant inside the seed, ready to shed its outer casing and stretch to brush against the sun.

Fully awake, she didn't want to chance turning toward him to watch him sing, because then he might stop. Keeping her heart motionless like a vole in the mouth of its den, she listened, every sense trained on him even though she ought to be paying attention to the road. But it was four in the morning; no one else was driving. No one but her and an angel singing along with the radio.

It ended. He sounded pleased. "You're awake now."

An intense nausea spread through her at his song's absence. "I didn't know you could sing." It was the stupidest thing she could have said and yet the only words to present themselves in her mind. What she could have meant was anything, anything at all: *I didn't know you could set my heart on edge,* or *I didn't know a banal song could do that to my soul,* or *Why am I homesick when you sing?* His spoken voice didn't create earthquakes, so why did the addition of melody slice a rift through her heart?

After the station call jingle, which Martin refrained from singing, came Queen's "We Are the Champions," which to Tessa's simultaneous surprise and relief, Martin did sing. Sang, she realized, in multiple parts. As in, all the parts. Again she felt transported by that sense of her spirit unfolding, pushing its way out. It intensified her hunger to get home, but at the same time her house wasn't really where she wanted to be.

With only blocks to go, the song ended. Martin said, "You're nearly there."

Throat tight, Tessa couldn't speak at all. She couldn't even cry.

"I always thought that was half a song." Martin sounded thoughtful. "It's supposed to be paired with 'We Will Rock You,' and I doubt Freddie Mercury intended them to be split. Of course on the radio they do split it because of the constraints of their format. But when they have twofers and play two songs by the same artist, it feels as if they cheat when they play those two together and move on to the next. In my opinion, the station still owes you a song."

Tessa's voice wobbled. "Angels pay attention to that stuff?"

"We notice everything. I don't spend hours analyzing your music, no. It can't withstand that sort of treatment. Nor, I'll add, could I. But," he added, "at times while on assignment there's not a lot to do, and some of the world's oddities are so obvious that I have to wonder why humans don't comment on them too."

Tessa turned on her blinker (no reason why, since no one would pass this way for hours) and pulled into her driveway. Martin tingled with emotion, once more exuding wonder but now also a question mark.

Was she detecting uncertainty from him, who'd always been certain? He didn't know how to tell her goodbye, and even worse, he didn't want to. But at the same time, he must realize her familiarity with him meant they'd encounter on a regular basis in his future, so he could release the moment without fear. He'd have more. Only despite himself, he was reluctant.

Why the surprise? Why this off-balance? And yet here, in an early Martin, she'd encountered awe.

All the same, she couldn't let this riddle keep her awake for hours. She'd only get ninety minutes of sleep as it was. "Thank you for getting me home."

"I'll walk you inside," said Martin, which sounded reasonable.

"Are you my date?" When he didn't reply, Tessa added, "Thank you. You're a perfect gentleman."

By the time she slipped her coat onto the hook, Martin had disappeared. All around her ghosted the sparkles of an angel's excitement, though, and within her churned the froth of a human's questions.

NINE

If Tessa had thought about it rather than dozing on the train ride home and then delivering a baby, she'd have realized everything would go to pieces as soon as they left Pryce's house.

She and Gary didn't have a chance to speak about the interview during the day, between caring for her clients and caring for her children. That night while she baked corn bread and then made white beans with sage leaves (plus a salad), she helped Eric with his kindergarten homework, supervised Brian's music practice, and listened to Mark rehearse a presentation for science class.

At the same time, Gary cranked out a column on sailboating and conducted an interview with a speech-language pathologist about how to best help children who stutter.

After nine o'clock, with all the boys but Joe in bed, Gary emerged from his office. "If you've got a few minutes, I need you to hear something."

Gary clicked around on his computer. "At ten o'clock this morning I got a phone call from one of the two veterans remaining to be interviewed."

Gary's face and tone gave Tessa all the information before he even clicked on the recording.

The audio picked up in the middle of a heated conversation: "—not going to talk to you and listen to ridiculous accusations—"

"If you'll let me speak," Gary was saying.

"You don't need to speak. You need to listen." The voice had a sharper pitch than Pryce's, lacking any sort of smoker's gravel. "I'm canceling our interview. I don't know what you're after, but I'm not helping you destroy anyone's good name."

"What would be destroyed?" Gary said. "I'm writing a piece for Veterans Day—"

"I want nothing to do with it. This interview is cancelled."

There the phone call ended. Gary frowned without looking up at Tessa. "My guess is, Pryce or O'Mara are burning up the phone lines."

Tessa bit her lip. "What are we going to do?"

He shrugged. "Well, at this point I have enough information to run an article, and I plan to. That may flush out the other two. I've also got a list of relatives of the ones who have already passed away, and I may be able to ask questions of them. And finally," he smiled, "I have something for you."

He opened a new window and had her come look. "Look at this: a contact in Barlassina."

Tessa paused. "Who?"

"A relative of yours, a DiOrio." He tapped a couple of times, then handed it to her. "I would have to construct a family tree to figure it out exactly, but I think she's a second or third cousin."

Dear Mr. Testerman, the email began. *I was so surprised to read your letter about the article you are writing for a magazine about our town and our church. I am glad to hear you are married to one of my own relatives, and this explains your interest. Our church isn't very well known even in Italy, but that is why you found out.*

Tessa tucked up in the seat to read the rest of it.

I'm sorry if my English is not very good, but I hope you will help me improve as we talk more. Also please give me your wife's email so we can write. I used Google Translate for some of this, but I don't trust it in total.

Tessa said, "Google Translate works best if you already know the language."

"No doubt," Gary said. "A few years ago, a Spanish gentleman wrote me a letter, and in the middle of a perfectly normal sentence was the word *overcoat.* Turns out he wanted *sobretodo,* or 'overall.'"

She grinned.

I am more than happy to send photographs, her relative continued. *The church is in a bad state now, and no one can decide what to do, but time decides for us. I will answer your questions too when I speak to my relatives. I know only stories and I should not get it wrong if you are going to print it. I will write you again tomorrow after I speak to my mother.*

Sincerely,
Alessandra DiOrio

Tessa swiped up, and there she found the pictures.

"Martin," she whispered, but she hadn't needed to.

She was already sitting, and that was important because her limbs turned to jelly with the backwash of his grief when she saw the ruined church.

She blinked past her own tears (or were they Martin's tears? Could angels cry, or did they need a human to cry for them?) and tried to sort out what she was seeing.

The Church of the Holy Cross had been an imposing stone edifice. She wasn't a good judge of height. (Inches, yes. She could measure pounds with her hands. Spill fluid on a chux pad and she could estimate within a tenth of an ounce how much it was—but once you were in feet, all bets were off.) Still, she guessed the church was maybe a fifty-foot structure, all stone on the front and sides and with a stone staircase leading to the massive gap where there should have been front doors.

Every window was smashed. Over the front should have towered a rose window and instead was only a circle (again, boarded from the inside). Brambles crawled over the facade, and trees grew alongside the walls.

It was going back to nature. What the soldiers had failed to finish, rain and time would complete in their stead.

The next photo was one of the side. Here you could see better the tarps lashed over the roof. The two windows at the very back of the building remained unbroken, perhaps because they weren't part of the nave, and they looked incredible. The whole building looked beautiful, in fact, and if she hadn't kept fighting the urge to curl around herself in despair, she might have found the ruins fascinating.

Alessandra had sent three more photos. Instead of looking, she handed Gary the tablet. "I'm sorry. I can't."

Martin sparked angrily in her mind.

Later. Give yourself a break.

He insisted. She sank into the chair and let him insist.

It popped into her head that he could look at it any time he wanted.

Then go right ahead, she thought. *Do it without me. I'll look later on.* Later, maybe he wouldn't be with her and she could study the pictures without his grief. Something in those photos might help her identify what went wrong all those years ago. But now? With him all over her heart like that?

You don't torture someone with things they can't change. Midwifery was about taking in hand the things you could change, then managing all the factors so the natural systems could work themselves out. Midwifery was about recognizing when nature wouldn't do the job on its own and needed extra help (usually in the form of a medical referral to someone with surgical experience).

Whatever nature was for an angel, nature wasn't doing the job now. Or at the very least, adding injury to injury couldn't promote healing, even if it seemed at first to alleviate the symptoms.

Gary said, "I've asked permission to run her photos. Once I've gotten that and her mother's letter, I'll submit the article and we'll see what that stirs up. We may be able to flush out the thing from wherever it's hiding."

Tessa bit her lip. "It's such a long shot."

"Not really. Once the story runs, then I can approach other publications for a much more in-depth story. *Atlantic* likes investigative pieces without clear answers, and at that point," Gary said with a grin, "I can get amazing interviews. A church historian at Boston College would talk to me about the process of verifying relics, and there's an antiques dealer in Brooklyn, NY who was willing to be interviewed about selling relics and the underground sale of stolen goods."

Tessa said, "So in the long run, Martin may well have handed you a book deal."

Gary laughed. "Should I pitch a literary agent now, or wait until the first article publishes?"

"Maybe wait until you have more than a thousand words worth of material." She sighed. "I'm heading to bed, though. It's been a really long forty-eight hours."

"No joke. You had what, an hour of sleep last night?" Gary checked his watch. "It's too early for the Italians to be awake yet, even with all the coffee they drink. But hey," he said, "I sent your cousin your email address, so maybe you'll end up hearing from them too."

Martin pushed into her thoughts when the lights went out.

Tessa was so tired that she could have slept on a picket fence, but Martin was really insistent. He'd be able to keep her awake, and she desperately needed sleep. "Really?" she whispered.

Garry was cuddled beside her. "Hmm?"

"Nothing." She braced herself. *What is it, Martin?*

Information flowed into her: she had no right to "protect" him from information he deserved to have. He would be the decision-maker as to what he could handle, and she should rest assured he was capable of handling quite a bit.

You were really sad seeing the pictures, she thought out into the darkness. *It was awful for you. Do you think I didn't feel that?*

Yes, of course he was sad seeing the damage he'd known about compounded by the damage of passing decades and the totally unnecessary damage done by vandals and looters, plus the sealing off done by the local authorities. Would she expect anyone not to be sad?

It was too much, Tessa sent. *You needed a break.*

No, he hadn't.

Then I needed a break, she sent. *I couldn't deal with how devastated you felt.*

No response. She tried to relax muscles that had unconsciously tightened while Martin was speaking to her. He'd been devastated an hour ago, but now he felt angry. Although the last time she'd said he been angry at her, he'd said he wasn't.

She couldn't tease apart what angels called different emotions. Someone in the midst of correcting her behavior usually sounded angry or offended, so she'd handled it that way. Nothing she'd ever heard indicated that angels couldn't get angry. In fact, if she remembered Sunday school correctly, angels could get very angry in ways that involved burning cities to the ground or harvesting human souls off the face of the earth. Or telling John the Baptist's father to shut up for nine months. She'd prefer not to find out the limits of Martin's capabilities, so de-escalating him was the best response.

More information came to her: Martin hadn't realized she was picking up that much of his emotions, and in the future, rather than trying to limit his information, she should instead tell him to stem what he was projecting.

You can control that?

The emotion from Martin was so strong that Tessa actually rolled her own eyes. Yes, he could control that.

Well how was I supposed to know? It's not like you ever told me. She sighed. *It felt cruel to keep looking at the photos. Satisfying my curiosity was hurting you, and that would be selfish.*

A thought rose in her head: she coached laboring moms through contractions. Her vocation itself was geared away from administering painkillers to women in labor, but she didn't consider that unfair. Instead she considered it normal and natural for the body to work through the pain to the reward.

And your reward would have been...?

Information. Reality. Knowing what he was up against.

You can have all the information you want. Go over there.

No, he couldn't.

She tensed up again. He couldn't just go overseas? She'd assumed all along that he teleported around the globe just by thinking about things and being there. How could all this time have passed and he not have stopped back at the building? Or did he know what he could handle, and he couldn't handle that?

Instead of cogitating, she just said, *Why not?*

A jumble of weird restrictions and information welled up and then back down in her head. Something about assignments and authority and restrictions.

That was odd. His assignment was getting the relic back home again, so why wouldn't that count? Not having the authority to look at the church seemed like a major impediment to completing his assignment. Angels needed to come with user manuals, although with Tessa's luck it would be one of those badly translated manuals. *"Please not put finger on touch button too long to avoid touch sensor become not that sensitive."*

When she didn't reply, Martin pushed further: when she woke up, she should look at her email and see the remaining pictures Gary had forwarded. Martin would make sure not to overwhelm her when she did it.

Now who's deciding what someone else can handle?

Martin bristled in her thoughts, another jumble of facts that left her with the very strong sensation that angels looked out for human souls and not vice-versa; it was wrong to upend the natural order.

Her mouth tightened. It didn't matter if something was the natural order. Just because he was an angel didn't mean she should go out of her way to hurt him.

Again there was that sensation as if staring into a high wind: how dare she judge whether he was adequate to the task he'd been assigned? He was capable. He was an archangel.

Wait, what does that mean?

That he wasn't one of the lowest order of angels. Even the lowest of the angels was a higher-order being than the highest of the humans. But she was setting herself up as judge over an angel of an even higher order.

Your ability was never in question, Tessa replied. *I was looking out for your feelings.*

He pushed harder on her heart: don't soft-pedal him. He was strong enough to see this through. He'd get everything done, but she had to let him do it.

Okay, she thought. *Okay. Fine. I'm sorry.*

She focused on relaxing the muscles in her shoulders, then her arms, and then she worked on her face. She was frowning and her teeth were clenched, and she shouldn't fall asleep that way.

Abruptly she felt Martin one more time: that he forgave her.

She didn't even know what to reply. But then her exhaustion overtook her, and she fell asleep.

TEN

For the next week, they waited. Maybe Martin was skipping the boring stuff because she didn't hear from him. Having received Alessandra's mother's information, Gary submitted his article. Karen printed up lawn signs and made sure every one of their clients had as many as they could place. "Say NO to H.8937!" Gary moved on to contacting editors about getting some attention on the legislature.

"A few editors don't want me writing the piece myself." He'd called Tessa at work between client appointments. "But tell Karen they're willing to provide lots of coverage. She just has to do something newsworthy."

Tessa shuddered. "I'm not telling her that. She'll climb the flagpole at the state house!"

"A rally in Copley Square, though. A nurse-in by protesting homebirth moms." He rambled a bit, thinking out loud through a few other ideas, then added, "Just so long as it's interesting enough that you can run a picture with it. Fill that news hole."

"Will do."

Tessa's next appointment was with Amanda, now at twenty-seven weeks. "How's the sciatica?" she asked as Amanda took off her shoes to step on the scale.

"So much better! Those stretches totally did the trick, or maybe it was the compresses. I have no idea." She giggled. "It's kind of bad science to try everything at once, isn't it?"

"We weren't trying to conduct science," Tessa said, writing down the number. "We were trying to make sure you could walk up and down the stairs. Weight's awesome. Let's get your blood pressure and put some hands on that baby."

Amanda's great attitude was the reason she'd ended up here rather than at an obstetric practice. She'd wanted a medical provider to give advice, to tell her what milestones were coming up, and to observe without interfering. With a first-time mom's natural trust in her own body, she'd plunged into the pregnancy only to be shocked by the frozen reception at her local obstetric practice. They didn't want her to deliver in a tub, told her she couldn't deliver squatting if she wanted, and reassured her that an episiotomy wasn't so bad and everyone had them. "From what they said," Amanda reported later, "I had a ninety-five percent chance that someone in their practice was going to deliberately cut me open."

Now she traveled forty-five minutes each way to the Milliston Common Birth Center, and by all accounts she was having a blast. "My husband feels the baby move while I'm sleeping," she said as Tessa measured her belly. "I'm completely unconscious, and the baby keeps kicking his side."

"No beating up Daddy," Tessa said in a low voice to the belly. "He's going to be contributing to your college fund."

"Such a disobedient baby," Amanda said, and they both laughed. She'd asked during her ultrasound not to know the gender, so Tessa hadn't bothered looking at the results herself.

"Measuring fine," Tessa said. "Let's get the heartbeat."

Five whoosh-whooshes later, the Doppler got a number and she switched off the machine. "Heartbeat is great. Now, tell me in general how things are going."

Amanda sat cross-legged on the bed while Tessa moved to the rocking chair, and they talked about a recent tussle with her mother-in-law ("She says the baby has to have real food from a bottle rather than breastfeeding, otherwise, the baby will die") and then asked about whether it was safe to co-sleep. Tessa pulled out a flyer with the most recent guidelines. "Awesome," Amanda said. "My mother-in-law is also convinced the baby will die if we don't have a crib." She rolled her eyes. "Cribs are magical talismans against SIDS, right? That's why it's called 'crib-death'?"

Tessa said, "Babies can die in beds too, but that's why they developed safety guidelines. No water beds. No thick comforters. No pillows near the baby's face. Never, ever sleeping with the baby if you've taken anything that would impair your ability to wake up. No siblings in the bed."

"No mothers-in-law standing at the doorway to wake you up every hour to make sure the baby is still breathing?"

Tessa frowned. "Will your husband stand up to her if she tries that?"

"I don't know." Amanda sighed. "She's kind of a force to be reckoned with. He doesn't like to do it."

"You're a force to be reckoned with too," Tessa said. "Don't let him choose her over you. If he sacrifices you and your baby to keep the peace, that's exactly what he's doing. But if you think about it, *she's* the one disturbing the peace, not you."

"He caved to her and won't let us put up a lawn sign about H.8937," Amanda said. "It's our front lawn. She doesn't even live near us, but maybe she does drive-bys to make sure I haven't put it back up."

Marital dynamics were always tricky. Tessa had done as much marriage counseling in her midwifery practice as nutrition counseling, and she'd suggested more couples go to counseling than she'd ever had made referrals to Dr. Cravey.

"My mother-in-law already thinks not seeing a real doctor is 'jeopardizing the baby.'" Amanda sighed. "She's like a tornado. Like the sciatic nerve thing. 'A doctor should have fixed that,' she said."

"You fixed it yourself." Tessa smiled. "No doctor in the world could have prevented it from *starting*, but once you knew what to do, you helped yourself. I know the limits of my job. When and if you need to see a doctor, we've got a good one on call."

"I think I met him once in the waiting area!" Amanda said. "Older guy, soft voice? He was really nice."

"He's also sharp as a tack and has thirty years of experience. He's one of the only doctors in the state who will evaluate women for a breech delivery, and I trust his judgment." Very few people knew what kind of compliment that was, coming from Tessa. "If I had a daughter and she needed an obstetrician, I'd send her to him. Instead I send you guys."

Amanda nodded. "I just don't want all the extra stuff. If I'm safe to deliver here or at home, why wouldn't I?"

"Not everyone is comfortable with that. Midwifery is more than about the place of delivery," Tessa added. "It's about the mindset. Obstetrics is about statistics, numbers, risk-aversion, and specific outcomes. It draws guidelines from theories about the general population. Midwifery is about watching and waiting, observing the individual, and sometimes about getting messy. Obstetricians tend to think about winning and losing. Midwives tend to think about cooperation and commonality."

"She'd never get that." Amanda rolled her eyes. "It's too philosophical."

Tessa leaned back in her chair. "It's just a different philosophy. Medical care is all about treating things. If this symptom happens, you treat it. If that symptom happens, you treat that one too. Midwifery, on the other hand, is about healing." Tessa took a deep breath. "It's about removing the impediments so your body can do whatever it does best and heal itself. Sometimes it needs a little help. When it needs a lot of help, then we change your model of care. But for now, our job is to get any physical issues out of the way and let your body bring its own resources to bear."

Amanda chuckled. "You treated my sciatic nerve."

"You relaxed the muscles tensing up around the sciatic nerve," Tessa said, "and by doing so, allowed your body to heal itself."

The morning Gary's article appeared on the *US News* website, Tessa sat with her coffee and the tablet open.

I'm reading it now, Martin, she thought out into the big empty world, and when she didn't feel a response, she went through it on her own. She had today off, so she lingered.

Martin had taken the emotional backflow issue seriously. What he'd done, in fact, was cut off any sense of himself. He hadn't appeared since their late-night chat, nor had she picked up any stray feelings from him.

Most likely he didn't need her help right at this moment. The interviews were done, and although she was emailing with her relatives from Italy (in a combination of mangled English and Italian, plus some help from Google Translate), none of that would be pertinent. He'd skipped the boring stuff, as he'd said he would. Either that or he'd just tightened the locks on whatever mechanism he used for communication.

It was a really good article. Gary had changed the soldiers' names because no one wanted four nonagenarians (that's what came after octogenarian, right?) to get court-martialed over an alleged theft that might have taken place seventy years ago on another continent. Gary would handle things if he got a phone call from a four-star general. Until then, names were changed to protect both the guilty and the innocent.

He'd done such a compassionate write-up, though. He had quotes from both soldiers regarding how hard it was in the final weeks of the war, their exhaustion and their longing to get home. With a few paragraphs and a few well-placed quotes, Gary had set up a scene of young men pushed well beyond their limits in an environment that was hurtling them still further beyond what they could endure. No one would walk away from this article thinking them monsters.

The photos elicited no emotional response from Martin. Neither did the writing. Neither did her next act, which was sending the link overseas to her very-removed cousins.

Maybe Martin had never existed at all. Maybe she'd hallucinated the whole thing.

Tessa opened another window on her browser and typed, "What is the difference between an angel and an archangel?" Martin had been emphatic on that point: he was able to handle this because he was an archangel. Why?

It turned out that everyone had different answers, but the overall story seemed consistent: angels were messengers sent by God and had a certain type of power; they guarded human beings from the dangerous and stupid situations they got themselves into. Archangels, by contrast, got the big jobs. They guarded entire countries. They served as patrons of organizations and cities and categories of people. And, according to Martin, they served as guardians of specific churches.

How much protection did a church need? But maybe that was the wrong question. Up until recently in Europe, the church would have been the center of a town, or a group of churches at the center of a city. People would marry there, enroll there, socialize there, and be buried from there. The church would have a school. The church would be the focus of many careers. It would serve as sanctuary and lighthouse. If a church went to the bad, doubtless it would take the town with it.

Martin had said as much. With the church derelict, Barlassina was dying.

Oh! She flipped back to Gary's article and looked at the photo of the relic in its ornate reliquary. Something Martin had said suddenly made sense: he'd made a glancing reference to the guardian angel of the town of Barlassina. That would have been an archangel too. If the town was dying because the church had died, and the church had died because of Martin's mistake, then that other archangel might be keeping Martin away as punishment. Right? That would explain why Martin had been reduced to looking at the photographs her something-cousin had emailed.

"We celebrate Mass in the monastery chapel," her something-cousin had written. "We are there, in the shadow of the old church. But many people worship somewhere else."

Or, Tessa supposed, they left entirely. A dying town had little industry. A dying town that gave you no reason to stay soon became a dead town. A town with no school was a town with no children, and a town with no children became a ghost town.

Gary had queries out with several magazines. Illicit trade in relics could net him an article, as could a deeper investigation to the stolen relic of St. Peter of Verona, as could a discussion of the place of relics in the Roman Catholic and Eastern Orthodox churches. She'd begun to suspect he was really enjoying this, having plumbed a subculture he'd never even heard of before Martin showed up.

As to what Martin would ask for next...well, who knew what that would be?

She sent the link off to Mom as well. Mom replied within five minutes. "I heard from my brother," she said. "He sent me some things. I'll be over in a bit"

A bit meant half an hour, and that was enough time to get the coffee going, put muffins in the oven, and make sure the bathroom was fit for human use. (With five boys, even daily cleaning didn't always suffice.) Mom arrived holding a cardboard box still festooned with priority mail stickers.

"He's a rip," she said as she set the box on the kitchen table. "I ask him for any photographs from Italy, and he needs to send me everything your grandmother ever touched." Given the size of the box, Tessa found that unlikely, but Mom went on. "He sent me a pair of teacups he took from her house, plus a speeding ticket he got on vacation in Rome ten years ago and paid off by giving the policeman a bottle of wine. I bet Cecilia made him send these just to clean out her house."

Tessa snickered. "Aunt Cecilia's a bit of a neatnik."

"She's got a good heart and a tidy home. I'm not sure how those two things fit together. Here we go." Mom pulled a folder out of the box. "This is the important stuff, the thing Gary will want."

There, right on the top, was a black-and-white photo of the relic.

Tessa sat forward, finally eye to eye with the wild goose Martin had her chasing. "How big would this have been?" she heard herself saying, but actually the workmanship fascinated her. The frame around the relic didn't know what it wanted to be: locket or monstrance or statue or work of art. It was ornate metalwork, lace made with wire wrapped fully around the frame, parting only for the base that held it upright. Gold or silver, Tessa couldn't tell. It was much more decorated than her twenty-first century American tastes preferred, but she recognized fine craftsmanship when she saw it.

By contrast, the relic itself seemed ridiculous. Her midwife's eye glanced at the fleck of linen fabric and immediately judged it medical waste. She dealt with bloody gauze and torn human tissue on a regular basis, so seeing a black spot on old linen meant nothing to her, even if it lay on velvet behind a glass oval. She discarded more than that after a healthy birth. If she'd found this at a garage sale without knowing its value, she'd have cleaned out the bit of fabric, tossed it into the trash, and found something pretty to put in the frame.

Mom said, "Oh, it was probably the size of your hand if you stretched out your fingers. You saw that First Holy Communion photo. Here, check this picture." She flipped through until she found one with a nun. "See how they kept it on a side chapel, along with a painting of St. Peter the Martyr? Plus all the votive candles. And the statue. Italians never overdo anything when they decorate," she added with a grin. "It was a little thing, but with that much glitz surrounding it, it's no wonder the soldiers realized it was valuable. It fit right into a pocket. Who wouldn't take it?"

Through all this, Tessa picked up no sensation from Martin whatsoever. She found it disconcerting. No, not disconcerting. Horrible. He could be feeling anything whatsoever, and she'd have no cue to stop torturing him.

Mom went through the other photos until she found a priest holding the relic aloft. "He was probably blessing the people."

"I really don't get the fascination with relics," Tessa said.

"Me neither." Mom chuckled. "But boy, did they love this one. Peter the Martyr was their own personal hero. Grandpa had a prayer card he kept taped to the wall beside his bed, and he'd pray that prayer every night. It had this gruesome picture, with a sword in his head, and he's got his eyes turned toward heaven." She shuddered. "Every year, we went to church on his feast day—I'm forgetting now, was it April 6th? April 29th? And heaven help if the priest didn't celebrate the Mass in his honor. Oh, you Barlassinesi, he'd say. Such a thorn in my side."

Tessa laughed. "I inherited my thorniness, didn't I?"

"From all the way back in time, absolutely." Mom looked back through the box. "He sent me some of Mom's jewelry that Cecilia had gotten after she died. I guess he thinks I should give it to you, or maybe his daughters don't want it either. This is good, though." Mom smiled. "Are you ready for this?"

She removed a handkerchief and a note card from a paper envelope and handed them to Tessa.

"Who made this?" she asked.

"It's not about who made it," Mom said. "The note says this is a third-class relic of St. Peter of Verona."

Tessa dropped the handkerchief. "What?"

"I had to look this up myself. A first-class relic is what you've been calling a relic all along, a part of the saint's body." When Tessa nodded, Mom said, "A second-class relic is a thing the saint owned or which was related to the saint. So the axe that chopped off Peter the Martyr's head would have been a second-class relic, or if we still had Peter the Martyr's Bible."

Midwifery was all about classification, and hey, it sounded like the Catholic Church was doing that too. "Oh, so it's one degree removed."

"Right, like the difference between saving Grandma's gravy recipe and gravy spoon versus Grandma's hand that she used to stir the gravy."

"Yuck." Tessa chuckled. "That still sounds so odd."

"Well, a third-class relic is something that was touched to a first-class relic."

Mystified, Tessa said, "Why would that be important?"

Mom opened her hands and shrugged. "Beats me. But it's a category of relic, and this handkerchief was, apparently, turned into a relic of its own by touching it to the relic of Saint Peter the Martyr."

Tessa unfolded it and smoothed the deep creases. Clearly no one was going to dry tears or worse with it now, but it would have been too nice a handkerchief to do that anyway. The center part was only four inches by four inches of linen, with the rest festooned in a deep halo of lace.

As Mom made herself more tea, Tessa spread out the photos. *Martin? Are you seeing this?*

How did the time-travel thing work? For that matter, how did regular travel work for these guys? Could he hear her from a long distance with some kind of psychic cell phone connection to her thoughts? How was he even hearing her thoughts? But what if right now he was actually on Wednesday afternoon? No, that didn't make sense either. Maybe later on he popped in, checked her calendar, and then jumped over to whatever time her mother had arrived.

Martin? she asked again.

Abruptly she felt more awake and very alert.

Okay, that probably meant he was around. *I can't tell if you're here looking at this stuff, but you probably want to see it.*

Agreement.

She wrinkled her nose. *You know, it's a good thing you didn't try contacting me this way the first time, or I'd never have come to believe you existed at all.*

Mom said, "Are you okay? You look irritated."

"Mildly. I have some strange relatives." And some strange visitors too, when it came down to that. "I'm still having a hard time believing soldiers would destroy a church just because someone shot at them. It was a war. People shoot."

Actually, I'm irritated at you, she sent to Martin. *Having you talk to me this way is going to lead to miscommunications.*

Inside he felt puzzled. She didn't reply. No, she was not playing this game. He wanted the relic, so eventually he would have to concede this point and actually talk.

That didn't happen until late that evening. After she'd kissed her mother goodbye and Gary had gushed over the photographs, after dinner and chores and two loads of laundry, after all the kids were in bed and Tessa was changing into pajamas. Then Martin appeared.

He said, "How will that lead to miscommunication?"

It took a moment to backtrack the conversation, which clearly Martin had just left off, stepped fourteen hours into the future, and continued without pause.

"Because if you put a feeling into my head, I have to interpret it, and I'm going to interpret it through the lens of what I expect to hear." She finished buttoning the front of her flannel pajamas, then said, "You'll think you told me absolutely not ever to go into that house over there, and I'll think you want me to. Then you'll be even angrier because I openly defied you, whereas I thought I was carrying out your wishes."

Martin folded his arms. "How is this a better system? I'm projecting sounds into your head in the form of a mutually-agreed-upon vocabulary, which one would note is also open to interpretation."

"*Don't go in there* is pretty straightforward," Tessa said.

"So is this," said Martin, and Tessa jumped back from her own closet door, terrified and filled with loathing.

The feeling vanished, and Martin shrugged.

"Angelic communication mostly operates on that level," Martin added, while Tessa's heartbeat returned to a normal pace. "It's how an editor takes a second look at an article that isn't the best fit for his publication."

"And yet *I* don't operate on that level very well."

Martin shot back, "So I've discovered."

"And that going totally silent? Not acceptable. I want to know when you're around."

Martin said, "How about you assume I'm always around and behave accordingly?"

She said, "Or you can dial back the silence, that way I sense where you are and what you'd like me to look at. I've already said I'm not going to protect you from yourself because you don't think I should care about you."

Martin looked annoyed. "I don't need your protection."

"I'm still learning the rules," Tessa said. "Speaking of which, how come you can't go to Barlassina but you can go to an editorial office in Washington, D.C.?"

Martin shook his head. "I didn't go there. I reeled in a favor. A friend of a friend asked his guardian angel to lean on him, and that's permitted."

Tessa blinked. "And you had the nerve to say Italians were bad about one hand washing the other?"

Martin smirked at her. "Who do you think taught me how to do it?" He was getting better at giving the visual form its own body language cues, something Tessa realized abruptly were humans' own form of nonverbal communication. He really was trying to communicate with her via every avenue possible. But he also demanded she meet him halfway.

Oh, now there was an interesting question. Were those two things her thoughts, or were they something he wanted her to think?

Then she wondered something else: had she been chosen because her own guardian angel, whoever that was, owed Martin a favor? That must have been a big one too. Martin might have said to himself that despite all her drawbacks, she was the best chance he had at retrieving this thing because this other angel owed him the moon. What kind of favors angels did for one another was way beyond her comprehension, but for now she'd let that go. Maybe they subbed for one another in choir. Maybe they jumped ahead in time and jumped back to say, *Hey, next Thursday? Don't go there. It's a mess of epic proportions, and you don't want to fix it in time too soon.*

She studied him. "Okay, so you guys have this series of interlocking permissions and authority systems, but you can network with one another for help. What happens next?"

Martin looked thoughtful. "The article is putting information into the world now, and that information is awakening strands of memory that will begin to touch on the relic's presence. This is trickier than you detecting when I put emotions into your head, but those memories should begin leading to actions. The actions should set in motion events that lead to the relic's reemergence into time."

"Do you have a relic of your own?" Tessa leaned forward. "A piece of the church?"

Martin hesitated. "Why?"

"Did you keep any broken glass or stone?" She opened her hands. "A key? Something to remember it by?"

Taken aback, Martin said, "That's very materialistic."

"It's a material church."

"I have plenty of memories." He settled back down. "One more isn't required."

Fair enough. "And what about the handkerchief?" Tessa asked. "Since it's a third-class relic, shouldn't I send that to Barlassina?"

"They won't find it important. Most of Barlassina counts as a third-class relic by now. They'll want the actual item."

"So we're waiting for someone to call us with an offer on a stolen relic?" Tessa ventured.

Martin said, "Not that. Wait two days."

She forced a smile. "Now you're just showing off."

"Parlor tricks." His eyes wrinkled. "Set an alarm for 1:23 p.m."

This time her laugh wasn't forced. "Oh, did you set your stop watch?"

"Hardly." Now he looked amused too. "I just read the timestamp."

ELEVEN

At 1:23, Tessa got a text from Gary that he'd gotten the most interesting email. "It's from one Giorgio Monterosa."

She was too slammed to call him and find out what was in the email. *Oh, wait,* she thought at Martin. *When you said the timestamp, you meant the one on my text message, not on the email itself. For a minute there, I thought you might possibly have made a mistake. Carry on.*

Since she hadn't actually accused Martin of making a mistake, he didn't reply. She hoped he found it funny, at least.

The phone stayed mute in her pocket during working hours. No one wanted a midwife glued to a phone screen, and Tessa needed to be fully present for her clients. Still, between appointments she checked messages. She got a text from Amanda and then replied that since Amanda's mother-in-law was so wrapped around the axle about the birth center being unsafe, she could certainly come and have a tour of the facility and a rundown on all the safety precautions. She also got two more texts from Gary. "People are angry," he texted. "Even better, they're angry in Italian."

She texted back, "Threats?"

After a few minutes, she got a reply: "Oh, probably."

Gary at least seemed sanguine about the possibility of a hit ordered from across the sea. He'd been threatened before. She'd just have to trust his judgment.

She'd also have to trust Amanda's judgment when she wrote back, "Jeffrey's mom wants to come to an appointment."

A regular appointment was not the time for a meddlesome person to get into her face about perceived safety risks (Tessa also had been threatened before) so she texted back, "Call in for a 28-week appointment. We'll start you on the every-other-week rotation sooner rather than later."

It made sense to give Amanda one extra appointment, that way her bulldog of a mother-in-law could waste the whole hour on her anxieties without taking away from an actual appointment.

That evening, Tessa got a look at the other angry party in her life: the Monterosa family. "They don't even know I'm a DiOrio," she murmured while looking over the English diatribe of the first email, composed by one Giorgio Monterosa. "Imagine if they did."

The writer had included in his impeccable English, however, a thorough character assassination of the entire DiOrio lineage. "Did you know you'd married a whore?" she asked Gary.

"I'd always been disappointed that I hadn't," Gary said, leaning back on his office chair, "so you can imagine my relief at uncovering this new information."

She snickered. The gist of the letter was buried in a paragraph at the middle.

Journalistic standards demand you interview all parties involved in the church's continued plight. Your DiOrio informant quite squarely laid the blame on my father and the decisions our family has made for the good of the town, but a mere phone call would have provided information that would shed light on the DiOrio family's obstruction tactics. Every attempt at restoration has been blocked by them for the most spurious of reasons, and we have extensive documentation.

"Apparently both sides are at fault," Tessa said.

"He's correct that in a deeper piece of investigative journalism, I would have interviewed his father, who happens to be the mayor. Given that the focus was on the American soldiers, I didn't need quotes about the family feud."

"But for the next article...?"

Gary nodded. "For the next article, these folks will provide a wealth of source material, and I intend to use it. I haven't gotten these two letters translated," he said, gesturing to his inbox, "but as soon as I do, I'll reach out to them as well."

Tessa heard Martin's voice: "Have him show you the letters."

Tessa reached over Gary's shoulder and clicked on an email. "Dear Gary Testerman," Martin said, "What kind of rancid garbage did you print in an American magazine about my family?"

Tessa said, "Wait, stop. What?"

Gary looked at her, puzzled.

"Repeat this to Gary." Martin shrugged. "He can't read their dialect, but I can."

She looked up at her husband. "Martin's translating."

Gary's eyes widened. "Well, that's convenient."

One sentence at a time, she repeated back Martin's translation of the letter. "I'm giving a dynamic, idiomatic translation," Martin clarified at one point. "A literal translation would require the use of several terms I'm not comfortable saying."

"Tell him that's fine," Gary said to Tessa after she related this. "I wasn't planning to quote this work of literature in my piece."

"You can tell him yourself," Tessa said. "He can hear you."

"Oh, right." Gary leaned back. "Well, keep going. I want to learn more about my limited intellectual capacity."

The overall thrust of this letter, other than the uncomplimentary assessment of Gary's character traits, was that he didn't know the whole story and shouldn't lie unless he wanted to suffer the consequences. Gary then moved on to the next letter, from a Pietro Monterosa.

Martin's eyes glinted. "This one's better."

Dear Mr. Testerman,

My family is in an uproar about your article, and I understand some are writing to you. I apologize for writing in Italian, but my English is clumsy. I am sending this from my son's email account.

Please don't judge my family on the basis of their letters. We are not a bunch of brutes, but you know how it is. The loudest speak first and draw the most attention.

Gary said, "I take it Martin's being less dynamic right now."

Tessa said, "Talk to the angel. He has ears."

"I don't have ears," Martin said, "and yes, this letter requires less summarizing. She's much more measured in her tone."

Tessa froze. "Wait a minute. You're not a mammal."

Gary laughed out loud. "No!" She pivoted to look at Gary. "Think about it! He's— Martin doesn't have hair and won't produce young and doesn't have a spinal column."

Gary said, "He's a bodiless creature. You knew that."

Martin sighed. "Technically speaking, *having* a body is the anomaly here. Humans are embodied material creatures with souls. I'm a pure spirit, which is the original state of being."

He smirked at her, and she wrinkled her nose. "Well excuse me," Tessa said. "Keep translating. I'll just have to get used to the fact that I'm bantering with a hairless, bloodless creature without a body temperature."

Martin huffed. "You make that sound much more awful than it is. I've worked hard to acclimate myself to the way you're lugging around a material form subjected to entropy and pinning you to a specific space and time."

She glared at Martin, who grinned as he said, "See? I can play that game too."

Gary snickered. "I have no idea what he just said, but I'm very glad I'm not the one who said it."

Martin kept translating while Tessa tried to make sense of what had just happened.

Those of us who aren't screaming are appreciative of the story, although we wish you had condemned the soldiers for theft. Isn't looting and burning a war crime in America? Regardless, we understand your need to protect your countrymen, and we are glad that you shone light on a very old crime.

I have attached a picture of the relic, as I want to draw attention to something you did not touch upon, perhaps because you had only a grainy photograph. The reliquary itself was a work of art, and doubtless the reason the soldiers stole the relic in the first place. The reliquary was designed by Ercole Monterosa, a goldsmith of some renown in the 1800s. You can find his work in museums all over Italy and France, as well as in the Vatican itself. The ornamentation is his signature style, and in a letter to the local bishop, he declared that because of his love for Peter the Martyr, he fasted and prayed for forty days before even attempting this piece. He considered it the best work of his lifetime.

The loss of the artwork is, as you can imagine, as great a blow to Barlassina as the loss of the church.

My plea to you is this: please follow up this article to let the American public know how much we desire the return of our relic. My loud relations may sound crude, but it is a crudity born of loss. If your article can make us whole again, that would mean everything.

Most sincerely,

Maria Contessa Monterosa

Tessa finished repeating after Martin, but Gary was already typing into Google.

Martin sounded thoughtful. "Maria Contessa. I remember her. She was baptized a couple of years before I left, and I remember her guardian angel being so enthusiastic about his brand-new assignment. Poor thing."

Tessa looked at him, brow furrowed.

Martin said to her, "Think about the difference between parenting before you have a child and afterward."

"Oh!" Tessa chuckled. "So you're wondering whether her guardian has become disenthralled and cynical?"

"I'm not wondering that at all." Martin folded his arms. "The only question is how much."

"Ercole Monterosa," Gary was muttering under his breath. "I don't know why I didn't think to look up the designer of the reliquary. I focused entirely on the relic, not on the container."

Martin said, "To be fair, the reliquary exists only so you can focus on the relic."

"Stealing artwork from the enemy has a long tradition," Gary continued, staring at the screen as he clicked on a few different search results to open them in new windows. "The Germans did it. We're not supposed to."

Tessa said, "On the other hand, since the Americans blew up the church, maybe stealing the relic was the best thing they could have done."

Gary looked up. "How so?"

"It would have been crushed or burnt."

"I assume metal would survive a fire," Gary said.

"Depends on how hot it is. Our autoclave gets pretty hot, but there's an upper limit. Gold melts easily," Tessa added.

Gary said, "I don't think that's true. It's soft, but—Yeah, Google says nineteen hundred degrees Fahrenheit. The relic would have burnt," he added, "but the reliquary would have survived unless it got crushed when the ceiling caved in."

Martin said, "That part of the ceiling didn't collapse."

Tessa said, "But the theft saved it from the flames. So after it gets home, it may end up being in better shape than it if hadn't left. Isn't that the law of double effect?"

Martin's wings tightened. "Ethics 101. You can't do evil so that good may result."

Gary said, "I think you're talking more of a happy accident. They weren't taking it in order to preserve it. If preserving it were their intention, they'd have preserved it much better by not burning the church in the first place."

Tessa shrugged. "I'm not saying they were right. Only that in the long run, it might be better."

Martin said, "God brings good out of evil. It's the ultimate frustration of evil actions, but that doesn't mean the evil action was desirable or even acceptable. It only means God is stronger and smarter than any evil brought to bear against you."

She looked at him. "Is that Theology 101?"

Martin shook his head. "I need you to believe the thing I'm about to say next: in a thousand years, I heard a lot of homilies."

Tessa laughed. Gary said, "Nice to laugh at evil, hon. Oh, wow. Look at this."

He swiveled the screen so she could see an image. "Check out that metalwork! That's on display at the Vatican museum. She's right about her ancestor. Apparently Ercole Monterosa had a good deal of fame in that part of the world. Oh, and he was a priest too."

"More than that," said Martin, and Tessa related this to Gary. "Do you remember I told you about a DiOrio marrying a Monterosa? Those were his parents. Ercole was the second son in the family, and he contemplated the priesthood while also developing his art. The monastery laid claim to him, but they gave him a free hand in doing whatever art it took to keep him in the order."

Gary said, "That's impressive. So he wasn't kidding about the fasting and praying stuff. He was the real deal."

Martin said, "Iconographers have done that for thousands of years. They still do. Tell him."

Tessa repeated so Gary could hear it. He jotted that down. "Thank you. The more depth the better, but this is a whole new area to explore. The missing masterpiece of Ercole Monterosa."

He stopped then. "I may need Martin's help to write back to Maria Contessa."

Martin said, "Well, I figured he wasn't going to learn Italian overnight."

Tessa kissed Gary on the cheek. "He'll help you. No worries."

But by then Gary was lost in his research, and Tessa slipped from the room without him noticing.

TWELVE

Tessa had heard, at least a hundred times, "You don't get a medal for delivering without an epidural." The thrust was always that the speaker thought her clients, usually a specific client, craved suffering as a form of maternal heroism. In every single case, bar none, the client's decision to birth with a midwife was none of the speaker's business, and in most of those cases the speaker was unnecessarily defensive just because a woman was making a different decision than she had.

Tessa's usual response was, "You don't get a medal for delivering *with* one either," as a means of de-escalating the situation.

Today, Tessa wanted to respond, "Perhaps Amanda should get a medal for delivering without punching you in the face."

Amanda's mother-in-law was the most overbearing individual Tessa had ever dealt with, and that included herself. The woman found fault with everything, walked in with a sheaf of medical studies proving that midwives were all human rights violators, and disputed any opinion other than her own.

Tessa said, "I appreciate that you printed out the studies. I've read the Calgary one before, but the methodology was flawed. They lumped unintended, unassisted homebirths in with women delivering with a midwife after nine months of prenatal care."

"And this one?" The woman held up another article with an inflammatory headline.

"That's from 1985." She'd seen all of them before. It was almost too easy. "The study had too small a sample size to extrapolate any statistical significance."

Amanda looked unnecessarily meek beside this cyclone of a woman.

"You're endangering women and babies with your wild-west approach to delivery," said the woman. She had a name. What was it again? Oh, right, Suzanne Erickson. It was a wonder Amanda had gotten through her first appointments with the clinic. Tessa wanted to tell Amanda, next time, just don't tell your bulldog relatives where you're delivering until after the baby's born. That cuts down on the argumentation.

"I'd actually argue that it's more of the wild west in a hospital," Tessa said. "With MRSA, mandatory interventions with no statistical benefit to mother or baby, an episiotomy rate that's 100% higher than ours: that sounds more like taking your life in your hands."

Suzanne raised her papers. "There's a body of evidence that says you're wrong!"

"There's a body of evidence that says those studies are wrong." Tessa opened her hands. "If your only objection is, *But what if something happens?* then I'll ask you this:

What might happen? And what if that same issue happened in a hospital?"

Suzanne folded her arms. "Membranes rupture and the baby's head comes down onto the umbilical cord, crushing it in the pelvis. That happened to my cousin. The baby can die in seven minutes."

"The most likely cause for that situation is rupturing the membranes on a floating baby," Tessa replied, "and we don't rupture membranes unless the baby's head is fully engaged. Most of the time, we don't rupture membranes at all. Many hospitals do amniotomies to speed things along, so they're causing the issue you say you need a hospital to avoid."

Suzanne said, "And if it does happen?"

"If it does happen, what do you think the hospital will do? They don't have a surgical suite prepped and a surgeon ready to go at all hours. The surgeon is at home, twenty minutes away. The suite needs to be prepped, and that takes ten minutes. And here's the worst part: a woman in labor is usually checked by her nurses every fifteen minutes." Tessa sighed. "Things that go wrong have fifteen extra minutes to go really wrong before they're caught. Here, no one will leave her alone during active labor. The ambulance is two minutes away. We call them and we call the hospital, and then she'll arrive at the hospital before the surgeon."

It wasn't helping. A reassurance visit worked best when the concerned third party thought out-of-hospital birth meant delivering in a wheat field attended by an untrained flower child who crooned out encouragement in between baking loaves of bread. Nervous husbands were Tessa's favorites: they loved seeing the clean facility and the under-bed niches full of the same equipment you'd find in a hospital.

This woman had come for a fight, and it didn't matter what evidence Tessa produced. Suzanne didn't want to learn; she just wanted to win.

"Here's the thing," Tessa finally said, cutting Suzanne off by raising her voice and just speaking over her. "The prenatal monitoring she receives is exactly the same. Our attitude and culture are what's different. We also do nutrition counseling. We spend forty-five minutes on each appointment, as opposed to fifteen. We see clients more often. She's getting *better* prenatal care than she would at an OB, so your objection hinges on the actual birth. Our care is geared toward making sure low-risk women stay low-risk, and we refer high-risk women out to the surgeons they *should* be delivering with. The only things an OB can do that we can't do are epidurals and c-sections, and if she needs either one, she goes to the hospital, and we go with her."

Suzanne folded her arms. "You've brainwashed her."

Fine. It was time to shut this down. Tessa said, "I take it you're pro-choice?"

Suzanne said, "Of course I am!"

Tessa smiled. "Then respect her choice."

Suzanne glared.

Behind Suzanne, Amanda looked both horrified and startled.

Tessa said, "I know you disagree with her choice, but the burden is on you to respect her decisions about her body."

Suzanne actually geared down a bit at this point, so Tessa escorted her back through the birth suite and showed her the equipment again, plus the autoclave, plus the recovery rooms. She gave them a handout with all their standard safety precautions, and finally she ushered the pair of them out the door.

In her office she should have been making notes, but instead she thought to Martin, *I don't know if you were here just now, but wow that woman was a battle-axe.*

A sense of surprise blossomed over her. Tessa blinked.

"Are you going to show yourself?" she said. "Or should I just pretend you're here?"

Martin appeared by the exam bed, decked out in the white robe and with no readable facial features.

Oh! An early Martin. This was awkward.

She said, "And don't sound all smug, like now I know how it is dealing with me."

Martin replied, "I wouldn't say that. It would be more politic just to think it."

The angel streamed out emotions. He was just as thrilled as before, but beneath his delight thrummed a certain degree of calculation. Martin was absorbing every detail, and he was making decisions. The backflow of his sensations astounded Tessa after such a long dry spell: he was piecing together how this unexpected familiarity had come about, and when it might have started, as well as weighing what he could do with the situation.

She felt it inside: a beam of light. He had an opportunity to achieve something he very much desired.

This was a huge problem. What did early-Martin know, and what should she not let slip? She couldn't use his nickname because he hadn't known she'd give him one. She shouldn't mention the relic because the first time had to be his mention. But then what could she talk about?

Martin had no such conversational problems. "You've faced down worse clients."

"She's not a client. I won't be surprised if she makes Amanda sign up for OB shadowcare." Tessa shrugged. "Total waste of money, but it's her money."

"Then I won't scruple to confirm that you've guessed correctly. Amanda has retained an OB as well, and she sees him between your visits."

Tessa nodded. "So when the birth comes, she either has an easier transfer or she just goes to the surgeon. That's fine. It's happened before."

Martin's image dimmed. "You know it's not fine. You're protecting her, so it's disappointing if she can't be honest with you."

Tessa's nose wrinkled. "Don't you have a moral code where you can't tell me other people's secret guilt?"

Martin's wings fluffed. "It's not really secret. She'll tell you herself shortly."

What was "shortly" to a being who could step a few weeks forward in time? He was going to need some adjustments to think like a creature that was chronologically linear, but even so... No, this was ridiculous. Just ask. "How 'shortly'? Her next appointment is in two weeks."

"Her next visit is in three minutes because she only drove far enough to convince her mother-in-law she was going home. Amanda turned around at the gas station." Martin's image remained standing at attention, and his face revealed no emotion. "Therefore our conversation will terminate in approximately a hundred eighty seconds. If you have a request, now would be an opportune time to ask."

Both his phrasing and the way his image failed to fully sync to his words were fascinating.

Martin sounded tentative. "So, why did you ask to see me?"

He was famished for information. For once she'd flummoxed him, and he wanted it resolved. Underlying that, though, burned a huge question. God had handed him a tremendous gift. How should he use it?

Tessa blinked. No, not *using* her. Working with her. She could tell the difference. He thought in some way his plan would benefit her as well.

Unfortunately, without being able to talk relics and churches, she didn't have a reason to summon an angel. "I thought you liked touching base with me after difficult situations."

Still off-balance (well, no, a bodiless spirit wouldn't need *balance* as such, stupid English idioms), Martin said, "I do," in a way lacking all conviction. "But you've handled worse without touching base. What do you want me to do?"

Tessa said, "I don't suppose you can hit our friend Suzanne over the head with a cast-iron skillet?"

"That wouldn't be allowable by any stretch of the imagination."

He didn't look horrified. He should have.

Tessa smiled at him. "Way outside the scope of your authority?"

"Very much so. I wouldn't even be allowed to let the air out of her tires. I could, if you like, warn you if she attempts to interfere again in your realm of authority."

Tessa's eyebrows shot up. "How would you know that?"

"I'd feel it if she encroached. You'd understand it as similar to the way a violin's strings vibrate the wood of the violin."

She would understand no such thing because it made no sense whatsoever. "Well, if it's allowed, I'd like it if you could warn me, thanks."

Stiffly, Martin's form nodded.

Tessa ventured, "How far does your authority extend?"

"It's situational, and in some respects authority changes based on a subtle network of connections and requests." Martin paused, as if figuring out how to explain very simple concepts to a very simple mind without sounding condescending. Somehow, he succeeded. "In this case, your client is your responsibility, and since she'll entrust the information about shadowcare to you anyhow, I'm within boundaries."

Tessa leaned forward. "How do you get your assignments?"

"From God," he answered, somewhat surprised. "Although if you're asking about sub-assignments, many of them happen in the course of working on your main assignment." He added as an afterthought, "Much of doing the will of God consists in doing the good work that's right in front of you."

Tessa smiled. "I like that."

"I knew you would. That's why I said it. Your client is here," Martin said, and his form blinked out.

Okay, that was really weird. Weirder than usual.

Tessa stepped into the waiting room and so was right there when Amanda opened the door.

"Oh! You startled me. Um—"

Tessa pointed to her office.

Amanda glanced around, nervous. "How did you know I was coming back?"

"A midwife knows these things." Amanda sat on the bed, and Tessa closed the door. "I've got ten minutes until my next appointment, but you can have them all."

Amanda stared at the floor. "I'm sorry she was so rude to you. She's not usually that rude with me."

"The word you're looking for is 'badgering,'" said Tessa, "and I will warn you now that her disrespect for your boundaries will extend into every area of your life for as long as you allow it."

"I'm not *allowing* it," Amanda muttered. "She's unstoppable."

"She's stoppable. She's not an angel who can override your free will and force words into your head." Tessa flinched the moment she said that, but it was already out. Anyhow, she'd enforced boundaries with Martin. "If you hung up the phone whenever she harangued you, or if you walked out of the living room when she dictated your decisions, she'd realize her lack of power."

Amanda said, "She'd get far worse. You should have seen her about our wedding."

Tessa said, "Did you give in to her on every point?"

Amanda looked aside.

"And did that make her happy? Or did it just create more demands?"

Now Amanda looked really uncomfortable.

"This is going to come to a head in future years." Tessa went to her bookshelf. "Your marriage will suffer if you and your husband don't set firm boundaries and mutually maintain them. Your husband has to not only take your side but actually go on the offensive against his mother's bullying."

Amanda snorted. "Yeah, that'll happen."

"If you don't lay down the law now," Tessa said, pulling out the books she needed, "you're going to be back here in two years, pregnant with your second, telling me about how your mother-in-law is dictating where your firstborn is going to preschool, deciding whether you will go back to work, and vetoing the name you picked."

Amanda closed her eyes.

Tessa turned, holding two paperbacks. "Tell me the truth because unlike her, I will respect your decision. Are you getting shadowcare from an obstetrician just to shut her up?"

Amanda swallowed. "How did you know?"

"Didn't I just say midwives know these things?" Tessa kept her voice clinical. "What I don't know is, are you planning to deliver with her obstetrician? Because if you prefer to birth her way, with her chosen care providers, I will photocopy all your records right now and consult with the other provider to transfer your care."

"I want to stay with you, but she's all over me. I keep telling her it's perfectly safe, but she doesn't listen. I think she means well, and I went to her doctor just to reassure her."

"But it's never enough until she gets exactly what she wants, and then she'll ask for more. That's called 'moving the goalposts.' She's a classic bully." Tessa handed the two books to Amanda: *Boundaries* and *The Dance of Anger*. "Read both and then tell me she's not a bully."

Amanda couldn't meet Tessa's eyes.

"The answer is either strong boundaries or moving two thousand miles away." Tessa sighed. "I don't want that for you. You asked me to be responsible for your baby, so I'm informing you of a threat to your baby's well-being. When there's long term third-party interference in a marriage, it often leads to divorce."

Amanda still wouldn't look up, so Tessa sat in the rocking chair. "I'm not angry at you. You're in a bad situation."

Amanda nodded.

"You have the power here, and do you know why?" When Amanda looked up, Tessa said, "You have what she wants. You have her grandchild."

THIRTEEN

Tessa's phone had only this mysterious text from Gary: "We have a guest for dinner."

Clearly he wanted a text back along the lines of, "Isn't it inhospitable to devour a visitor?" But no, Tessa had an exam room to clean and supplies to restock. He was cooking, so let him figure out how much rice to put in the steamer. She'd figure it out when she arrived.

Let's see: it probably wasn't Mom, unless he was poking fun at himself for forgetting to tell her last time. It most likely wasn't the Pulitzer Prize Committee, although she'd gladly make room at the table for twenty business-suited journalists once they realized what an excellent writer Gary was.

Tessa turned to put towels on a shelf and found herself face-to-face with Martin.

She jumped back, gasping.

"Aren't you going to ask who it is?" Martin said.

Tessa steadied her racing heart. "Won't I find out eventually?"

"So you're not even a little curious?"

When was this Martin? He wore a robe as in the early days, but the fabric had some motion to it. He also looked excited, so whenever in his own timeline he was coming from, he'd had practice manipulating his facial expressions.

"Not even a tiny smidgen of curiosity." She closed the cabinet. "I cannot think of a single reason I'd hasten the unmasking of this unexpected dinner guest."

"You keep surprising me." Martin rubbed his chin. "Gary thinks it's fun to tease you, and he knows you pretty well, so in effect you're surprising him as well."

Tessa said, "Is it my state legislator? Is it Amanda's mother-in-law, Suzanne, armed with a subpoena and five deputy sheriffs?"

"Perhaps we could play charades." Martin sounded thoughtful. "I'll render the full explanation for this individual's presence in a sentence with a hundred thirty-four syllables, and you get to work on the first one now. First word, one syllable, rhymes with 'knee.'"

She turned to him, but he hadn't yet nailed down the art of the smirk. "Sir Angel, I do believe you're mocking me."

"Madame Midwife, I do believe you may be correct, but it's a friendly mockery between allies." Martin waited, but when she didn't go on, he said, "It might be about the relic."

Okay, so that nailed down a rough time-period he might be from. He knew she was cooperating about the relic, but this also wasn't after the Monterosa family's email barrage.

Still, when was he? He must have already told her his name, so the next thing she said would be safe. "You quoted me back to myself. I just realized today, about an hour after I said it."

"I may have." Martin was clearly enjoying himself. "Your own words are the best way to get through to you while in a state of high emotion because you already find them familiar."

"I hadn't said them yet."

"In some respects it works better that way. Humans take comfort in their own voices, so when you hear something phrased the way you'd say it, you trust it."

"Don't you find that manipulative?" Interestingly, she had no idea whether Martin-now was before or after the Martin who had accused her of doing exactly that.

"I wanted to reassure you. I'd just scared you terribly when I hadn't meant to. But you still haven't replied to Gary. I think he really wants you to ask who's your dinner guest."

She texted Gary. "Should I be worried about this guest?"

Gary replied immediately. "Not at all."

She showed Martin the phone. "He's leading me on with a trail of breadcrumbs."

Martin's eyes glinted. "You know, your next text could be asking whether it's someone very specific, and he'll wonder how you knew."

She raised her eyebrows.

Martin offered, "Midwives just know these things...?"

"He'll know it was you. I love him in part because of his massive intellectual prowess."

Still, she texted Gary again. "Does this guest have fur and four feet?"

His reply: "Hasn't mentioned either."

Martin said, "Ask if it's another angel."

"You're having way too much fun with this." Still, she texted Gary, "Celestial being?"

"Maybe sent by one."

"Tell him no," said Martin. "I felt it would happen, but I had no idea when."

"So you jumped ahead to find out about it," she said. "You're like a little kid who can't wait for Christmas and goes peeking under the wrapping paper."

Martin recoiled. "Everything had to be made straight, and I needed to know what to straighten."

She chuckled as she texted Gary. "That would be a negative. Is it a high-ranking official from the local school district who is curious as to whether our sons' parents are both feral?"

"As opposed to only one of us?" Gary asked. "No."

With the suite straightened, she returned to her desk. On the way there, Karen intercepted her with a pink phone message slip.

"I'm not impatient," Martin said as she carried it into her office. "This work is important, and I detected a change in advance of when it was coming."

She shut the door. "Something you thought was very good, and you didn't want to wait."

"I don't have to wait. I can just look. That's not impatience. It's prudence."

She paused. "Are you offended? I'm sorry. You liked joking with me last week. I'll back off." She went to her filing cabinet and pulled out the folder for the client who'd called.

Her client was having early pregnancy exhaustion issues and wanted to know if she could be anemic. In

Tessa's opinion, without even opening the file, of course the woman knew if she was anemic. She checked the bloodwork, noted the iron number, and then called her back. *Your numbers were borderline before. If you want to take a gentle iron supplement, I think that's for the best. You're in Hopkinton, right? If you go to the compounding pharmacy on 85, they've got a liquid iron supplement that a lot of my patients have had good results with. We could do another CBC if you like, but in a case like this, I think it's best just to supplement first and see if that helps. Call me in a few days if you don't feel any improvement.*

As she hung up the phone, she thought to herself, *Impatience.* Martin would, later in his timeline, disclose that his injudicious time-hop was the reason the church got destroyed. She'd just accused him of what he believed about himself, so her teasing was anything but teasing. No wonder he got offended.

She couldn't see him anymore. "Martin? I'm really sorry. I have no idea how you guys move back and forth in time, so I shouldn't have joked around."

He reappeared. "If you don't understand the basic mechanics, kindly don't accuse me of character flaws I don't have."

"I thought, because you were joking with me about texting my husband, that we were having fun and not being entirely serious. I would never criticize your virtue or your skill."

He considered. "Thank you."

"You're welcome. Now if you don't mind, I have a husband to keep tormenting."

Martin didn't join again in the textual jousting, which Tessa found oddly disappointing. Odd because it had felt comfortable and correct to have him there, egging her on. Martin liked Gary. Whenever they interacted, in that slantwise interaction where Martin had to pass through her to get to Gary but not so in the other direction, she got the sense that Martin was pleased with Gary and all his efforts.

Martin should have singled out Gary in the first place, regardless of whatever reason he thought mandated selecting her.

Martin's banter with Gary solidified that approval. Gary was a good man. She'd always known that. It was why she'd fallen in love with him: that straightforward heart with its constant focus and unwavering belief. She'd driven most of the changes in their marriage, but always he'd come onboard with an enthusiasm and a strength she'd never experienced from anyone else. Martin's easy relationship with him, inasmuch as the two of them could relate, meant Martin recognized it too.

But she didn't point that out as she got into her car for the drive home. Instead she just texted Gary with, "I'm on my way. If you found the Abominable Snowman, you'll have to surprise me at the door."

He replied as she turned on the engine: "Shorter, warmer, and slightly less abominable than reported."

Tessa let herself into the house only to be tackled by the kindergartener. "Mommy!" Eric exclaimed. "Mommy! He's a real soldier! He has pictures and an old uniform, but he doesn't have a gun!"

"I need to take off my coat," Tessa said. "Who's a real soldier?"

Gary met her at the entrance. "In the kitchen. You've got to meet him."

Sitting at Gary's place was an old man with a straggly grey beard and sharp brown eyes. "Well, ma'am," he said, "pardon me for not getting to my feet, but my legs aren't quite what they used to be."

"Don't worry." She crossed the kitchen to shake his hand. "My husband said we had a guest, but he didn't tell me anything more."

"No, that's our secret!" The man laughed, Gary laughed, and Martin might as well be laughing too because that would complete the set. "I'm Howard Masters, Sergeant, F Company, 304th Infantry Regiment of the 76th Infantry Division."

Tessa inclined her head. "Pleased to meet you. Thank you for your service, sir."

Gary said, "Sergeant Masters saw my article and had some information that might point us in the right direction."

Tessa pulled out a chair. "But you weren't part of the platoon in question."

"No, ma'am." Masters had a southern accent both delicious and imposing. "After Montecassino, I met up with what remained of their platoon and took them into my own. The group of them kept to themselves, kept their heads down, and did their jobs. It was on the way home that one of them pulled out this pretty bauble and asked what I thought he should do with it."

Tessa's eyes widened. "Do you remember which soldier?"

"Not at all. I didn't know these fellows very well or for very long. Toward the end, you tended not to," he added. "The new guys straight out of basic training, if they lasted the first week, you'd start warming up to them. Most of them just went out on the line and died."

Tessa shuddered. Masters shrugged. "It was part of the way the brass figured they'd win the war: throw enough of our young men at the Germans and keep replacing the dead guys with fresh ones. Anyhow, one of them pulled out this bauble and said, 'Now what do we do?'"

Gary returned to cooking, but his phone lay on the counter, recording audio. Tessa said, "Did you get a good look at it?"

"It looked like big ugly jewelry to me, and I'm not much of a jewelry guy. I asked where they got it, and they said their sergeant took it from a church up north. He was dead now. They'd pulled it from his gear."

Tessa nodded. "Did you touch it?" If Masters had held it, did that make him a third-class relic?

Masters shuddered. "I wanted nothing to do with it. It's papistry. I told them to throw it out the window of the train because it's just an idol. Going through Italy, we were surrounded on all sides by statues of this and that saint and Mary this and Mary that, and I was sick of it all. If they blew up a church, good, just one fewer brothel for the Whore of Babylon, you know?"

Tessa didn't know, but she could read his tone. "Blowing up a church can't be right."

"We flattened Montecassino, and that was a monastery." Whatever things you could say about Masters, plagued by deeds of the past was not one of them. "One more headless statue or one more burnt-out church didn't make any difference to me. So I told them, chuck that thing out the window. It's an idol. One of the guys went no, no, it's valuable, and he made like he was going to take it home and sell it. Another guy said you can't sell these things because God will get mad at you, like God isn't mad at people for worshipping body parts of other people in the first place." Masters laughed out loud. "They kept bickering. None of them liked having it around, but none of them wanted to get rid of it either."

"Did they say why?" said Tessa.

Gary was listening the whole time, and she wondered momentarily whether this wasn't his plan: use her to get maximal information from Masters because she just happened to have that knack with people. Even Martin had opened up. Maybe she'd suss out something Gary hadn't already.

"It was a war," Masters said. "Guys didn't ask too much. These soldiers, they were close and you could tell they'd been through a nightmare. Wasn't my place to pry. I could have ordered them to hand it over, since I ranked them all, but I let them have their trinket. It wasn't doing them any good anyhow. They'd all been through hell by that point. If they went to hell for keeping an idol, it'd be no different anyway."

His theology bugged her, but Tessa chose not to question it. "By that point, you must have been through hell too."

"Sugar, I was ready as anything for the war to be done. I wanted hot meals and dry feet and no one shooting at me." He nodded. "We all were. I signed up to do my duty by my country and by my God, but I had no idea how hard it would be. Every day, every stinking day, waking up and wondering who you're going to shoot today and whose orders you follow today and whether you live. The Italians, they didn't make it easy on us. They couldn't have mismanaged things worse if they tried, and you know how Italians are? Three Italians, five fights. They'd disagree with you just because they wanted to. They'd help you and then turn around and work against you in the same breath. Cowards and traitors. If someone stole their precious thing, then fine. Steal it. Steal it all. Just don't worship it."

Tessa snickered. "Surely the soldiers weren't worshipping the relic?"

"Nah. If they'd prayed to the thing, I'd have crushed it under the train wheels myself. They took it to get revenge, so I let them have it."

Tessa leaned forward. "Revenge? For what?"

"They'd been ambushed. Someone led them in and said they could stay overnight, have a hot meal, sleep in a bed. The people seemed nice enough. But then the fascists shot one of them, and the sergeant had enough. The went out into the street in pursuit."

Tessa said, "But if it was just the two fascist sympathizers—"

"Is it, though?" Masters shook his head. "Do you ever know how many there are? You get lured into a house. A family makes you a meal. You're thinking about maybe sleeping where no one's going to kill you. Then someone takes away the only comfort you're likely to have for months." Masters snorted. "I'd have snapped too. The disappointment is worse than anything you could imagine. You lure me in and then you shoot me? Unfair, unfair."

Tessa's heart quickened. "Was it all a ruse, then?"

"I don't know. I wasn't there. Sometimes civilians were real nice. Sometimes they'd betray you without a second thought. And our boys snapped. They used grenades, and the sergeant let them loot the place. He took their pretty little relic, which your article said was the *heart of the town*. A heart made of poison for a town full of venom."

Tessa couldn't breathe.

Masters said, "If that was their heart, no wonder they betrayed those men."

Tessa could only manage, "Wow."

She couldn't agree. She couldn't disagree, though. What if that really had been the plan all along? She'd assumed from the start that the Barlassinesi, the Monterosas and the DiOrios both, were innocent of the initial insult.

But her own relatives could have been the betrayers. Her people could have been the reason for the massacre, and thus Martin picked her to make it right. It was fitting, in a horrible way. If her people ruined it, then her people had a burden to set it right again.

"Now, sugar, don't look so shocked." Masters chuckled. "Those Italians, we didn't expect anything good. They'd shoot themselves in the foot to get out of service. The Germans though they were slippery cowards, and I never saw anything to say otherwise. So our boys, I told them to get over it. Take the thing home and sell it. Or throw it in the trash. I wasn't going to turn them in to anyone. The southern part of Italy was starving to death and the northern part was in chaos. What's one more horror in a war full of horrors?"

Across the kitchen, Gary met her eyes. She said, "Need any help?"

No, she was the one who needed help, and he saw it. He said, "Actually, could you please set the table?"

Masters said, "When I saw your article, I said to myself, 'These people, they need to know the real story.' So I took an Acela from Union Station in D.C. and rode in style. Tell them you're a World War II veteran and suddenly there's an upgrade, especially if it's near Veterans Day." He laughed. "I tried that at the grocery store, and it didn't work there. Then when I got to South Station, I called my worthless grandson to pick me up, and then I got to surprise you."

"I didn't know he was coming until the doorbell rang," said Gary.

Tessa said, "Lucky thing you were home, then."

Yeah, said Martin's voice in her head. *Lucky.*

She snickered as she got down a stack of dinner plates.

You should invite his worthless grandson over for dinner, Martin added.

Tessa said, "Your grandson, where is he?"

"I sent him to find a coffee shop where he can waste his money on fancy coffee and play with his phone."

"Have him join us," Tessa said. "He can play with his phone here."

Masters pulled out his own phone and texted. "What are you having?"

Gary said, "Chili and corn bread."

"Should be illegal for your northerners to make chili." Masters sighed. He texted again, then said, "He's coming."

Tessa set the leaf in the table and added two chairs. Masters looked like she imagined a fisherman would look: thick beard, dark eyes, weathered face. He had plenty of opinions and not much tact. And what was with his open hatred for Catholicism and derision of Italians? She'd need to harness the older boys before dinner so as to avoid putting this soldier in the midst of yet another war.

But by the same token, she could hear that vulnerability in the memories. He'd gotten on a train from Washington, D.C. in order to disclose something he could have said over the phone. Why?

With the table set, she went upstairs and warned all five boys that they were to let the guest say whatever he wanted. "He's got some rather strong opinions, and you're not going to agree with most of them."

Alex frowned. "You always tell us to stand up for what we believe in."

"I also tell you to pick your battles. The man's in his nineties. Do him the courtesy of allowing him to be wrong."

She got back downstairs in time to hear Masters telling Gary that the problem with vegetarians was how those tenderhearted loonies ate bird food, but a man needed a good steak. The doorbell rang, and she answered it to find a Lexus in the driveway and a man in his early thirties wearing a suit and tie.

She didn't say, "Oh, you must be the worthless grandson." She didn't. It was very hard not to, but she didn't.

"I'm terribly sorry," the visitor said, "but my name is Jason Masters, and I believe my grandfather is holding court in your kitchen?"

"Come right in. Dinner's almost ready, and we're pleased to have you both."

"Oh, good. I thought perhaps he'd invited both of us over. He's rather a strong personality." Jason left his coat and hat on a peg, then accompanied Tessa into the kitchen. "He didn't want me coming in with him, so I went to the Panera to work on a report."

Tessa said, "We have an open-door policy for dinner. Come in and enjoy yourself."

Once the boys found out Howard Masters was a veteran, they unleashed a barrage of questions. Jason Masters sat in stoic silence, offering brief answers whenever Tessa tried to include him in the conversation. He was an analyst who worked with a public policy firm that advised the governor's office. *Some worthless grandson,* she thought toward Martin. The guy drove money, dressed up with money, and most likely was used to hanging out with money. His table manners were impeccable, and he complimented the meal while his grandfather made sure to point out how it was nothing like the chili his wife used to make.

During a lull, Jason said, "You have a 'Say No To H.8937' sign in the yard. Would you mind if I asked why you oppose it?"

Tessa said, "Because women need midwifery services, and Bill H.8937 is going to curtail them."

Jason said, "What kind of services are we talking about? We've gotten a bit beyond women giving birth in the fields."

"That's why we have certification and licensing for midwives, and why midwives provide the same prenatal services women would receive in an obstetric setting. The philosophy is different, but the standard of care is the same."

Jason took a bite of corn bread. "How so?"

The boys sent up a chorus of protests. Gary said, "You'll have to excuse our sons. They were raised by wolves."

"Raised by birth-aware wolves," Mark muttered.

"Were these guys born at home?" said Jason.

Eric piped up, "I was! I was born in a pool! Him too!" Brian nodded.

Tessa smiled. "They're correct that I'll talk all night if you give me a platform."

Masters said, "It's relics all over this place. Papist relics and birth relics and bird food."

Jason tried to hide his flinch.

"And apple cobbler for dessert," Tessa added. "I didn't whip the cream or churn the butter myself."

Gary murmured, "We should keep a cow."

Mark said, "Goats. I keep telling you, goats. That way Mom can milk them, and I don't have to mow the lawn."

"And then you get to clean goat poo out of the pen." Joe shook his head. "Just shut up and mow the lawn."

Masters laughed. "Got to love a house full of boys."

"I do," said Tessa.

Jason said, "You have no daughters? So why that much advocacy for midwifery?"

Tessa said, "I'm a certified professional midwife."

"Oh!" He laughed. "Pardon me. I encounter advocates for so many causes that I assume everyone is an activist. You're actually a professional."

They made it through dinner without the boys having to defend their heritage. Masters shared more stories over coffee and apple cobbler while Jason parked himself in the living room with his laptop. Masters had plenty of tales about World War II, talking about life in the foxholes

("You'd die for your foxhole buddy. You'd do anything for him") and about the struggle to keep your feet dry during winter and mud season ("You'd drape your clean socks around your neck so they'd dry off while the ones you were wearing got soaked. At night you'd switch. They'd punish you for insubordination if you got trench foot, like you'd do that on purpose").

It was well past dark when Masters declared, "Now where's my worthless grandson? It's time to leave."

At the front door, Tessa handed Jason Masters his coat and hat. "You're with the Milliston Common Birth Center?" Jason said. "I took the liberty of looking you up on Google."

"That's us. You can contact me if you want more information."

Howard Masters said, "You're not married, Jason. Don't go having any babies yet."

Jason gave a pained smile. Tessa said, "But if you do, and if that bill dies, we'll be there for you."

Jason turned to his grandfather. "I'll warm up the car for you."

Masters huffed. "Fine, go do that." He turned to Tessa. "Coddled brats. You know his car has heated seats? They'll baby your behind the whole time you're cruising from one Starbucks to the next."

She chuckled as she reached for her coat.

"Wow, that coat's seen better days." Masters barked a laugh. "Midwives don't make any money, do they! I was wearing better than that in the trenches."

Tessa sighed. "You know how it is. There's always something more important."

"You don't need to wear rags that the Goodwill would throw away." Masters focused his dark eyes on her. "You know, I like you. You're good people. When I read that article, I wasn't sure because dragging up something from a war so long ago, what's the point? Trying to make money off a few old men's broken hearts?"

Tessa said, "Not at all. The relic needs to go home."

"With a few more dead bodies lying in its wake long after we thought the war finished taking bites out of us." Masters shook his head. "But I like you, so I'm going to tell you something. Men are dangerous. The most dangerous kind of man is the man who's ashamed of his own guilt."

Tessa shivered.

"Me, I've got nothing to hide anymore. I'm right with Christ, so I'm not going to hide anything from anyone. But people with shame, there's nothing they won't do."

Martin had said as much on the night he'd told her about the theft. Tessa said, "Do you think Gary is in danger?"

"I have no idea, but those men, what I saw there on that train was shame. They knew they'd done wrong, and one of them was already dead. Now they had this thing that reminded all of them of their guilt. You know why they didn't throw it away?"

Tessa shook her head.

"Because you can't throw away your shame."

She recoiled.

"It sticks to you. You can't set free your shame, so it eats you alive. That relic, they were going to hold onto it or hide it or pass it around, but they what they weren't going to do was let it go because you can't let it go. It would always be there, burning in their memory because they had to do something about it, only they didn't know what."

Tessa lowered her eyes. "That's awful."

"Lots of things are awful, sugar. But the only evil that destroys you is the one you carry with you, and those men, they carried a lot. Not their papist idol. They were carrying something else, and I don't know what it was, but that was the thing they couldn't let go. That idol wasn't about a saint. It was really the idol of whatever thing they did." Masters leaned on his cane. "One of them? He's still carrying it. Bet on that."

Jason returned to the door.

"Gary!" she called.

Masters shook Tessa's hand. "Thank you very much for the dinner, ma'am. And you, sir."

Gary came up behind Tessa. "Thank you letting me interview you, and thank you again for your service to our country."

Masters made a dismissive noise. He walked with his cane down the driveway back to his worthless grandson's hundred-thousand-dollar car.

"Thank you for getting him to open up," said Gary.

Inside, Tessa heard Martin as well: *I thank you too.* Followed a moment later by, *I'm concerned he's more right than he knows.*

FOURTEEN

*D*ear Mr. Testerman,
    Thank you again for your beautiful work about our relic and the tremendous loss to our town of Barlassina.

Gary had Tessa translating for him again, or rather had Tessa asking Martin to translate. Martin didn't mind. He'd done three letters so far, since Gary's newest piece had gotten disseminated through Barlassina all at the same time. This letter was from Maria Contessa Monterosa.

We very much appreciate the in-depth study, giving the history of Barlassina and the history of Peter the Martyr's relic. You will be pleased to note that some of the smaller-minded among us actually sat down and counted the number of quotes you provided from the Monterosas versus the DiOrios, and they're furious that you made it exactly even.

Gary said to Tessa, "If they really feel like compiling statistics, both families got the same number of words. That took a little skill, let me tell you."

"You know the saying that only Nixon can go to China?" Tessa said, wrapping her arms around his shoulders. "Maybe only you can go to Barlassina."

I noticed that you never explicitly delved into the animosity between our families, and you had each side tell their stories themselves. You are a clever man.

Gary leaned back in his chair. "I'm okay with each side thinking I'm on their side."

I will warn you that the DiOrio family is claiming you as one of theirs.

"Well, there goes that idea," Gary said.

You appear to have married one of them, which is unfortunate. But since you're not related by blood, and because you wife is separated from her clan by an ocean, I'm giving you the benefit of the doubt.

Tessa had to stop repeating Martin's translation at that point because she was laughing too hard. "I'm sorry." She wiped the tears from her eyes. "My clan. Thank goodness for billions of tons of salt water, separating me from the source of my evil."

"Don't forget the cleansing effect of my presence." Gary arched his eyebrows at her, then kissed her. "Surely that counts for something."

Please understand that neither side is blameless, but the Monterosas have been more than willing to permit the restoration work to go forward. Every time we've issued permits, the DiOrios have blocked it, either by withholding money or taking some legal action. We want the church rebuilt. But the DiOrios will neither rebuild the church nor permit its demolition.

This wasn't entirely true. Tessa had it from her DiOrio relations that the Monterosas liked to issue permits with impossible restrictions or unacceptable specifications, which the DiOrios would then protest. The permit would then be revoked and the matter tabled for another ten years, each side blaming the other. They'd created the perfect interlocking system where no gear could ever turn any of the other gears.

"Allow me to translate your translation," Gary murmured to himself, interlacing his fingers behind his neck as he leaned back in his chair, "Neither side is blameless, but it's completely not our fault at all."

Tessa chuckled. Martin continued:

As long as your reporting remains balanced and fair, we are interested to learn if any leads turn up on our relic. Again, no one in Barlassina wants the thieves prosecuted, but surely there must be some legal leverage to uncover the relic and bring it home.

"America," Tessa intoned, "the land of lawsuits."

"I'm talking to our congressman about passing a law that the relic needs to reappear." Gary grinned. "That ought to do it."

She closed with greetings to him and to his DiOrio wife, and Gary said, "So that whole thing about DiOrio women...?"

"Not my deal," Tessa said. "Remember? I was raised here."

He gave her a pointed look. "Apparently it's in your genetics. You're wild, and I never knew it. What was that phrase the other Monterosa guy used....? Subterranean street-walker?"

Martin had translated that phrase reluctantly, and Tessa knew he'd softened it.

"I love you, but my underground skills are a bit rusty."

Gary winked at her. "Need some practice?"

"The boys are still awake," she said, laughing at him. "And you've got work to do."

"Yeah, yeah. After I write next month's sailboating column."

Martin appeared in the kitchen while she was preparing tomorrow's school lunches. "I'm moderately concerned about the Italian side," he said. "It was a concern from the start that the DiOrios might claim Gary as one of their own, but there was no way around that. At least Maria Contessa established contact with Gary prior to the DiOrios poisoning the well."

"Gary's also pretty good at keeping things smooth." Each of the boys had his own specifications for lunch. Joe made whatever he wanted, but she still assembled the others. The school's lunches weren't worth talking about, but every so often one of the boys resorted to the lunch line. Then the next day it was back to Mom. Spanakopita. Yogurt. Veggie lasagna made in a way that the boys could pick it up and eat it as a block of cheesy yumminess, and not coincidentally done in a way that horrified her mother. Tessa couldn't cook that when Mom was around, not again, or risk disownment.

"You should write to your relatives and ask them to back down."

Tessa laughed out loud. "You worked with these families for a thousand years. Would that have ever worked, ever, with any of my relatives?"

Martin said, "Fair point. I wonder if there's a way you could trick them into backing off about you."

"You did say they'd taught you all about manipulation and trickery."

"Did I?" Martin sounded amused. "Then I'm probably right."

"See? We're useful for some things."

Martin folded his arms. "I never asked for humans to be useful."

She put a note into Eric's. Brian liked getting notes, but this year he'd told her he was too old for it. No, he wasn't too old for notes, but his friends were on his case about it. Thus went all the wonderful things of childhood. Either the kid outgrew them or else his friends outgrew them, and then they were cast aside until whenever in the future they'd be rediscovered.

That didn't destroy the role of motherhood. It only meant you had to cultivate different skills, a clandestine code of *I-love-yous* that the other kids couldn't decode and mock even though they probably had a similar code with their own mothers.

Martin added, "God isn't as interested in having us use one another as in having us love and be of service to one another."

Tessa paused. "That's...not what I would have thought you'd say."

Martin chuckled. "What would you have thought I'd say?"

"I mean, you're talking to me for a specific purpose. We're trying to get back the relic."

Martin said, "In all fairness, you consented to help locate the relic because you thought I would be of use to you with the anti-midwifery legislation."

"Right, so that's a mutually beneficial association. Clearly there's nothing wrong with making an agreement."

"God doesn't end things there. He didn't assign angels to work with humans because it in any way benefits the angels to do so."

"But you have a scorecard in your head." Tessa felt Martin's surprise, and she added, "You count things as wins and losses. I tend to be fuzzier. I like meeting in the middle. You know, like a midwife does." She grinned at him. "You'd be an obstetrician. One of the good ones, but still. Statistics and scorecards."

"That's not at all true." Martin frowned. "God gave me an assignment, and I'm doing it, but we're not trying to score points and level up."

"I get that. You're obedient, and it's nice." She zipped up Eric's lunch box. "Don't read too much into it. I was joking about humans being useful for teaching angels how to engage in subterfuge."

She set the lunches in the fridge, then gathered the containers to put them away

Gary came up behind her and wrapped his arms around her waist. "Hey, babe. So, are you going to be telling me about those subterranean tricks?"

Martin was saying, "It's not exactly subterfuge if you're up front about using someone's weaknesses against their own self interest."

Gary breathed into her ear, but she pulled away. "Um, maybe not now?"

Martin said, "Oh, I'm sorry. You wanted to have intercourse with your husband. We can talk more in a while," and he disappeared.

Gary sounded confused. "Why?"

"Never mind. I—" Okay, that was weird. It wasn't that Martin was embarrassed. He just...well, it was practical. "Martin was talking to me, but he left."

Gary snuggled back into her. "I have good timing?"

She turned to face Gary, and he pulled her close. "No, more like he said, go have intercourse with your husband."

"My man Martin!" Gary exclaimed, and Tessa laughed. Gary kissed her, and although still a bit confused, she relaxed into his arms.

On her day off, Tessa sat with a cup of coffee while Gary filled the kitchen table with photographs, note cards, and sticky notes all about Barlassina and the missing heart of Saint Peter of Verona.

"This is fascinating, but what do you think this accomplishes?"

Gary kept moving items. "Sometimes when an article won't come together, I do this to get the ideas reframed without rewriting the whole piece. I was wondering if we couldn't rejigger the questions without getting more threats of lawsuits."

Tessa straightened. "More threats?"

"Oh, yeah, I forgot." He didn't look up. "Ellen Ashland sent a cease and desist letter from a bottom-feeder attorney, plus threats about suing us for libel. Nothing with teeth." He sounded unconcerned in the extreme. "They can't sue for libel because first off, I haven't named her father in any of the articles, and secondly, everything I documented is backed up by facts. If she files, her father has to be named in the suit. Once he's named, it's public record, which is exactly what she doesn't want."

Tessa frowned. "Does her bottom-feeder attorney know that?"

"Doesn't matter. The magazines all have their own attorneys on staff, and I'm sure at least one of them is writing back at five hundred dollars an hour to inform her that if she feels like wasting her money, they're more than happy to expose her father's name to the world."

Tessa's nose wrinkled. "It doesn't seem fair. She's only protecting him."

Gary said, "We haven't harmed him. I made sure of that when I wrote the article." He hummed. "I wonder if your mother will come back next week with more photos from her brother's house."

Mom had made arrangements to visit New Jersey. Maybe Aunt Cecilia had more junk she wanted to unload. Who knew? Maybe after all this searching, it would turn out the relic was in a box of junk Aunt Cecilia had made Uncle Joe stash in the attic twenty-five years ago.

Tessa walked around the table to look at how Gary had arranged everything. It unfolded like a pictorial map of a world-spanning tragedy. He'd placed the relic's photo at the center, then arranged other tidbits in clusters, then sticky notes to draw arrows connecting one thing to the next.

"You could use a whiteboard for this," he said, rubbing his chin as he moved one paper to the opposite side of the table. "This feels more mobile."

She found herself back in front of the very old Barlassina photos, and without thinking she reached for Great-Aunt Alicia's.

"Everyone's in long black coats," Gary said. "Must have been the fashion."

Looking at the First Communion photo, Tessa didn't answer. She'd had never had a daughter. All five times, she'd wondered what it would be like to raise a little girl. She'd thought about the things she'd say and what values she'd teach, and how she'd tell this girl in very strong terms to be proud of her body and everything it could accomplish. Women too often were treated as though their bodies were shameful, as if they were faulty versions of the male template. But if anything, midwifery had shown Tessa the value and the power of a woman's body.

Every time, after she gave birth, it had been a boy in her arms. She'd been overjoyed every time, of course, but in a way it meant that her clients became surrogate daughters. Those women were the ones she told to respect their bodies.

How did she die? Tessa thought to Martin, unsure if he were there right now.

Her oldest son was a priest at Holy Cross. Martin sounded subdued. *She was desperate to make sure he was safe. When the shooting stopped, she ran for the church. I wasn't able to help her. She had her youngest boy in her arms. When she rounded the corner, she surprised a soldier.*

For a moment, Tessa saw images as though looking at living photos. Her great-aunt Alicia, black coat flapping in the wind and a preschool-age child on her hip. Gaunt face, high cheekbones, eyes just like Mom's. Hair tight back in a bun. And then the image of a soldier staring at the woman on the ground with blood all around, a soldier horrified at what he'd done, shocked by a small boy's shrieks. The soldier had screamed at her. Martin hadn't heard it well, or maybe the words weren't coming through in his memories. The soldier was angry, hysterical, urgent. It could have been "Get up!" or "Why did you do that?"

Tessa closed her eyes. *Did her son survive?*

The little one, yes. The soldier fled, and the boy stayed at her side until someone got him. The older one, the priest? No, he died in the church.

So senseless. So much waste. So much trauma and heartbreak for a little one.

Eric was little like that. Her heart nearly broke in two, thinking of how Eric would be devastated to see her dead right in front of him.

I couldn't keep her indoors, Martin sent. *I didn't have the authority. I couldn't clear the street to get her there safely.*

I don't blame you, she thought. He sounded so sad. *I just wondered how it all happened.*

The phone rang, and the images dispersed. Caller ID didn't give any information. She left it ringing.

Get that, said Martin.

Yeah, I need another credit card offer, she thought, but she answered anyhow.

"Is this Teresa Testerman?" said the voice. "This is Jason Masters. You had me over to dinner last week."

"Oh! Hi, Jason. Is everything okay?"

Gary looked up, surprised.

"Everything's fine, but I wanted to let you know how grateful I am for your hospitality to my grandfather. I know he's a bit much to take."

Tessa leaned against the wall. "Please, he was no trouble. You and he would be welcome back if you wanted to come again."

"I'm sure he was quite a big deal of trouble, based on just the little I heard. He got home just fine, so now he's Virginia's problem again." Jason laughed. "Regardless, I wanted to give you a heads-up that H.8937 is going to have a public hearing with the Joint Committee on Public Health next Thursday at the state house."

Tessa said, "What?"

"I made a couple of phone calls. Both you and Karen Meyer now have VIP status to speak to the state house."

Tessa blinked rapidly. Karen would have killed for a chance like this. To speak directly to the committee members? To do it in a public session with cameras rolling?

Tessa said, "Wow. Um..."

"Fair's fair. I can't guarantee any of them will listen to you because they're all pretty much decided to begin with, but at least you get a chance. It will be an open session, so anyone can speak, but I've guaranteed the both of you slots. I'll email you more information, and of course it's up to you whether you address the committee, but I strongly encourage you to do it."

"I...I will. Thank you!" Tessa lowered herself into her kitchen chair. Public speaking. She could do that. She taught third graders for all those years. How much worse could a bunch of elected officials be?

Jason said, "And thank you again for dinner. It was great meeting all of you."

She got off the phone, breathless. Gary said, "What's going on?"

"I'm talking to the state house." Her ears started ringing. "About the midwifery bill."

"Really?" Gary beamed. "I've always wanted to write a political speech!"

FIFTEEN

Sitting in bed in her pajamas, Tessa was reviewing her speech when the phone rang. Caller ID said it was Amanda.

"Hey, my twenty-nine-weeker," she said. "What's going on?"

Amanda said, "I feel really silly, but the baby's not moving much, and I've been nervous all day."

Martin appeared and sat at the foot of the bed. Tessa glanced at him, puzzled. "When was the last time you felt movement?"

Amanda replied, "I don't know. I've been moving around all day, and I haven't been paying attention. After dinner I started getting worried, and now I'm really anxious."

"Twenty-nine weeks..." Tessa glanced at the clock. 10 p.m. Most babies kicked into gear when mom turned in for the night, so if Amanda drank something sugary and lay down, she should start getting some serious movement.

Martin said, "Don't."

She squinted at him.

Amanda said, "Twenty-nine weeks, four days. I'm so sorry to bother you. But I just keep feeling anxious, and I've had a lot of contractions today."

"Hang on," said Tessa, and she lowered the phone.

Martin said, "Her baby is dead."

Tessa's heart stopped.

Dead? Dead? Amanda's baby?

She choked out, "What? How?"

Martin looked sad. But he didn't retract his words.

She picked up the phone. "You know what? You don't live that far from the birth center. Why don't you meet me there and we'll do a quickie ultrasound?"

"No, I don't want to bother you! It's just—"

"I went into this job to be bothered. I love being bothered. Come to the birth center. I'll be there in fifteen minutes." She grabbed her clothes off the chair where she'd just discarded them. "I can't let one of my moms worry all night."

Amanda hesitated. Then, "Thank you. I'm sorry."

"Don't be sorry. Midwives do these things. Fifteen minutes, okay?"

She disconnected the call and then whirled on Martin. "Fix it!"

He started. "What?"

"Fix it! Go back in time! Fix whatever it is that happened!"

Martin raised both hands. "That's not how it works. This isn't my sphere of authority!"

"But surely it's in *someone's*! The birth center's guardian angel has some authority, right? The baby's guardian? Someone does! Figure it out and send them back in time!"

"I can't fix it," Martin protested. "The world is broken. Evil happens. Tragedy happens."

"Are you saying God couldn't give that baby life?" Tessa exclaimed.

"God can do whatever He wants," Martin shot back. "I'm not God, and I can't do anything for Amanda's baby."

Tessa grabbed her crocheting bag and her phone. "And then what good are you?"

Downstairs, she found Gary in his office. "I'm going to be gone the rest of the night."

Gary recoiled. "What happened?"

"Martin says a client's baby is dead. I'm trying to make him fix that, but he refuses." She grabbed her coat and her homebirth bag. The birth center would have supplies, but she had no idea what she was doing. Her head was spinning. At this point even her autopilot reflexes were on autopilot. "I'm sorry. There's no telling when I'll be back."

Gary met her in the hallway. "Hey, it's okay. This isn't your fault."

"I know it's not my fault!"

"It's not Martin's fault either." Gary hugged her. "I'm sorry. I'm really sorry. Do you want me to drive you there?"

Her eyes blurred. She shouldn't be driving, but Gary... No, Gary would have to come back and get her later. It wasn't fair to him.

He grabbed his coat and his keys. "I love you too much to let you wrap your car around a tree. I'll just take you."

She huddled in his car as he drove, her brain whirling with nasty things she could say to Martin, and in the back of her head rage at everything else. Rage at a world where babies died even though their mothers took excellent care of themselves. Rage at celestials that sat idly and watched as it happened. Rage at herself for not identifying the problem in advance.

Amanda had gotten better care than most mothers. She'd had that extra appointment with her mother-in-law in tow. She'd been having shadowcare with an OB who'd done an ultrasound at every visit. With more than twice as many visits, plus nutrition counseling, plus everything else she'd done, there was no reason for her baby to die. None at all.

They waited at a light, and Tessa still couldn't find any words. This wasn't fair.

It wasn't fair in the way so many stillbirths simply weren't fair. It was like a SIDS death in utero: the baby just stopped. She could explain why it happened in general terms: something in the baby's DNA wasn't right. Something hadn't developed properly. Something couldn't sustain life, and the baby had hung on as long as he could, but in the end it just wasn't possible.

Martin couldn't fix that. Martin couldn't rewrite DNA and probably couldn't go back in time seven months to selectively destroy the defective sperm cell that gnawed its way through Amanda's egg first. Or maybe it would take destroying the defective egg before she ovulated. But why not? She kept thinking of the question she'd detonated in his face just before leaving her bedroom: *And then what good are you?* Totally unfair but at the same time completely legitimate. Why would God create all these insanely complicated and powerful beings and dispatch them into the world like personal bodyguards but then deny them the ability to do anything meaningful when it came to life and death?

Gary pulled up in front of the birth center where lights were on in one of the suites. "Karen's still with a family," Tessa murmured. "Good. I'll need her."

Gary squeezed her hand. "I'm so sorry."

"It's worse than that. Amanda doesn't even know yet. She just thinks he's not moving as much."

Gary flinched. "So you have to tell her?"

Tessa bit her lip. "I've done that before." Too often before. Well, twice before. She'd confirmed plenty of miscarriages, but only two stillbirths. One had been a baby the parents knew had a fatal defect. The other had been like this, a baby perfectly developing all along and then one day...not.

"Thank you for driving me." Tessa kissed him. "You're right. I shouldn't be driving right now."

"It's fine. I love you."

Her voice broke. "I love you too. I'm sorry."

Sorry for making him drive. Sorry for not being able to save the world.

Gary waited until she got inside before pulling away.

She found Karen in a birth suite. "When you get a minute," she said before going to prep the second suite.

Amanda arrived two minutes later, and by then Karen had the ultrasound machine ready to go, so they were all together when Tessa turned the screen to face Amanda and her husband. Then she gelled up her belly and palpated the baby to figure out the exact position to place the probe.

Martin, seriously, if there's anything at all you can do, anything, do it now. Right now. Before I confirm it.

She flipped on the machine, and the screen revealed the tiny form. Unmoving. Totally still. No heartbeat.

Amanda's husband said, "Is everything okay?"

Amanda let out a thin, "The heart's not fluttering."

After three pictures, Tessa had enough images from a medical standpoint, but she zoomed in and out. Karen held Amanda's hand while Amanda stared at the screen with tears sheeting down her cheeks. Jeffrey had his face in his hands, sobbing, but Tessa didn't point him toward the tissues. At some point she realized she herself was crying.

She turned off the machine, and she toweled the gel off Amanda's abdomen. When Amanda sat up, Tessa hugged her, and Amanda sobbed into her shoulder.

Karen's voice was very soft. "If you want, sweetie, you can stay here tonight. We can start the induction process and try to get things going, and in the morning we'll bring you over to the hospital with Dr. Cravey. Or you can go home and sleep in your own bed, and we can start in the morning."

Tessa said, "If you want, though, the other option is to call your shadowcare OB. They may offer you a dilation and extraction procedure rather than induction of labor."

Karen tensed. Tessa hadn't told her about the shadow.

Amanda looked at her husband, who said, "Anything you want, sweetie."

She turned to Tessa. "I want to be with you. I want the baby born in one piece. I want to hold my baby. I'm sorry. I know this is terrible, and I don't want to put you through this, but—"

"It's not about me. It's about you." Tessa hugged her again. "Karen will get Dr. Cravey on the phone. In the meantime, let me check you for dilation and see what's been going on with those contractions."

Amanda lay like a deflated balloon while Tessa checked her cervix. She was at two centimeters but not at all effaced, so Tessa oiled her gloves with evening primrose oil and gooped her up pretty well. She wouldn't strip the membranes with the cervix that long and tight; it would hurt and wasn't likely to trigger full-blown labor anyhow. She inserted a Cervidil tablet and had Amanda remain lying down while they waited for Dr. Cravey.

When had the little one died? For Amanda to already be contracting, had it been all day? When had that last movement been, the one when her baby said goodbye?

When Dr. Cravey arrived, he sat with Amanda and Jeffrey. With his soft voice and gentle eyes, he apologized that they were meeting under such circumstances; he gave his personal assurance he would do everything he could. Then, without any pressure whatsoever, he explained all Amanda's options. He reviewed her choices, and he answered their questions. Amanda remained firm in her conviction that she wanted to induce labor, do it now, and hold her baby after birth.

"Very well." Dr. Cravey patted her leg. "I'll have the hospital prepare for the transfer. You keep lying down, and I'll let you know when they're ready to receive you."

Through it all, Tessa had remained by the door. Jeffrey blurted out, "Wait. Before you go—is it a boy or a girl?"

The next day, Tessa would remember his urgent question and burst into tears. But now, she only choked out, "You didn't want to know, so we never checked."

Jeffrey said, "Oh. I didn't realize. I figured you'd know. I thought it would...you know, just kind of help..."

Amanda squeezed her husband's hand. "Tessa didn't want to slip and tell us by accident."

Tessa flipped on the machine again, and they both started. "Let's find out."

It took two minutes. Amanda and Jeffrey's baby was a boy.

"A boy." Jeffrey swallowed hard. "We wanted to name him Benedict."

"We should save that." Amanda sounded broken. "You know. Because."

"You should name him whatever you want." Tessa rolled the machine back into the corner. "He's your baby, and you love him. There's so little you can give him, that you might as well give him the name you love."

Sixteen

When it came time to go to the hospital, Tessa drove them in their own car. They were no more fit to drive now than she'd been earlier, so fueled with coffee and care, she'd offered. She walked in with them, and there she stayed.

Dr. Cravey brought one of the nurses and introduced her by name, then assured Amanda this nurse was trained in bereavement issues and would take care of her as if she were his own daughter. "I'm sorry to say, you are not the only one. We will support you however you find us most helpful." He pulled a chair closer to the bed. "I understand, it shouldn't be up to you to tell us what you need at this time. But we're going to be guessing based on what helps many women. If we guess wrong, please correct us so we can do better."

Amanda nodded. Her husband, sitting alongside her on the edge of the hospital bed, wrapped his arm around her shoulders.

Cravey explained the induction process and gave an estimate of how long it would take and everything she should expect. He told her what would be normal and then told her what he wanted to know about immediately if it were to go wrong. "We will make sure your pain is controlled at every point," he said, "but we will warn you if any of the medications might leave you groggy. We used to medicate mothers so they didn't remember. But remembering will be part of your healing, and we don't want to deprive you of even a single memory with your little guy."

He stayed with her while the nurse set her up with an IV. Tessa said, "It will take a while for labor to start. Your cervix isn't prepared for birth, so while everything is in a slow stage, you might want to try to sleep."

Amanda choked, "I'll never be able to sleep again."

Tessa said, "Do you want to maybe close the lights down and see what happens? I'll stay in the hospital the whole time. I'm not leaving you alone, but I think it will be better in the long run if you get even a few hours of rest."

Jeffrey said, "At some point, I'm going to have to call our parents."

Oh, dear heaven no. Not Suzanne. That freight train of a woman was going to charge in here with her anger and accusations, and just at the time they needed support, they'd have to defend themselves.

"Not until morning." Amanda closed her eyes. "Wait until everything's started and it can't be changed."

Jeffrey hesitated. "Should we call your mother at least?"

Amanda hesitated. Then, "No. Because then your mother will blame you for not calling her too. Just wait on both of them. I'll try to sleep. Tell them that's why: because I was sleeping."

Tessa didn't offer a sedative, and Amanda didn't ask. She did close down the lights and then took up a position outside the room. She pulled out her crochet bag and prepared to spend hours. Hours during which she could have spoken to Martin. Could have, but didn't.

In the morning, with Amanda sixty percent effaced and three centimeters dilated, Jeffrey phoned both sets of parents. First he called Amanda's father, who lived furthest away, followed by Amanda's mother. Tessa didn't go into the patient consult room where Jeffrey had retired to make the calls. Instead she stayed with Amanda, who was staying on top of the contractions but working too hard to keep this up for the duration of labor. Jeffrey phoned his parents last, and he checked on Amanda again before he did it.

Interesting. He didn't want to talk to them either.

While he made the last call, Tessa said, "Pitocin contractions are harder than regular contractions. They don't warm up, peak, and then drop off. Plus, they're not coming at a frequency dictated by your body. So the minute you feel like it might get too hard for you, let us know."

Amanda gave a brave smile. "I'm good for a little while."

"Don't wait until you can't handle it." Tessa squeezed her hand. "It takes about forty-five minutes to place an epidural. If you think you want it, I'd rather you get it too soon than too late."

Amanda swallowed hard. "It's not like... I mean, it's not like it will hurt the baby now. I didn't want it. But I might as well. I mean..."

"You don't have to change your mind." She shrugged. "Popular culture treats epidurals like they're a vest you can snap on. It takes time to page the anesthesiologist, and then it takes a while for the anesthesiologist to find the right spot. You'll need to hold still during several contractions for the placement, and then we need to make sure it's working. I love you, and I don't want you to suffer."

"It's too late for that." Amanda sagged into her pillow. "I wish. I just..." She looked up. "Could I walk around maybe? Before it gets too much?"

It took a few minutes to work a second hospital gown around her IV line (backward, to keep her covered), and then Tessa found a pair of hospital-issued slipper socks. "They're bright yellow," Amanda said.

"So you'll have something to look at if a doctor puts you in stirrups," Tessa said. "Dr. Cravey won't make you push flat on your back, though. I'll show you how to push upright, and he's great about catching in that position."

Amanda said, "He's been very nice."

"He's got a midwife's soul." Tessa chuckled. "He still hasn't caught a baby while the mother is standing over the toilet, though. And I suspect he prefers it that way."

In the hallway they heard Jeffrey arguing into the phone. Amanda tightened her grip on Tessa's arm. "I hate her. I hate her, and she's going to be terrible to me."

"You did nothing wrong," Tessa said. "Whatever she says to you, you did nothing wrong. There was no way you could have caused this and nothing you could have done to prevent it."

"But why? I mean, was his cord wrapped around his neck? He's not deformed. We didn't have an amnio, but maybe it was genetic?"

"You may never know," Tessa said. "I hate it, but you may never know."

Before they reached the end of the hallway, a baby started squalling, and Amanda froze in place. She gripped Tessa's arm, and then she started to cry.

For five minutes, Tessa held her right there, not daring to guide her back just yet. Jeffrey saw her crying into Tessa's shoulder and said, "I'm hanging up now. She needs me," and rushed to them both. He was able to guide Amanda back into a walk, and when he got into the room, he closed the door.

Amanda choked out, "I don't want to feel anything anymore. I want an epidural. I want all the drugs they can give me," so Tessa pushed the button for the nurse.

There is no epidural for the human heart. Nothing would make the heartbreak go away, but they could at least numb her body.

Twenty-five minutes later, the anesthesiologist arrived. Amanda was sitting on the edge of the bed, leaning on Tessa and breathing together with her as she weathered a strong contraction. The anesthesiologist went over all the informed consent stuff, then had her lie on her side with her knees to her chest so he could get a good look at her spine. Tessa crouched alongside the bed and held Amanda's hands in hers. Another contraction started, and Amanda squeezed, then started breathing hard. Tessa breathed with her, face-to-face.

"I've got the right spot," said the anesthesiologist. "Stay very still. I'm numbing you for the insertion."

The door blew open, and in marched Suzanne. Jeffrey stepped toward her. "She's getting an epidural and can't move right now."

Suzanne said, "Well I'm glad at least she's in a hospital."

Tessa focused on Amanda as she struggled to stay still. The anesthesiologist was talking in a low voice, but Amanda had to be hearing the sharpness in her mother-in-law's tone, the anger, the blame. Grief came out all sideways sometimes. Sorrow was so hard to hold that people turned it into accusations and defensiveness, excuse-finding and denial.

Worse still was helpless sorrow, when there was no way out except crawling through it. People might fumble to offer comfort to the grieving parents. *God needed another angel* seemed like rotten theology (she ought to ask Martin) because if God actually needed anything, how could He be God? And if God somehow did need another angel, why not just create one more?

There was also *You can always have another*, so cruel in the way it assumed one human being could substitute for another; it was even more cruel to parents who might not be able to conceive again. And then the glorious one, *There must have been something wrong with it,* which made the parents feel even worse because someone had labeled their baby defective merchandise. Some comfort that was: you shouldn't have loved your broken baby anyhow.

Amanda's grip eased up on Tessa's hand. "Okay. Okay. It's better."

"One or two more," Tessa whispered. "Then the meds should start to work." She stood alongside Amanda and watched the anesthesiologist finish with the epidural placement. Contractions came every three minutes. Amanda would need to ride out a few more, but after that she should get significant relief.

Suzanne said, "And you found out last night? Why didn't you call us?"

Jeffrey said, "She needed to sleep, and nothing was happening anyhow. It didn't make sense to wake you up at midnight."

"I'd have come!" Suzanne exclaimed. "I'd have come right away! This isn't the kind of thing you can do alone."

Tessa glanced at the monitor. The last contraction had double-peaked. Poor Amanda. She was being a trouper, though.

A hand crashed onto Tessa's shoulder. "You!" Suzanne exclaimed, clamping down on her like a bear trap. "You *dare* come in here after what you did?"

"What?" Tessa stepped backward. "What did I do?"

"Mom, she didn't do anything!"

"She killed my grandson with her frontier medicine!" Suzanne took another step forward, but Tessa didn't step back. The nurse came around from the opposite side of the bed, but the anesthesiologist was saying to Amanda, "Don't move. Really, don't move."

"You think you can treat pregnancies with herbs and acupuncture, and my grandson is dead because of you! You're as good as a murderer!"

The nurse got between them. "Ma'am, you need to calm down."

"I don't need to calm down! This woman has no place here, and I want her gone! She's not a hospital employee.

She's a madwoman who needs to be brought up on malpractice charges!"

Another contraction was beginning. She dropped back to her knees alongside the bed and grabbed Amanda's hands. "Breathe with me."

Suzanne shook her by the shoulder. "I'm not done with you!"

"I'm taking care of my patient," Tessa said loudly, "and if you touch me again, I'm calling security to have you removed."

"You wouldn't dare!"

But the hands came off, and Tessa looked right into Amanda's eyes. Her patient was crying. It wasn't just the pain. It was everything, and Tessa knew it, but right then Tessa's maternal instincts and her midwifery instincts surged hard enough that she hungered for violence. Claw that woman in the face or slap her across the mouth, drive her away. Make her disappear. Amanda was focusing on her to ride out the contraction, though, and Tessa focused on Amanda to ride out her rage. Suzanne was hurting her patient. Suzanne had barged into the sacred space of a birthing woman and polluted it with her hatred. Tessa had to focus now. Focus or else she'd lose her professionalism.

Tessa murmured, "Doing good. Doing good. Just a little bit longer," and Amanda stayed with her. The epidural timing had been absolutely right. Another hour and Amanda would have been in agony.

The contraction ended, and Tessa steeled herself. She stood.

Suzanne said, "You have no right to be here."

"I'm with my patient."

Suzanne folded her arms. "We can order you out of here, and you have to go."

Jeffrey stood looking helpless. Thank God for Gary, a strong man who knew his own mind and who would stand up for her if ever she needed him to do it. But with a mother like this one, what chance would Jeffrey have had to develop a backbone? One thing was certain: he wasn't going to stand up for his wife.

"As it turns out, you aren't employing me. Amanda is. Amanda gets to decide who is in the room, and Amanda has asked me to stay."

Suzanne said, "Amanda, tell her to leave."

With closed eyes, Amanda lay still. The nurse said, "Please, ma'am, you're very agitated. She's been through a lot."

The anesthesiologist was taping the tube to her back. "You can move again," he said, but Amanda didn't uncurl. It had to be the most uncomfortable position in the universe to labor in, but she didn't move. She just kept her eyes closed and her tears soaking into the pillow.

"Tell her!" Suzanne insisted. "Tell her she has to leave! She's the reason your baby is dead! She brainwashed you with her quackery and her snake oil. She let everything go wrong, and now you're the one who has to pick up the pieces! I told you this would happen!" She turned to her son. "Jeffrey, man up! Tell this woman to get out of here!"

Jeffrey looked at Tessa, then at Amanda. "Um," he managed, "maybe you should go?"

Their marriage wouldn't survive this. How could it?

Tessa pitched her voice nice and low. "I will leave only if Amanda tells me to go. Until she fires me as her provider, I'm here for her."

Amanda reached for Tessa's hand, and she squeezed. Tessa squeezed back.

Suzanne strode forward and pulled Tessa's hand out of Amanda's. "Why do you insist on staying with this woman!"

Tessa turned to the nurse. "Bernadette, please call security."

"Don't you dare!" said Suzanne, but Tessa pushed the call button. "Please send security to Room 402."

Suzanne was shouting. Amanda started another contraction, but this time Tessa didn't dare take her eyes off that woman. Jeffrey made mollifying noises, and the nurse rushed to the door. The anesthesiologist hurried to get all the equipment put away, and through it all, Tessa couldn't do the only thing she was there to do: care for her patient.

Security arrived after Amanda's contraction ended. Suzanne ranted at them, but Tessa said that because she'd been grabbed and pushed, the woman needed to be removed until she could calm down.

"I'm going to sue you," Suzanne snarled. "I'm going to take your entire livelihood and shut down that clinic. I'll find your car and slash your tires. I'll burn your house to the ground. You're going to regret this forever."

The security guard said, "Ma'am, please come with me."

Tessa did turn her back this time, and she took Amanda's hand.

It paid off. Suzanne lunged for her, and because of that, the security guard intervened. A second guard grabbed Suzanne by the arms, and the two of them pulled her from the room while she kept shouting. Tessa was a murderer, she yelled. That woman was a murderer, and the hospital wasn't doing anything about her.

Behind her, there were noises. Someone left the room. She wasn't sure if it was Jeffrey's father, or Jeffrey and his father together. She didn't check.

Tessa stayed next to Amanda. "Sweetie, if you want me to leave, you just tell me. I'm not going to stay against your will."

"Stay," she whispered. So Tessa stayed.

Seventeen

After twenty-two hours of labor, Amanda delivered her baby boy. A volunteer photographer came to take pictures of her and Jeffrey with baby Benedict, and Tessa got them handprints and footprints. They dressed him in little outfits and wrapped him in a hand-crocheted blanket a local church had donated. Tessa pulled out the little cap and booties she'd crocheted for him, and she settled the cap on his head with a kiss. "I love you, little guy. I'm so sorry."

Dr. Cravey had been a marvel. "I'm not allowed to let Tessa deliver your baby in the hospital," he'd said, his voice low and soothing. "I know you wanted her to, but the lawyers make such a fuss. She's right at your side the whole time, though, and if you want, I'll show you how to catch him yourself."

Amanda had gotten a little more sleep. Her mother and father had both arrived, and whatever animosity they shared for one another, they set it aside for the sake of their daughter. Jeffrey stayed the whole time, without even the benefit of the few hours of sleep Amanda had gotten.

Jeffrey's father had called from outside the hospital: he and his wife were going home.

Jeffrey then started getting phone calls from his aunt and his cousins and apparently some family friend who hadn't talked to him in six years, each accusing him of being horrible to his own mother.

Tessa didn't bother feeling sorry for Jeffrey. He could have earned those attacks by being a righteous man and standing up for his wife. Instead he was getting henpecked by his own mother to the point where he turned off his phone, and then he turned off Amanda's too.

For now, though, they had time with baby Benedict. They admired his perfect face, his tiny hands, and his teeny feet. They touched his sweet-smelling skin and inhaled the scent of him. He weighed two and a half pounds, and he fit into the crook of Amanda's arm.

"Take lots of photos of your little love," Tessa said to the grandparents. "You'll want them later. You'll want photos of his face most of all."

After checking to make sure Amanda's uterus was shrinking at the right rate, Dr. Cravey said to Tessa, "You need some sleep, my dear."

She shook her head. "I need to go back to the birth center and take care of my patients."

"It will be a service to every one of your patients if you have someone else take care of them today." Dr. Cravey rested a hand on her shoulder. "You've been awake well over thirty-six hours. Your patients deserve a midwife who is awake. Please, go home."

Tessa texted Karen. "I'm finished up here. Do you need me at the center?"

Karen didn't reply right away, so Tessa packed up her things and got a cup of coffee from the nurses' station. At the half-hour, when Karen's appointment ended and before her next began, the reply came: "Sarah's got your clients. Get some sleep. You're on call tonight."

Dr. Cravey met her in the hallway. "Say goodbye to them. I'll drive you back to your car."

"My car is at my house. I'll call Gary."

"Then I'll take you home."

The wind slammed through Tessa's time-eaten coat when she stepped into the parking lot. It was too much, too long, too everything. Baby Benedict's death alone would have been as much as she could handle. A patient's relative getting violent would have been as much as she could handle. Staying awake for two days straight would have done it too. All three? How was she still upright?

Dr. Cravey plugged her address into his GPS, and the robot voice guided them home. Tessa kept her eyes closed, fighting against the urge to correct the guidance system. *If you go that way, you have to make a pretty bad left because you can't see oncoming traffic. It's better to turn one block sooner.* All the words swirled in her head. The coffee hadn't kept her awake. She was just as sleepy, only jittery and filled with a sense of dread.

She forced her eyes open when the GPS said her street name, followed by, "Destination is on the right."

"Thank you for the lift."

"Thank you for staying with your patient the whole time. She's a treasure, and I wish her the best."

"I may never see her again after that altercation with her in-laws."

Dr. Cravey chuckled. "You know the truism. Whether a patient stays with her practitioner is determined in the first ninety seconds after the diagnosis. You'd have to pry her out of your practice with a crowbar. I can see how much she trusts you, and she knows you love her."

Tessa left her coat on the hook, and in her bleary-eyed state, she admitted it did look ratty, after all. How many of her things looked ratty? There was always money to buy new for the boys. You couldn't outfit any one of them just in hand-me-downs, and the secondhand shops were so unpredictable. Pants never survived from one boy to the next, and shoes barely made it through the one they were bought for. She and Gary got the kids outfitted and fed, and then they put off buying themselves new boots, and they mended the hole in this thing or reinforced the threadbare patch of that.

Gary met her with a hug. "You've been wrung out and hung up to dry. You should get some sleep."

A note in his voice made her look up, puzzled.

He sighed. "I've been contacted by one of the monsignors in the diocese of New York. He's got some fingers in the underground sale of church memorabilia, and he wants me to meet one of his contacts tonight."

Tessa's heart skipped. "That's dangerous."

He shook his head. "We're not talking about the Mafia. I'll be meeting someone who works for the Metropolitan Museum of Art and who happens to be the Church's point of contact with people who are selling religious contraband. He's as dangerous as a bunch of daisies and probably walks with a silver-tipped cane. But he'll have information on the underground movement of relics."

"And you're seeing him tonight in New York?" Tessa glanced at the clock. 9 a.m. "What time do we leave?"

"*We* aren't leaving. If I hop in the car around eleven, I'll get there in plenty of time, and then I'll get back around midnight."

Tessa squinted at him. "Shouldn't I go?"

"You've been on your feet for far too long. I arranged a playdate for Eric for after school, so you'll just have to get him from Melissa's at three o'clock." He waved her away. "Go."

Tessa staggered back into her bedroom, remembering as she did the last time she'd stood in here. Martin had been right there, at the foot of the bed. She'd yelled at him.

But she'd deal with that later, and instead just dropped into bed.

"You have to go with him," Martin said.

Tessa closed her eyes. "I have to sleep."

"I'll help you stay awake, but you really should be in New York."

Tessa didn't reply.

Martin pushed into her mind harder.

"You go with Gary," Tessa said. "You like him better anyhow. I'll stay here and sleep."

"You were willing to go back to the birth center and see clients all day. This would be less work, and you can sleep in the car. Go with Gary."

Tessa rolled onto her back. "When are you? Do you remember anything from my past two days?"

"Amanda's baby. An induction. You putting yourself in physical danger in a way I truly wish you wouldn't."

"It was calculated, and it paid off. But speaking of physical danger, are you aware that humans can die of exhaustion?"

"I've been told about sleep deprivation torture, although I've been fortunate enough never to witness it. Humans die if they don't sleep for five days straight. You'll develop hallucinations long before dying, and based on the random hours you were able to doze at the hospital, I estimate you have at least a hundred and four hours before death occurs. Go to New York."

Tessa frowned. "You're really serious?"

"Mostly serious. I'm not going to let you die. Get up."

She went back downstairs to Gary. "Don't argue with me because I've had enough arguments. I'm under orders to go to New York."

Gary looked up, something of anger flashing across his eyes. "Would it help if I argued with the order-giver? What if I refuse to take you?"

Tessa's stomach clenched. Martin versus Gary should never happen. "No, don't try. I guarantee you the car won't start or there will be highway closures all the way through Connecticut."

"I'm doing a lot of work to locate something he loves." Gary folded his arms. "It's not too much to ask that he respect the one that I love."

"I can sleep in the car."

"You can sleep in the bed too."

"I asked you not to argue with me." She went upstairs and got in the shower.

Martin possessed a certain clinical presence that reminded her of herself. *"I estimate you have at least a hundred and four hours before death occurs"* sounded an awful lot like something she'd say to a forty-one-weeker complaining that she would be pregnant forever. "By most definitions, *forever* will last longer than two weeks, but at the end of two weeks you'll have delivered." She wouldn't say that to just any patient, of course. Some patients didn't have the self-awareness to focus past their frustration. She only joked with the ones who could take it.

She showered off the smell of the hospital and dried her hair, then collapsed into bed to nap for at least an hour. She didn't set an alarm. If Martin could read time and manipulate the universe, doubtless he could wake her before Gary left.

It turned out he could. She snapped to awareness all at once at 10:50, got on her shoes, and trudged to the kitchen where Gary was standing beside the coffeemaker.

He grimaced at her. "Tell Martin I'm not very pleased with him."

"He can hear you."

"Well, he's not listening. If you collapse, I'm taking you to a hospital, and the relic hunting stops."

"He says I'll be okay. I think any sleep at all resets the clock, so I'm back to five days before brain death." She reached for a thermal travel mug. "I'll sleep in the car, too. If not, I hear they sell really strong espresso in New York."

Despite not wanting her to go, Gary had arranged for Tessa's mother to watch the kids after school. "Joe and Alex will be fine. Mark's got practice until five. She'll be here for Brian when he gets off the bus, and Melissa says she'll drop Eric here instead of making your mother pick him up. So if you're determined to do this, let's head out." He pointed to the kitchen table where he'd stacked all the things he was bringing to New York. "Also, I unearthed my travel pillow and a blanket."

Tessa kissed him. "What, no teddy bear?"

"I'll pick one up on the way."

Baby Benedict had a teddy bear. It was soft and with big eyes, and it had come from the hospital gift shop. Poor Amanda. Poor Jeffrey. Amanda would be in a crash-sleep right around now. Jeffrey would be dealing with his parents. The hospital machinery would be in motion, other women delivering down the hall while a nurse phoned whatever funeral home would handle Benedict's transport. Tessa had talked Amanda and Jeffrey through their options about burial and cremation. She didn't know what they'd decided. They'd probably decide on whatever Jeffrey's mother wanted, on the grounds that it didn't matter anyhow, and then regret it later. She'd hear about it at the postpartum checkup. Or she'd hear about it when they filed a medical malpractice suit at the insistence of the same woman.

She tucked into the car with the travel pillow and the blanket and her insulated coffee. She closed her eyes and took the temperature inside her insulated heart. So awful. She hated losing a patient, and hers was the worst profession in the world for that. Thirty percent of confirmed pregnancies ended in miscarriage, but her clientele tended to use fertility awareness methods and therefore the number climbed. They knew they were pregnant, and then not pregnant, before the point where pregnancy could be confirmed by a blood or urine test. Birth defects claimed a percentage in the middle trimester, and then in the third, the rarest, came the unexplained stillbirths.

She'd never had a baby die during birth or just after birth. She couldn't imagine the guilt and pain, the second-guessing and the inevitable reluctance to attend another birth. And how many women would pay the price for it afterward, if she tried in every subsequent birth to correct for whatever mistake she thought she'd made in the tragic one?

Her mind wandered as they drove, and every so often she'd rise to wakefulness to find the car on a different road, surrounded by different traffic. Worcester turned into Hartford which turned into Meriden, and at some point she found herself registering the beautiful bridges dotting the Merritt Turnpike, and then the crawling traffic of the Bronx.

Half-asleep as the tires consumed the roadway, Tessa thought about Barlassina as though she were there herself. The buildings were whole, a crisp sheet of snow overlying everything, with people congregating near the church. It seemed right and perfect, and she felt protective of them. Among the people, she'd drift through and touch this one or that, nudge another. But then she shifted to another day, and now she was frightening them away, sending them to safety, making them worried enough to shut themselves inside their homes. She pushed on the priest in charge of the church, but he wouldn't change his mind about locking the doors, so she circled all around the church building again. It was beautiful, and she loved it. In one moment without waking up she'd be aware of the traffic, and that she was in the Bronx. A moment after, she'd be back at Barlassina. This person. That little corner of the church. The orange-red sunrise over a beautiful mountain peak.

Oh. Oh, it made sense. Her half-asleep brain was picking up Martin's thoughts. The road. The past. The road again.

Then she found herself atop the church, oddly separated from her own senses. Smoke rolled up from the broken roof, and cries rolled up from the street. Shouting. Sadness. Grief. She hovered on the roof—Martin, she was Martin—looking down at the people who'd rushed to the church to see its destruction. Every voice set her nerves on edge, and the crunch of glass under the people's feet made her want to scream. She'd done all she could. She felt bound, a sensation she disliked as time tugged her forward. She fought it, but her work was done. She glanced back at the broken roof and the smoke. It was finished. She'd failed.

Failed. Failed everyone.

Tessa jerked with a gasp. Traffic was stalled, and a sign overhead said Pelham Parkway.

"If you want to eat," Gary said, "you might want to do it now. I don't know when you'll get another chance."

Tessa shook herself away from the memory, but her stomach was tight. Her eyes felt hot with tears.

Martin had just watched her deal with a professional failure. He'd responded by remembering his own.

Tessa opened the cooler. Gary had packed caprese sandwiches for them both, although he'd already eaten his. As they left the Bronx and cut through part of Queens, she ate hers. They crossed the Queensborough Bridge only to end up in a traffic impasse in Manhattan.

"I always forget how much I hate driving in Manhattan," Gary muttered.

"I can't imagine why." Tessa tucked the container back into the cooler. "I always remember."

They inched across the borough until they found a parking garage, and from there they walked to the New York archdiocesan chancery on 56th and First. Gary asked for the Reverend Monsignor Joseph Callahan, and after a quick phone call, the receptionist said he'd be down momentarily.

Gary squeezed Tessa's hand. "You hanging in there?"

Tessa smiled. "Much better."

The elevator doors opened, and out strode a man in his fifties wearing a priest's black shirt and pants, plus the white dog collar. "Mr. Testerman!" he said, shaking his hand. "Thank you so much for all the good work you've done researching the relic of Barlassina." He turned to Tessa. "And would I be correct to assume you are Mrs. Testerman? A pleasure to meet you."

Suddenly she felt conscious of how rumpled she felt, how awkward and outclassed in this beautiful Manhattan office, standing in front of people who jetted around visiting presidents and popes. She was a woman who cleaned up bodily fluids and wore a coat so old that the tailor wouldn't repair it any longer. "Thank you, Monsignor Callahan." She tried not to shrink as he shook her hand. "You can call me Tessa."

"Of course, and please don't worry about my title either. Call me Joe." He gave an easy smile. "Come with me. My friend wants to meet us at the Met, and we can talk on the way."

Callahan both walked and talked quickly, weaving through pedestrians with an unconcern that left Tessa believing everyone in New York City developed their own personal radar. "In order to be certified, relics need to have a pedigree," Callahan was saying. "There has to have been a documented chain of possession all along that gives us assurance the relic belongs to the saint they claim it does. Officially the Church does everything possible to verify it. People tend to be gullible. Would some Catholics want a relic of the Blessed Virgin Mary? Of course they would. Are there any? No. I've personally been involved in three cases where people have claimed to have one, and we've had to rule them unsuitable for public devotion. The validation process is rather exciting, actually." Callahan beamed at them. "But then you end up with situations such as with your relic, where the chain of possession is interrupted due to theft or general social upheaval, such as when someone hid a relic in order to protect it. Those are the interesting cases."

Callahan talked like this most of the way to the museum, enthusiastic and knowledgeable and with the occasional anecdote thrown in for good measure. Gary must have been gnashing his teeth not to be able to write all of this down or otherwise record it all.

Tessa said at one point, "So after you've validated a relic, that's when you can put it into a church for the people to use?"

Callahan looked pained. "People don't *use* relics per se. The faithful aren't required to acknowledge them at all. They're visible reminders of the ways ordinary people have responded to God's grace in an extraordinary way, and therefore they're a means for us all to take courage in our own journeys. Relics put us in touch with our past, and at times of stress, we can take comfort in that. It's like an inheritance." He nodded. "Did you ever receive something from a grandparent or a parent, and when you want to be reminded of them, you touch it? People are physical beings. We're the perfect amalgam of soul and body, and God Himself said physical creation is good. Our physicality demands we have sensory reminders of God in our lives. So when we worship, we look at beautiful things, hear beautiful sounds, smell beautiful smells, and yes, we honor the physical reminders of those who went before us in faith."

Gary said, "So are you saying Catholics worship with their bodies?"

"Absolutely!" Callahan laughed. "Haven't you ever heard the joke about Catholic aerobics? Sit! Stand! Kneel! Stand!"

Tessa laughed out loud.

Callahan said, "The Second Person of the Trinity became incarnate as a human being. There's nothing wrong with physical existence. And as physical beings, we respond to one another's physical presence."

Tessa said, "Then why would a relic be important to an angel?"

It just slipped out before she thought better of it. Stupid exhaustion.

"I imagine because if something is important to God, it's important to an angel too." Callahan, for what it was worth, hadn't missed a beat. "I'm sure you care about things that Gary cares about, even though you wouldn't if you didn't love him."

"I think it went more the other way." Tessa snickered. "I've swayed him over to the things I'm passionate about."

"You're selling yourself short," Gary interjected.

"Regardless," Callahan continued, "there's plenty of Biblical evidence that relics have a history in both the Old and New Testaments, and that the practice dates from the very earliest days of the Church. A man touched Elisha's bones in the Book of Kings and was healed. Was that idolatry? Obviously not, since God healed him. In Acts 19:11, you have people touching handkerchiefs to Saint Paul and carrying them away to touch the sick, and the sick were healed. Again, no one was worshipping a handkerchief, and God honored their intent by granting the healing. Obviously they wanted to worship God, and they recognized His blessing was on Saint Paul."

"Blessings are transferrable?" Tessa said.

Callahan said, "There aren't limits on God. If He wants them transferred, they go."

Gary said, "We had someone in our kitchen who thought relics and idols were the same."

Callahan snorted. "I get hate mail just about every day from someone who wants to know why Catholics keep idols, but obviously we're not worshipping the thing. If people can read the Elisha story and not recognize it's a relic, then they either don't know what relics are, or else they're so mired in their hatred of Catholicism that they can't read their own Bibles. Neither is incurable," he said, "but writing back to argue is seldom a fruitful effort."

EIGHTEEN

At the Met, they went in through the main entrance and then peeled off to the side, where Callahan greeted one of the guards by name and asked about his children, then led them through several corridors to an office stacked all around with crates, cardboard filing boxes, and random artifacts.

"Have a seat." The curator nodded at Callahan, then shook Gary's hand and Tessa's. "It's a pleasure to meet you. I was so pleased with the articles Joe sent about the Barlassina relic. You show a very compassionate touch in your writing, and I could feel what a great loss it is to both the religious and the art worlds that our troops may have taken it. Have a seat."

The curator was Allen Edgerheim, and even after he got warmed up, he was a bit more reserved than Monsignor Callahan. "I understand you wanted information about the underground trade in relics and other religious objects, but I may have something else for you." He leaned back in his chair. "As you can imagine, stolen antiquities are of great concern to us all. My specialty is artifacts of the Ancient Near East, but I've dealt in more than my share of contraband from the early Middle Ages. These works are stolen, resold to private collectors, and often end up in the collections of the extremely wealthy who don't ask too many questions. Our job is, frequently, to rescue these objects without rewarding the thieves, and then either to display the objects as they deserve or to return them to their homeland. Recently you may have heard of mummies being returned to Egypt after a couple of centuries of being gawked at by carnivalgoers."

"Ramses II?" said Gary.

"He was one of them. A terrible shame, such a great man being paraded about that way." Edgerheim shook his head. "Here's the problem, of course. The museum doesn't want to become a black-market consumer of rare pieces, but at the same time, we don't want valuable works floating around in the wrong places. So much has been lost."

Callahan said, "The Church is in the same position. If someone makes it known to us that he has a connection to a seller who claims to own a relic of Saint Francis, we might be interested, but we can't cut him a check for what's most likely stolen property."

Gary had his recorder going, but he was taking notes on his laptop at a speed that made Tessa wonder how his brain worked that quickly: moving all ten fingers, processing the information, and at the same time formulating new questions. "But there's definitely an underground market for these things?"

"In recent years, we've see two or three organizations crop up in the United States in order to combat the problem. Because of them, eBay has backed off on the sale of relics, not because it's immoral but because they forbid the selling of body parts." Edgerheim shook his head. "Regardless, there are some sellers who know people who know people. We've managed to infiltrate some of these networks with buyers of our own, and that's why I wanted to talk to you."

Callahan nodded enthusiastically. "You see, your article wasn't the first we'd heard of the Barlassina relic."

Tessa sat up. "How?"

"Many years ago, a collector contacted me on behalf of an anonymous seller," said Edgerheim, "asking if the museum would be interested in a reliquary from a medieval church in northern Italy. I started asking questions, and it became obvious that the anonymous seller didn't know the object's entire provenance."

Edgerheim opened a folder, and Tessa gasped aloud even before he'd handed the photograph across the table. The faded Polaroid revealed the reliquary standing on a kitchen table, countertops behind and a checkered table cloth beneath.

"He started by telling me it was a family heirloom. Obviously it's not." Edgerheim sighed. "The collector then reframed it that the seller's ancestors had safeguarded the reliquary after escaping from certain death, but clearly that's not true either."

Gary snapped a photo of the photo in Tessa's shaking hands. She couldn't take her eyes off it.

Here. Maybe forty years after it had last been seen, here was the relic. They'd just gotten forty years closer to it in time. Still thirty years away, but maybe reachable.

Martin, can you jump back in time to whenever this was taken? She flipped over the photo and checked the date stamp. Thank you, Polaroid: 1986. *Is this time pocket big enough for you to get back there?*

A negative impulse flowed through her, but it almost didn't matter. She couldn't stop devouring the photo, a feeling that had to come from Martin. She didn't stop him.

The little round of glass shielding the relic had broken so it looked like a three-quarter moon, but the part covering the relic was intact. She noticed the pattern on the tablecloth, the tone of the laminate on the countertop behind them, the angle of the sun, and the height from which the photograph was taken. There was the white handle of a mug on the counter, but no identifying features. Martin would be noticing the fingerprints on the photo and the vintage of the dust trapped in the thick folds of the photograph.

It was here. As of 1986, the relic had been here, and it was safe.

She felt her attention drawn to the bit at the center of the broken glass circle: exactly the same location and shape as the one in her uncle's photograph.

So the relic itself is intact, then.

Inside she felt relief and agreement.

Well, it was intact thirty years ago.

This time she felt resignation.

Still, someone had kept it safe and was looking for a buyer, meaning they'd recognized its value.

Gary brought up his copy of her uncle's photograph. "This is one of the only photos of the relic before its theft."

Edgerheim and Callahan both pushed forward to get a good look, but Tessa kept gazing at the one in her hand. What Martin wouldn't give for this. Just a chance at it.

Gary settled his laptop back in his lap, and Edgerheim reached for the Polaroid. Reluctantly she returned it.

"I never spoke with the seller directly. All of this went through the seller's agent, but I was given to understand that the seller was ill and needed money." Edgerheim sighed. "This isn't unusual, by the way. Every seller is ill and needs money for treatment, or his wife just died and he needs money to bury her, or his mother is trapped in a war-torn country and he's selling his most precious possession to bring her to the States." He shrugged. "The sob stories get quite creative, and I assume the seller's agent fine-tunes them for maximum impact. It's just as well for me I have a heart of granite." Edgerheim smiled dryly. "At any rate, the agent told me the seller's asking price, and it wasn't as outrageous as you'd think. I stipulated we'd need to see the object first, and it was in the midst of negotiations that the seller's agent rescinded the offer."

Gary huffed. "Who did he sell it to instead?"

Edgerheim said, "There's a catch here. Before we go any further, I'm required to obtain a promise from you that these specific details will be off the record."

Gary said, "In what way?"

"Anything up to now is on record," Edgerheim said, "but after this point, none of this should appear in your story."

Gary studied them.

Callahan sounded firm. "I promise this is worth your time."

Martin sent, *Tell him to do it.*

Tessa, who had no intention of telling Gary how to do his job, sat with her mouth closed.

Finally, Gary said, "Agreed." He shut his laptop, then returned it to his bag. Edgerheim waited, and Gary also turned off his recorder. Callahan asked for Gary's and Tessa's phones, and they handed them across the table.

Edgerheim placed a call, then said, "He's agreed," and then placed the phone on the desk in speakerphone mode.

"Testerman? Are you there?"

Gary said, "Who am I speaking to?"

"That's not really important." The man had a Brooklyn accent that made Tessa smile in the same way a really thick Boston accent did. "I was the seller's agent for the Barlassina relic, and I've remembered it all these years because it was just such a strange thing. But I'm not getting quoted here, and I don't want you going and spreading around all the details. It was a long time ago, and everyone deserves to rest in peace."

"The relic deserves to go home," Gary said.

"See, now there I agree with you." That voice had smoked more than its share of Camels back in the day the relic was on offer. "I'm not in the same line of work I was in the 80s. Found religion and cleaned up a bit. But back then, a fence put me in contact with a man who had this piece he didn't know what to do with. The guy was dying, and he wanted it sold."

Gary said, "I'm given to understand that's a standard lie when selling stolen goods."

"Actually it wasn't. He had emphysema and was wasting away, and he had this thing he needed to unload that he'd been hiding since he'd come home from the war.

He didn't care about the money, not as much as I did. I told him I'd sell it at that price, but I wanted a bigger cut if he wasn't going for broke. He was good with that. Just wanted it gone."

Shame. Wasn't that what Howard Masters had said? The soldiers were carrying shame over what had happened.

"I put out feelers, and Edgerheim bit. Then one day, the guy's wife calls me. Guy is now in the hospital, and he doesn't want to sell the thing anymore."

Tessa's heart skipped. Gary said, "What? He wanted it buried with him?"

"One of his war buddies came to his deathbed, she said, and they'd argued. The guy badgered his friend on his deathbed until he agreed not to. He thought it was wrong to sell this thing, okay, but she couldn't tell me why or what exactly this guy objected to. It wasn't the money. I told her I could get a lot more money than he was asking for. Enough to bury him in a really nice coffin if he wanted, you know? She was having none of it. Finally she told me that the war buddy offered him the asking price in cash. Said he'd take a few days and get the money together, sell his car if he had to, but he'd buy it outright. So while Edgerheim and I were haggling over the price, the seller sold it right out from under us."

Gary grimaced. "You sound kind of disappointed about the commission."

The man laughed. "At the time? You bet. I don't care what war you fought in—don't waste my time! But the dying guy had gotten his money, so what was I going to do? I called back a week later, but by then he was dead."

Tessa met Gary's eyes. Gary said, "What was his name?"

"That's privileged. You're good about promising, but there's only so far I trust journalists."

"Fair enough." Gary smirked. "I understand agent-client privilege. But do you remember the name of the war buddy who undercut you?"

"Never found out his name, but I gathered they'd been in contact the whole time since the war, and the friend came for one last visit."

"The seller lived here?" Gary said. "In New York City?"

"Yes."

"And the seller's wife?"

"She's dead now too."

That was a literal dead end. Tessa had come to expect that, though. Enough time for a town to die was also enough time for aging soldiers to die.

"But here's the deal," said the speakerphone voice. "I'm good at reading between the lines. Obviously they didn't care that you shouldn't sell a blessed object. It wasn't that the thing *couldn't* be sold, because the war buddy came back with money and the seller sold it to him. Something the wife said cued me in. The war buddy didn't want it sold because the buddy didn't want anyone to find out. But the seller? Bet me he did. Have you ever heard of a deathbed confession?"

Gary said, "You think he wanted people to find out?"

"In my experience, yes. That was his halfway attempt. He couldn't admit to guilt. He actually told me at one point that he hadn't stolen the thing, but he'd got it from someone who'd taken it off the actual thief. I guess another war buddy. But the point is, he had that urge to confess and couldn't man up to doing it. A museum, though? They'd research it. They'd find out what it was, and they'd send it home without him ever having to confess to a crime."

Gary gasped. "That's why he couldn't just leave it in a local church somewhere! Because they wouldn't have the ability to research it."

"Right. But the Met? The Smithsonian? They'd unearth all the squiggly details. Who knows what else they'd figure out?" The seller on speakerphone chuckled. "This guy didn't care. He knew he was kicking off soon and wanted his affairs in order. The other guy? Well, my guess is he had a bit more time to run out the clock."

Tessa whispered, "Shame."

Gary said, "So the war buddy went to great lengths not to get outed for what they'd done."

"Could be. Could also be that he wanted his fair cut of the take. I told the wife that if the other guy wanted it sold, to give him my number since I had two potential buyers. Never heard from anyone else."

Edgerheim had no readable expression. Callahan, however, seemed sad.

"How much was he asking?" Gary said. "You said it wasn't much, but I've got no idea what these things go for."

"Five grand. I could have gotten him fifteen, but he wanted to move it."

For some reason, Gary wore a triumphant smile.

"So that's all I know. But it was weird enough that I remembered it when Edgerheim contacted me. Don't go trying to find out who I am," the man added. "I'll deny everything, and you've got no proof."

"You have my word that you're not being quoted or identified," Gary said. "There's no need to identify the seller, either."

"There'd be no point, since he's dead. I'm alive, and I've got a reputation and a family. Don't kick me in the teeth for helping you."

"I promise. I've never betrayed an anonymous source."

"Good to hear it. Good luck finding the thing."

The guy hung up. Tessa sagged back in her seat.

While Callahan returned their phones and Gary's recorder, Tessa waited for some kind of contact from Martin. There should be something, and instead she felt only silence. Was he angry? As much as everyone wanted to help, no one seemed to have the right information. How did it feel to be an angel assembling a ten-thousand-piece puzzle with pieces scattered across two continents and seven decades?

Edgerheim slid his phone back into his pocket. "I know that's not much, but now you know everything we can give you."

Gary said, "I really appreciate your help, thank you."

Ten minutes later he and Tessa were out on 83rd Street. "Let's get dinner here before we start the drive back," Gary said, and Tessa agreed. They ended up in an Indian restaurant, and after they ordered, Gary opened his laptop.

Tessa watched the headlights on the Manhattan street. "It's a shame they didn't have more to go on."

"Are you kidding me? We have so much information I don't even know where to start." Gary scanned back through his notes. "Okay, so the seller's name was Brent Fagan."

She dropped her napkin. "What?"

"We know where he lived, and we know what year he died. I have a list of all the soldiers in that platoon, and I'd already tracked down death dates for most of them. Fagan lived in Brooklyn. Fagan died in 1986. Therefore Fagan was the seller. We don't know who Fagan got it from, but he said it was from someone who took it from the sergeant who stole it."

Tessa's heart hammered. "And we still don't know who took it from him."

"Not yet, but Fagan and the seller were in contact. They were close enough distance-wise to visit multiple times over the years, and twice in the span of four days—apparently by train. That means the Northeast corridor or maybe out as far as Pittsburgh or Chicago. The buyer was able to get five thousand dollars in hand during that time. Did he sell a car? Sell other property? Take out a loan? There might be records of those things. Did he contact anyone else from that platoon? We've got all sorts of interesting avenues to pursue."

Tessa sat back while the server returned with their meals.

Gary looked like he couldn't wait for the server to drop the plates and get out of there, and he resumed talking as soon as he was gone. "Pryce and O'Mara would have been close enough, geographically. I'll have to check on the others. But here's something else to consider: if more than one of them went in on this, then the relic may have changed hands a fourth time. If the buyer came in with a thousand from Pryce, a thousand from O'Mara, a thousand from some guy in Kansas, and two thousand from a guy in

Indiana, then he might have passed it along to one of them."

Tessa shook her head. "That's getting complicated."

"It was already complicated," Gary shot back. "These were soldiers intent on keeping a crime under wraps. What I'm finding most interesting is how well they did at keeping the secret. The deafening silence implies a smaller group rather than a larger one. So, say, the buyer and one other. Or the buyer solo."

Tessa dug into her meal. Curry, a bit spicier than she was used to but still delicious. New York always struck her as having the most authentic food. She tolerated Boston's cuisine (and it was certainly better than Delaware's), but New York possessed a certain abandon with its ethnic dishes.

"At any rate, we've got leads, and you can point out to your invisible friend that I'd have gotten all that without you propped up at my side like death warmed over." Gary's eyes narrowed. "I had no idea they were going to put a fence on the phone with us. If we'd actually gone to a meeting with this guy, or ended up in a seedy shop in Hell's Kitchen, I'd be really upset."

Tessa said, "In all fairness, I wouldn't want you there either."

"Even so. I wasn't going to say it, but how long do you think I'd live if I were to publish any of that guy's personal information? That's why I didn't even want you speaking when he was on the phone."

Tessa went back to her meal.

"Sorry, but it's been a long day. Even longer for you." Gary's gaze softened. "We'll get home by midnight, and you can catch up a bit on sleep. Tomorrow, I'll start sifting through public records."

NINETEEN

At eleven o'clock they reached home. Mom had encamped on the futon couch, so they slipped upstairs without turning on the lights. Tessa took a few minutes to change into pajamas and brush her teeth, then checked on the boys. By the time she got into bed, Gary was already snoring.

She, on the other hand, felt wired. She'd napped in the car both to and from New York, and after five minutes, she found herself still awake.

You aren't keeping me awake to talk to me, are you? she thought in Martin's general direction.

If I needed to talk to you, I'd go to a time when you were awake and talk to you then. You're incredibly caffeinated right now. I can work on eliminating that if you'd like.

Her brow furrowed. *Can you just put me to sleep?*

Sure, but you'll wake up again in ninety minutes and be incredibly tense. It's better if I do it this way, but it will take ten or more minutes.

She chuckled in the dark.

Why is that funny?

Because you're a time traveler, and if you wanted to work out the caffeine, you could step back ten minutes and start it then. I know, I know, 'It doesn't work that way, Tessa.' It never works that way, which is why I think it's so funny.

It's actually not a time travel issue. His voice in her head sounded prickly. *It's a permission issue. I can't just reach into your body and start jacking up different hormone levels or consuming certain chemicals whenever I feel like it.*

She drew a deep breath. *Oh! That's the authority thing you keep talking about. So if I ask for help with caffeine or the fact that I'm falling asleep, you have authority, but only after that point. Or are you just picking out caffeine molecules and sending them back in time to that night when I asked for help staying awake?*

Very funny. He didn't sound amused. *But you see, Gary was worried about you being too tired, and now here you are too awake.*

Gary's angry at you, Tessa thought, *but he'll be okay with it eventually. He didn't want me in danger, that's all. But speaking of permission, I'm surprised you got permission to send me down there in the first place.*

A series of question marks paraded through her head.

This quest didn't need me there at all. That means my guardian angel put me in a danger for no reason. Or do I not actually have a guardian?

What's that supposed to mean?

His voice was sharp.

Tessa thought, *What did my presence accomplish? I could have been sleeping.*

I told you it would be fine. It was fine. And yes, for the record, despite what you may think, you do have a guardian angel, and he didn't put you into any kind of danger. Martin's tone stepped right over the line into anger. *Every indicator was that something more would happen. By all accounts, something decisive should have happened.*

Tessa tensed up. *What did you think would happen? They'd actually have the relic?*

Or they'd have gotten us much closer to it. I have no idea why this dead-ended. Then he seemed to gather himself. *At any rate, I had the authority to take you down there.*

I know that. You're the archangel and you're stronger than everyone around you. I'm just confused because you have leverage in all these things, but then other matters come up where it seems like you should be able to do something, only you tell me you can't take action. It makes no sense.

He sounded strangely insistent. *Don't question my commitment to my assignment.*

She offered a smile, figuring he'd be able to pick it up in the dark. *I would never question your commitment to anything. You put up with the shenanigans around the church for what, nine centuries? You dealt with my relatives. I know from my own limited experience how much commitment that would require.* She paused just long enough. *Or else you'd get committed.*

He'd backed down from the anger. *Caffeine and late hours make you a bit of a wisecracker.*

She thought in a teasing tone, *Then you probably shouldn't have started appearing to me after births that ended at midnight.*

You know why I did that. Once again he sounded unamused. *There were disadvantages, but I made it work.*

She didn't reply. But she wanted to. Why was it that when she thought they were playing, he'd get prickly and sensitive? She knew the basic issues to avoid, and she'd avoided them. But asking if he was sending caffeine molecules back in time should have gotten a witty rejoinder: "No, I'm gathering them up to donate to Forty Winks for Wisecrackers, a charity that keeps smart-mouthed midwives from falling asleep during overnight labors." And sometimes he did reply just like that. Was the banter a later development, except that she kept encountering earlier versions? Or more disturbingly, were the ready rejoinders an early attitude until over time he'd gotten more fed up with her?

I need a GPS system for your timeline, she thought. *You need to give me numbers in order whenever you appear to me, and then I'll know when you are in your timeline versus when you're appearing in mine.*

He sounded puzzled. *What good would that do?*

So I can track what you know and when you know it, or what you think about things, or what information maybe I shouldn't be sharing at a certain time.

You don't need to hold back anything.

But if I knew what other developments you were reacting to, I could figure out how to talk to you. Like when you said you always thought those two Queen songs shouldn't count as a twofer, if I knew you were speaking to me earlier than that, I wouldn't reference it because that would be rude.

I'm aware you're not fluent in how the timestream works, and I account for that.

She nearly said she didn't need him to be charitable about her deficiencies, but that wasn't even the point. She'd automatically phrased her request in a way that would benefit Martin. What she needed here was to be honest. *The real reason is it would benefit me because then I could understand how our interactions are developing. The indicators I was using aren't working anymore.*

Now he sounded surprised. *What indicators?*

Your body language, for one thing. Whether you assume I can hear you in my head. Whether you clamp down on your emotions. And one time you called me Terry, which I'm guessing wasn't a mistake but rather because it happened before I asked you not to.

That wasn't all, but it was enough.

Martin sounded stunned. *I didn't realize you were trying to straighten out my timeline. I should have, of course. You do think linearly and logically.*

I upset you at least once by making a joke that you took the wrong way because you thought it was an insult. I'd rather not have that happen again.

He replied, *And insulting me would have been okay if you thought I was younger than I was?*

Now he did sound annoyed. *For goodness' sake,* she thought, *I'm trying to avoid having fights, not start one now. This was a bad idea.*

How about we just try not mocking one another?

You're pretty funny when you're being just a little critical of human flaws, Tessa shot back, *so I assumed it could go both ways.*

If he was still pulling caffeine from her system, it wasn't making her tired. If anything, the interaction was waking her up. Why did everything always go wrong? Were the cultural differences between the two species just so much that every sensitive conversation would inevitably devolve into him getting angry? She should just treat him like a visiting dignitary. The Bible called the angels "princes," right? Prince Martin. He'd love that. He'd be irritated for days, but she'd never know which days because he'd pop all around in time.

You conned me into telling you exactly why the church was destroyed, Martin said. *Then you used it against me. You question my judgment and impugn my ability to do my job. In what way is that teasing?*

I swear on my heart that I was in no way trying to use that against you! I know your guardianship is a sensitive topic.

Then respect it. Her chest was tightening too, and her gut. That had to be backflow from his anger. In retrospect, she should have said, "You know, I'll just deal with the caffeine and sit up crocheting a baby blanket until three a.m."

He went on, *You have no idea what magnitude of failure we're talking about. This isn't like leaving your to-go coffee on top of the car. This is more like coming home to find you accidentally killed your whole family. And then you drag up my current assignment and imply I'm not up to this one either.*

That wasn't melodrama. He believed that. He'd been charged with a task by God.

I'm not saying to brush off the past like it didn't happen, Tessa replied, *but it's been decades. I assume it's been decades, at least. I don't know how soon you jumped ahead to me to get it sorted. But there's an element of self-forgiveness and grieving that you've overlooked.*

Self-forgiveness is an excuse.

For some people, maybe, but you don't have any compassion on yourself at all, and I think you assume I'm equally uncompassionate toward you.

What he said next boiled with real anger: *I don't need your pity.*

I have never pitied you, she replied. *But I think you assumed too much of the guilt and all the burden of reparation for something that isn't on only your shoulders.*

She'd said similar things to grieving mothers like Amanda. "Your baby didn't die because of you. You're a good person. This isn't your fault."

I made an irrevocable and fatal error in judgment, Martin sent. *Reparation is the best I can manage. I failed because I was exhausted. There had been years of war. Years. You have no idea what it was like.*

I don't, Tessa said. *How could I? Even reading about it isn't the same.*

Every day people in the church would pray for an end to the war. Endless funerals. Grieving mothers. Bereaved widows. Prayers for their young men to be safe. Their soldiers to survive. Prayers that their sons wouldn't be taken into the service or that the fighting wouldn't come here. Prayers that there would be enough food and the armies would keep avoiding this one little town. Every day, every day, for years.

Tessa's eyes squeezed tighter. *That sounds awful.*

It was grueling. But it wasn't endless because the angels in Barlassina knew when the end of the time pocket would be, and it was the same for every one of us. We could tell the war was winding down. I needed hope. We thought there was going to be peace. We thought the pocket would pinch off when peace came, and I was worn down to shreds.

The emotions pouring from him felt exactly like a tattered, weather-beaten flag, the colors washed out and the threads barely holding one to the next, the flagpole rattling in the wind over a barren landscape. For all that he'd just accused her of using his emotions against him, here he was ladling them out with even more prodigality than before. He'd held this inside for so long. Did angels confide things to one another? Did they form friendships? Socialization was an evolutionary adaptation to assist in survival of the species, but angels didn't breed and hadn't evolved and couldn't be killed. So did they need socialization? Did they even want it?

But when you were all alone for centuries or bearing guilt for decades, did you hunger for even one other living creature to acknowledge it because just like a world war, after years it became too heavy to carry?

I needed to go to a time when we had hope again. I needed whatever victory there was in stopping a pointless fight, so I jumped ahead. I'd been testing the waters, and everything felt fine. There was no threat. So I jumped all the way ahead and found myself in a devastated church. There was a dead priest and dead townsfolk, and it was my fault. I couldn't tolerate it any longer, and then everything was in ruins because of me.

Tessa thought, *It wasn't just because of you. It's like I told Amanda: this wasn't your fault. It was the soldiers' decision to shoot the people and burn the church. Some fascist sympathizer shot the Americans and then the Americans shot back, but none of that was on you.*

I told you, I could have minimized the damage. The altercation might still have happened, but I might have been able to protect my primary charge, the church.

Right, and Amanda can think that if she just didn't go to a nail salon in her third week or have a glass of wine before she confirmed the pregnancy that Benedict would still be kicking her bladder. Amanda can think that God killed Benedict because she wasn't thankful enough for him when she had the sciatic pain. Do you blame her? Should she blame herself?

Martin's anger blazed in her mind. *I'm not wrong, Terry.*

Tessa rolled her eyes. *Oh, I get it now. Whenever something bad happens to someone else, it's morally neutral, but when it happens to you, it's because you screwed up.*

That is not the point.

It is exactly the point. You can't see your own double-standard.

What if you'd cancelled Amanda's last appointment because you didn't think she needed it? You'd be lambasting yourself.

I wouldn't because she could have been standing in my office when the baby died and nothing I did could have helped him.

Martin blew off a cloud of frustration. *You are such a DiOrio!*

By which you mean I'm right?

By which I mean you're stubborn as a bull.

Only when I know I'm right.

I should have just put you to sleep, Martin muttered in her head. *You'd wake up in ninety minutes just as smug as you are now, but it wouldn't be my problem.*

Tessa laughed out loud in the dark. All Martin's sensations vanished, and then before she could ask if he'd left, they returned. He must have done the angelic equivalent of counting to ten. Maybe he'd flashed into the past, listened to the music of the spheres for a month, and only come back when he felt capable of dealing with her. Maybe he'd collared her guardian angel and dragged him into a different silent midnight, raged at him for a while, and then returned with a new sheaf of smart remarks.

On the guess that he was calmer now, she thought, *Even in this conversation, you've taken the blame for circumstances that aren't your fault. I was trying to straighten out your timeline in my head, and you say it's your fault you didn't realize what I was doing. I held back information, and you accepted the blame for that too. But the problem with assigning so much blame to yourself is that a lot of the time you sense it's not right, so then you reassign that blame to me. Can't some things just be misunderstandings?*

He didn't reply right away, but his presence remained steady.

Let me go on, she added. *Amanda's baby isn't less dead if she finds a way she's at fault. Moms do that, though. They blame themselves because that makes the baby's death more understandable. It's like handling something hot by putting on oven mitts. The trouble is, you can't live your life wearing oven mitts. Do that and you can't feel anything at all.*

Human psychology doesn't work on me.

I don't know angelic psychology, so I'm working with whatever is closest to hand. Angels also don't need oven mitts to handle a cast-iron pan. You can't get burned, but I'd get really burned and wouldn't be able to do my job if I tried to grab metal out of the fire. So sometimes they're appropriate, but afterward, you take them off. That's where self-forgiveness comes in.

Martin sounded more didactic than reactive this time. *Most of the time when people engage in self-forgiveness, they're forgiving themselves for wrecking their families or breaking someone's heart, or for perpetuating a family feud into yet another generation. Ercole Monterosa's reliquary brought a brief peace. Then people started up the fight again, with no one holding himself accountable. Their self-forgiving excuses brought evil. I want nothing to do with evil. Angels clean up the messes they make.*

Barlassina was a mess. Martin hadn't made the mess, but he'd never agree with that. Tessa reframed her thoughts.

The relic's theft was an injustice, she thought. *It should be returned for that reason alone. I'm concerned that if returning it doesn't work out the way you plan, you're going to feel adrift. If you return it and the church doesn't get rebuilt, or if you return it and the church gets rebuilt but the families keep throwing firewood on their animosity, will you still feel as if you failed?*

He didn't reply.

This was the first time Tessa ever wondered if she should have read up on moral theology, or at least gone deeper than her medical ethics class. Guilt was a healthy response to wrongdoing. Martin didn't seem to have done anything wrong. He hadn't wanted harm to come to the church or to the town. He'd wanted relief. Wanted? No, he'd hungered for peace with the intensity of someone starving to death. Guilt in the absence of wrongdoing seemed misplaced. Or maybe guilt minus wrongdoing became shame.

Shame lay at the root of anger. Shame led to blame-assigning. Maybe shame ended in relic-hunting.

But when you dealt with someone tied so tightly by shame, you couldn't ever call it that. They'd get defensive. They'd call it other things. They'd defend it to the end because in their mind, the more they defended it and renamed it, the less of their shame an outsider would be able to see.

I'm a midwife, so I don't view injuries as something you need to treat. Injuries need to heal. Bringing the relic home, that sounds to me like treating. Healing is something separate. Treating happens from the outside, but healing happens from within.

You need to go to sleep, bad girl. Martin sounded subdued. *We'll make this work, but you're starting not to make sense. And I'm not giving you a number every time I show up.*

Her attention started floating off in different directions, and she found herself thinking about relics and babies. The last thing she saw was a checkered tablecloth in the Brooklyn sunlight.

TWENTY

New York had been Tuesday. Wednesday she spent in the office and at 8 p.m. crashed to sleep. Thursday morning she would speak to the state house.

But first she hustled the kids out the door to their respective buses. Eric was looking for his snow boots when the phone rang.

"It's the notification line," Gary said, then answered and listened while Tessa finished packing Eric's bag. "Bad news. Kindergarten is cancelled due to a leak in the building."

She froze, then ran through every possibility. Gary had onsite work today at one of his business clients. Her mother was out of town. She had to leave in ten minutes to give her speech.

Gary pulled out his phone. "I could maybe reschedule, but we've already rescheduled twice."

"No, wait. Think." She shook her head. "He can come with me. Karen's coming too, and between the two of us, we'll be able to keep him corralled."

Gary said, "Really? That's not at all a good idea."

"It's the only one that's going to work. You need to meet your client. Eric's good at sitting if we bring a stack of activities and snacks. Karen and I are both competent to handle a child, and for the record," Tessa added, "he's photogenic. If I'm holding him on my hip, we'll have a thousand pictures in the paper."

"Well, there's that."

Tessa ran upstairs and found a relic of her own, from her activist past: a child-sized sweatshirt emblazoned with, "Ask Me About My Homebirth!" She loaded up Eric's backpack with coloring books, two puzzles, picture books, and a zippered plastic bag full of Legos.

Karen would be here in five minutes. Downstairs, Gary had packed snacks, and Eric finally had on his boots. Tessa went into the foyer to grab her coat and...it wasn't there.

"Wait, my coat. Where'd I leave it?"

She turned, and Gary stood at the foyer entrance. "Are you looking for this?"

In one hand, held up at shoulder-height, he dangled a brand-new knee-length black wool coat.

Her heart stuttered. "What? We can't afford this!"

"You can't afford not to wear it. Plus, I cut off all the tags because I'm a jerk. Try it on."

The coat felt like a dream. The liner wasn't torn. The big buttons gave just enough resistance as she pushed them through the button holes. She slipped her hands into the smooth pockets, and Gary had even transferred her gloves so they were waiting.

Blinking hard, she choked out, "Thank you."

"You're going to speak to the state." He kissed her. "You deserve to look as wonderful as you are."

"I love you."

He kissed her again, then said, "If I'd only known a coat would make you love me..."

Eric slammed into their legs and hugged them both, and they both laughed. A moment later, Karen rang the doorbell. They liberated Eric's booster seat from Gary's car, and two minutes later they were flying toward Boston.

With the radio on the classic rock station, Karen chattered about everyone who'd be meeting them. She'd arranged for a whole crowd of their supporters, plus the inevitable reporters and photographers. Media circus wasn't really the right word. More like a media carnival.

Still, it was a good drive. Rush hour traffic had eased, and Tessa ran her fingers over the edge of the wool coat. Now she could claim to be just like her relatives, all those Italian women with their black wool coats in the World War II photographs. At least the new coat didn't look like it also dated from World War II.

The song on the radio changed, and abruptly she felt Martin singing. She hadn't felt that in so long, so she closed her eyes to let the vibrations run through her. She couldn't hear his voice, but just the effect on her soul made her know what he was doing, as if he were picking up the notes and putting them forward. Inside them rang a deep keening.

Through the whole play set on the station, he sang. "More Than a Feeling" followed by "Caught Up in You," "Peace of Mind," and "Give a Little Bit." He just kept going, but why this, why now? When she focused on the sensation of his song, she picked up something else: nerves. Not that angels had an actual nervous system, but every part of Martin was on edge.

When the play set ended, she thought to him, *Martin, are you with me?*

Inside, she felt agreement.

Why are you nervous?

Amanda's mother is going to be there.

She tensed. "Really?" she whispered, and when Karen asked her what was going on, Tessa said, "I bet you Amanda's mother will be there."

"It wouldn't surprise me. The woman's a bulldog." Karen sighed. "We'll be okay. Trust me."

With no other option, Tessa looked back out at the road. *You're nervous about Suzanne? She won't try to hurt me when there are cameras going. There's some measure of protection in being out in public.*

I really don't like you heading into danger, and this feels like danger.

Tessa looked sideways out the window. *We're on the Mass Pike. That's dangerous too.*

Don't remind me.

He sounded uneasy. What would settle him down since he didn't trust himself? *I have confidence in my guardian angel.*

Confidence? He sounded disbelieving. *First time you've ever said that.*

She glanced at Eric. *His guardian will protect him too, right?*

Absolutely. As much as he's able.

The state house was a mob, but because of Howard Masters' worthless grandson, they had special parking and then an escort. Karen looked great for the cameras. Eric rode on Tessa's hip and displayed his sweatshirt to everyone who'd look, waving at the cameras with the enthusiasm of a five-year-old who suddenly finds himself the object of the world's attention. Brian would have died of embarrassment. Eric acted like he never wanted to live again any other way.

On the front steps, Karen faced the crowd that seemed most dense with her supporters. She waved her own Stop Proposition H.8937 sign and shouted, "Homebirth forever!" The crowd chanted back at her, "Women's births in women's homes!" The crowd itself was filled with pregnant women, women with children, and women wearing baby slings.

It was great optics. A reporter with sun-streaked hair and fabulous sunglasses made sure to get lots of footage of Eric and his sweatshirt. Sure, on the opposite side of the square were all the pro-H.8937 signs, the "Safety first!" and "What if something goes wrong?" But Karen's faction outnumbered them. So far, so good.

Their escort guided them to a waiting room. Hands shaking, Tessa looked over her speech. Eric set himself up at a big glossy table with a puzzle, and she also laid out his snacks. "I'll watch from the gallery," Karen said, looking as if she were enjoying herself. "I assume the first part will be boring."

Tessa pulled out her crocheting and watched on the closed-circuit TV. She couldn't get her hook to behave: she'd keep trying to get it into the next stitch and missing, or the yarn wouldn't catch on the head of the crochet hook. Finally she gave it up as futile.

Several other midwives and advocates had gathered in the room, and although they fussed a bit over Eric, Eric stayed as well-behaved as she'd ever seen him. That at least was a small miracle. Maybe his guardian angel was pleased by the recognition and this was his way of saying thanks.

Martin was nervous. Specifically, nervous about her safety, and that still didn't make sense to her.

Do you really think I might get hurt? she thought to him.

I don't know what to think. His reply didn't fill her with any kind of confidence. *I'm keeping an eye out. There's nothing huge like a bomb or a madman with a gun.*

Still, he'd said over and over that he could feel when something was about to happen, or maybe he'd jumped ahead in time and could see that something definitely would. Although he'd sensed something would happen in New York, and then nothing had. Nothing definitive, that was. What if the thing he'd sensed pertained to now rather than to before?

Of course. This was where she kept finding herself: time travel made no sense.

She turned her attention to the closed-circuit TV. They were allotted three minutes each to make their point. She glanced again at Gary's speech, which she'd darned near memorized. He'd had her deliver it over and over last night, finessing her timing, making notes in the margins. At two o'clock she'd awakened and recited the central paragraphs to herself.

Knock 'em dead, Gary had told her just before she'd left. Meanwhile Martin was worried that someone else would knock her dead. Terrible juxtaposition, there. She'd be on camera. That was the worst part: Eric would be watching on TV, and if there was violence, he'd forever remember the helplessness of watching his mother die across a screen. And that....

No, not Eric. Not for Eric.

Violence had destroyed Barlassina. And it wasn't even the kind of violence you could understand. Here at least the violence was about something that mattered: it mattered the way you brought babies into the world. It mattered that women had the option to give birth in the best possible way for themselves. It mattered that the person who assumed the risk had the privilege of making the decision. It mattered.

If I have to die for this, Tessa thought, *it's okay. It'll mean something. When my great-aunt Alicia died, she died trying to save her son. It meant something to her too. Her son died in the church, standing up for his faith. He gave up everything to serve the Church, and I'm willing to give up everything to serve birthing women.*

Martin thought, *Be careful about that kind of commitment. You wouldn't sacrifice Eric for this. And I daresay, if given the choice between never birthing another baby ever again, versus bringing Amanda's baby back to life, you'd resurrect her baby.*

Tessa looked down. *I don't know.*

I know you. You give and you give and you give. You'll hurt yourself to save others. That's why sometimes someone needs to step in and help you too.

The speeches were all what she expected. Lots of emotion, lots of statistics cited out of context, lots of sloganeering. This was from both sides. Her speech would avoid those pitfalls. Gary, with his talent for wordsmithing compassion out of the entries you'd find lying around the dictionary, had crafted a speech with an undercurrent of manipulation and the tug of reality. In his prose, statistics blended seamlessly with sensitivity. In his words and her delivery, you'd hear the voices of women who needed Tessa to speak for them. That was really all there was to it. They needed her. She'd be here for them. She'd be there to answer the call in the middle of the night. She'd be there when they needed a midwife to hold their hand. She'd be here today to speak on their behalf.

"Teresa Testerman?" said a staffer.

Tessa kissed Eric on the head. "I love you, big guy. Be good for the other moms."

"Good luck, Mommy!" He beamed. "I'll see you on TV!"

She had to figure out which camera was the internal one. She'd look him right in the eye across several rooms, and he'd know she was looking at him. He'd sit there with his puzzle and the new coat Daddy had bought for Mommy, eating the snacks they'd packed for him, and he'd be safe. She'd be the one in the teeth of the storm.

They took an elevator, and when it opened, she met Karen fresh from her speech. "Nice work!" Tessa said.

Karen grabbed her hand. "You're going to do great! Just keep focus."

The current speaker was an anesthesiologist, of course, and she wanted to make sure everyone knew that childbirth was dangerous, of course. Women could die! Babies could die! Terrible things could happen in just a second! Tessa listened to the hysteria, wishing that whenever someone spoke before a legislative body, they had to have a ticker underneath their image showing how much money they'd made (or stood to make) from whatever action they were recommending. Yes, Tessa's livelihood was also dependent on what she was about to say, but what did her little income matter to an anesthesiologist who routinely pulled down six figures?

Still, Tessa could take comfort in the fact that anesthesiologists generally practiced on people who were unconscious, and this one had developed her people skills to match the target demographic. She spoke in bland, chunky sentences. She barked her demands like a master issuing orders to the staff. Even when she gave her compelling anecdote about saving a woman's life by putting her under in time for a surgeon to section the baby, she sounded like a lecture hall prophet.

Tessa touched Gary's speech in her blazer pocket. It was good. She'd do fine.

When the anesthesiologist finished, people applauded politely, and it was time.

Before beginning, Tessa paused to smile at everyone. Her teaching and midwifery skills had always seemed to blend one into the next in so many ways, and she drew on her teacher presence now. There was an element of reassurance in the way you spoke, backed up with the rock-solid conviction that you never, ever, talk down to your listeners. They're smart. They're engaged. They want to hear you, even if at first they don't know they want to.

"I'm Teresa Testerman, a midwife with the Milliston Common Birth Center. I've delivered a hundred fifty babies, and I've been present at the births of over two hundred more. In that time, I've learned a lot about women, and I want to share it with you.

"Women come in many sizes and shapes and colors. They have different health statuses and different ethnic backgrounds and different physical abilities. This incredible diversity of women has left me awed over and over again, but the one thing all those women had in common was that they chose to birth with a midwife."

Tessa looked out at the crowd of lawmakers and reporters and spectators, making eye contact with several.

"Every woman had a different reason. Each woman had a different goal in mind, but every one of them had done her research. She'd educated herself. She'd looked into what it would take to have a healthy baby, and she found that a birth center delivery with a certified midwife gave her the best shot at achieving her goal."

Again, she looked out at the crowd. "What path each woman takes is going to be different. Many women will do best with a hospital birth and an attending obstetrician. But for those women who will do best in a low-intervention environment, with continuous midwife support and a very hands-on approach, they deserve to have their decision respected."

Here began the sections where Gary had worked hardest: the interleaving of statistics with spirit. For every statistic about midwife-assisted birth, he'd said, you want to leave them with a positive image. For every statistic about the hospital, leave them feeling neutral. They'll remember something about higher breastfeeding rates and lower NICU rates, but it will be vague compared to describing the triumph of a new mother laughing at the scale when her breastfed baby gained weight, the moment she exclaimed, "I made that!"

In this section Tessa took her time, making sure every sentence could sink in alongside the images. Gary had provided a thirty second cushion so she could take it as slow as necessary.

Eric would be watching. Eric would have something to talk about tomorrow at school, or else Eric would forget and assume everybody's mother spoke to the state house. That was fine too.

"It's not just about a better experience," Tessa concluded. "Preserving midwifery in the great state of Massachusetts is also about preserving the dignity of women. It preserves the dignity of babies, who deserve to be brought into the world in the way their mothers decide. Safe, certified midwifery recognizes a woman's autonomy and ability to make decisions about her own health and her own future. We have no need to pit women against their babies, nor women against the system, nor women against their own doctors. Women are, and should be, the primary providers of their own health care. Midwifery recognizes and assists this process. Please vote for respect, and please vote against proposition H.8937. Thank you."

Nice applause. Smiling, she gave a single wave to the crowd, and she turned to exit the stage with her staffer. Then she stopped in her tracks.

Walking onto the stage, with livid eyes, was Suzanne Erickson. She was dressed all in black and cloaked in an unholy rage.

She didn't push past Tessa as they crossed paths. She didn't look to her at all.

Suzanne took the podium Tessa had just vacated, and with her very first words, she threw down the gauntlet. "I hope you recognize," she began, "that you just applauded a murderer."

Twenty-One

Tessa didn't move, watching as Suzanne, in black head-to-toe, held up an eleven-by-fourteen picture that could be one thing, and one thing only.

"This is my first grandson, Benedict. He died under the so-called care of Teresa Testerman and her holistic, homeopathic, home-based birthing system. With their eighteen-hundreds mentality, Testerman and Meyer bamboozled my son and daughter-in-law into accepting snake-oil care. My grandson's death is the result."

Tessa's pulse pounded loud enough that she could hear it, but she didn't move from just off the wing of the stage. The crowd couldn't see her. It wouldn't matter if they could: she couldn't step forward and share privileged information about Amanda's care to defend herself. Amanda had received the best care possible, and this woman knew it. This woman was outraged, and in her anger over a death she couldn't control, she was standing up in front of a session of lawmakers to destroy something else.

Suzanne waxed on about the heartbreak of walking into a hospital room and seeing her daughter-in-law curled on her side, in agony. She said that even then, the Testerman woman had bullied her daughter-in-law, spouting lies to keep the hospital staff from helping. Suzanne claimed that in response to her very reasonable objection, Tessa had ordered her ejected from the hospital. She painted a picture of her son, helpless with grief but unable to change his wife's mind about the destructive path she'd charted for their family.

"Because of charlatans like Testerman and Meyer," Suzanne said in her crisp, precise language, "I will attend a funeral at ten a.m. Saturday morning. I will have to bury my own grandson. I will have to reassure my sobbing daughter-in-law that she did everything she could when I know full well that she didn't. But *I* am going to do everything I can." She paused. "I am going to urge you to shut this thing down. Take a stand and do your job by protecting endangered young mothers. Protect vulnerable women and their vulnerable babies. Vote yes on Proposition H.8937, and if you would dare vote no, please come on Saturday morning to Christ Church in Hopkinton. Stand up in front of my grandson's casket where you can tell everyone why."

Tessa pulled back from the door so she wouldn't meet Suzanne on the way out. "Let's go," she urged the staffer, and they reached the elevator before Suzanne was off the stage.

What a monster. What a horrible, monstrous, predatory woman. Protect other women? No, this was an exploitative snake who wanted nothing more than to win. She wanted to dominate: she'd dominated her son and now she'd find a way to dominate her daughter-in-law. She'd been unable to dominate Tessa in the hospital, but she'd found a way to do it anyhow. With that dark glint in her eye, she'd probably been glad Benedict had died when he did, just to get a cudgel so she could go on the attack.

Tessa had never believed in negative vibes, but as the elevator ascended, she wondered just for a moment if Suzanne's toxicity hadn't poisoned her own grandson.

Well, that settled one thing. Tessa's next stop would be the police department, where she'd file assault charges against Suzanne. There were three hospital-employed witnesses, including a security guard. That would be enough to get a conviction, for all a conviction would be worth at that point. Suzanne would get thirty days community service, if that, and Tessa would lose her livelihood and her ability to practice in this state.

That was the kicker: Suzanne knew she was lying. Persuasive speech was one thing. Outright lies, though, were another. Amanda had been under the care of an OB. In fact, her last ultrasound had been two days before Benedict died. Two days! She'd been in an obstetrician's office getting measured and tested two days before his death. She'd asked them if the baby's kicking should slow down, and in response the doctor had checked for problems, but everything had looked great. "It's just positioning," the doctor had said, which was in all likelihood what Tessa would have said too. "If you're worried," Tessa would have added, "let's talk about how to do kick counts, and if it still doesn't feel right, we can talk about further testing." She had no idea if the obstetrician had said that. Maybe. Probably.

Suzanne's depiction of what had happened in the hospital room was also an outright lie. Yes, Amanda had been curled on her side in agony when Suzanne had walked in. Why? Because that was the position you assumed while getting an epidural, and because contractions hurt. That was why you got an epidural in the first place: they hurt. The position you had to be in so the anesthesiologist could make the pain go away also hurt. Amanda was in that position because she had been receiving medical care, not because Tessa had been preventing it.

On and on and on. The lies were a bare cliff face she couldn't begin to climb, and HIPAA regulations wouldn't allow her to start. All Amanda's information, including the fact that she'd been under shadowcare, was protected. The privacy laws were there for the patient's protection, and Suzanne was exploiting that.

Tessa stopped in front of the restroom. "Give me a minute," she told the staffer.

It was a plush bathroom, for all that was worth. She washed off her makeup and took a drink of water. Gary would have been watching the speeches. An entire roomful of midwifery supporters would have heard all those accusations. Oh, no, Eric would have been watching too. Eric would think she was a murderer who killed babies by her ineptitude. He was probably in the waiting room now, sobbing. Sobbing and afraid, and who could comfort him if he was afraid of his own mother?

She couldn't go back in there. She couldn't face the women and the inevitable anger in their eyes. It wasn't her fault. She'd swear that until her final breath, but those women...

Eric. She needed to get Eric.

She squared her shoulders and returned to the hall, where the staffer brought her back to the waiting room.

Karen grabbed her by the arms as soon as she walked in. "That horrible woman! Are you okay? She stood there before God and everyone and slandered you without so much as blinking!"

Tessa looked around, but the anger on the women's faces wasn't anger toward her. It wasn't scorn or hatred. Every midwife in America had been accused of similar things. But baby Benedict was dead only a few days, so Amanda's tragedy was the worst sort of timing for the profession. It wasn't even Tessa's failure, but her perceived failure might well destroy their profession.

The women didn't see it that way. "We need to get those records open," one of the other midwives said.

"HIPAA," Tessa said. "I'm not leaking that to the press."

"Suzanne knows our hands are tied," Karen said. "If we could be brought up on murder charges, she'd have done it by now. If she could file a malpractice suit, she would. They're not going to. She knows that."

Eric looked up from his puzzle, but other than smiling because Mom was back in the room, he didn't react, just went back to his puzzle.

Tessa breathed deeply. That was what mattered. That witch might destroy midwifery in the state of Massachusetts, but she couldn't get between her and Eric. Nor between her and Gary.

"I need to talk to our attorney," Karen said. "I'll file against her for character assassination and slander."

"It doesn't matter." Tessa dropped into the chair at Eric's side. Some awkward insurance industry expert was giving a forgettable talk about premiums. "They'll vote on Monday. They'll vote with their emotions, and they won't care about reality. The truth won't have time to come out."

Suzanne made a good show, that was certain. Gary could have crafted the best speech in the universe, and it couldn't compete with her performance. It wasn't fair.

Well, life didn't have to be fair.

Tessa's phone sounded, and she reached into her bag to shut it off without looking. That could be Gary or Sarah or anyone watching from home. She didn't want to deal with them. Her phone might as well weigh a thousand pounds with the weight of the voicemail messages that would have poured in already.

"That phone was blowing up," one of the women said.

Eric said, "I didn't answer it. But it was a lot."

Well, they could just stay there, unread.

In her head, she heard Martin. *Check your messages.*

I would rather swallow a mason jar full of killer bees.

I would rather you check your messages. Please, Tessa.

That was more urgent than she'd ever heard him. Urgent and a little excited.

She unlocked the phone, and the screen filled with notifications. It was the last that caught her eye, with a Martin-driven focus. She brought up that one first, even before Gary's and Sarah's.

It was from Ellen Ashland, Pryce's daughter, the same woman who'd sent them out of the house with a determination never to speak to them again.

The same woman who'd threatened legal action if their articles ever so much as breathed a hint of incrimination about her father. That Ellen. Maybe she'd seen this on TV and decided to press charges anyhow.

Only this message wasn't a threat. It was something more than a threat, something golden and beautiful and amazing.

"Can you come up to Maine? My father wants to talk to you. I think he has something to give you."

Tessa's hands shook so hard she almost couldn't text back. "I can be there in a few hours. I'm in Boston without my car. I'll have to get hold of Gary."

The reply came immediately: "Not Gary. Only you."

Tessa texted, "Okay."

She closed her eyes and thought to Martin, *You didn't warn me this was going to happen.*

I didn't know it would happen. The words came into her head with a tremble midway between excitement and fear. *I've been drawn back into linear time.*

TWENTY-TWO

Amtrak had a Downeaster leaving for Brunswick, Maine in half an hour. Tessa packed up Eric and got out at light speed. A staffer paged her a car service to North Station, and Eric bounced the whole way. He wasn't in a booster seat, but the trip was short. Tessa hoped it would be okay.

She texted Gary. "Going to Maine. Amtrak. Pryce has something to give me."

He replied, "Are you serious?"

"I wouldn't joke about this," she texted back, even as his next text appeared.

Gary had texted, "Do you have tickets yet? I'll order them and send them to your phone."

She'd planned to pick them up on the train itself because they had so little time. She said yes, and the notification appeared in her email before she'd finished paying the driver. They found the platform with the train idling, only a few minutes before the train would depart.

"I want a window," Eric said.

"We'll get whatever we get," Tessa said. "The train might be crowded."

Through this all, she kept trying to feel for Martin, but it was a jumble. He was nervous and uncomfortable, but also excited. Hints of claustrophobia kept sparking up from the swirl, as if he wanted to skip ahead in time and figure out what was going on, or at least have the ability to do so. There wasn't time to ask him about it. Time. It was all about time. Decades or minutes, it was all about time.

The train wasn't crowded, so she staked out a section with four seats facing one another. Eric, his bag packed to entertain him for at least ninety-two hours, pulled out a handful of play figures. Kneeling on the train floor and using the seat as a table, he set up a barn and some animals. The animals began fully inhabiting their single-seat world as the train lurched into motion. Tessa clutched her own bag on her lap.

Can you talk now? she sent to Martin.

He appeared in the seat across from her. It had been a while since she'd seen him. As she'd grown comfortable with talking to him in her head, he'd stopped making an image for her to relate to. Until now, she hadn't realized that.

Regardless, this was quite obviously the latest version of Martin she'd ever seen. He'd developed a proficiency at manipulating the mental image, and today he came fully equipped with facial expressions, plus a nice outfit from the LL Bean catalog: jeans, a polo shirt, and work boots like hers. He looked thoroughly New England in a practical way. And on his face, she could read a kaleidoscope of feeling.

Can you explain the linear time thing to me? For once you can't see into the future?

"Not at all." His eyes looked somewhat desperate. "We've just exited the previous time pocket. I told you how those work, right? Toward the last bit of a time pocket, you get something of a funnel effect. It's harder to move around then, and you start to feel a pull that drags you toward the end of the pocket. You don't go into the funnel zone until you're done with everything you wanted to accomplish in that pocket of time, and then when you're ready, you allow yourself into the funnel. At the base of the funnel, you get tugged into linear time until it ejects you into the next pocket."

Tessa nodded. *And how long are you usually in linear time?*

"It varies. It's never been longer for me than, say, a week, although some angels have told me they endured really long stretches. It feels wrong." Martin's gaze dropped. "It's so restrictive."

"That's my life," Tessa said aloud. She tensed, but Eric didn't notice her. She raised her phone so at least it would look like she had a reason to be talking to herself. "But hey, it's a good sign, right? Your search is nearly over."

Again that sparkle overtook his expression. "I had no idea this would happen. I try to avoid funnels before I have to. The church was destroyed during a funnel. I knew you'd be speaking to the senate during the funnel, so I was focused on your safety."

"This is a good thing, then, even if it's restrictive. It's like labor," she said. "The baby gets squeezed, but then the baby is out and everything is good."

Martin smiled. "You're right. Ashland called you on her own. That's got to be a good thing."

Eric looked up. "Mommy? That very angry lady was talking about a baby who died. What happened?"

Tessa's heart sank, and she set her phone in her lap. "I was the midwife for her grandson, baby Benedict. But Benedict died, and there was nothing I could do to save him."

She opened her arms, and Eric climbed up into her lap. She kissed his forehead.

"She said you could have helped him."

Tessa squeezed him. "No, sometimes you can't help no matter how much you want to."

Eric cocked his head. "Then why was she mad?"

"Because when something terrible happens, some people get angry." Tessa bit her lip. "Even if it doesn't make sense, they feel better angry than they do sad, so they get angry."

Eric thought. "Oh, I know. Alex gets mad when he's sad."

She nodded. "And Brian gets quiet when he's sad."

"Dad fixes things when he's sad," said Eric. "Mark gets mad too, but he gets mad at himself."

The kid had nailed everyone in the house so far, and Tessa wasn't willing to hear his assessment of herself. "What do you do when you're sad?"

He frowned as he puzzled it out. "I think when I feel sad, I'll just feel sad instead of feeling something else. That way I don't have to feel two things."

Tessa smiled. "That's probably for the best."

"But you have to feel two things," he said. "I could feel sad, but I'd still love you."

Tessa let him wriggle down from her lap. "You're right. I do feel sad about Amanda's baby," she said. "And I love you too."

And with that settled, Eric went back to playing with his farm animals.

Tessa pulled the clip from her hair to hold in her teeth, then tugged her hair back and twisted it into its familiar bun. She wasn't dressed for travel. She should be wearing jeans and work boots, but here she was in a long black skirt, black riding boots, and a white blouse. Her new coat slumped on the seat at her back, and it felt like a hug from Gary. He was so thoughtful. She couldn't help but feel as if she'd let him down because even though his speech had been amazing, in the end it had been delivered by her. All along she'd been the weak link in the midwifery legal defense strategy.

The conductor scanned the phone screen, then left two tags for them and tore three train stickers off a roll for Eric. He stuck them to his shirt sleeve. *Ask me about my homebirth!* He wasn't dressed for a visit either. With any luck, Pryce would forgive their fashion errors.

Through all this, Martin hadn't disappeared. She met his eyes, but she couldn't read his expression.

"I love you," he said.

She tensed. "What?"

He nodded. "You've done so much for this cause. You've brought your husband onboard, and you've connected with so many people because I asked you to. I appreciate that. I haven't been able to help as much as you wanted with Proposition H.8937, but you kept persisting anyhow. I love your strength of spirit and your warmth."

"Thank you." She looked at the floor. "I'm going to miss you when it's over."

He recoiled. "What?"

"When the relic goes home, you'll go home with it, right?"

He shook his head. "Oh! No, that assignment is done. I'll leave when I present myself before God to close it out, but I can do that while you're asleep. Then I'll be back to finish this one. Don't you have any trust in me at all?"

"Why wouldn't I trust you?" Tessa's brow furrowed. "Your assignment is to retrieve the relic."

"My side quest is to retrieve the relic. My assignment is protecting you," Martin said. "That's what a guardian angel does."

"Wait, what?" Her eyes flared. "You're *what*?"

He started. "What? Yes, I'm— You didn't know that?"

"You never said that!" She leaned forward. "You said— You didn't say you were guarding *me*! Archangels don't get personal jobs. You get countries and churches and alternate dimensions or really important things."

"Right, and at first I thought that meant my assignment was the biggest no-confidence vote by God in the history of creation." Martin looked directly into her as though seeing her soul. "Then I realized you were a DiOrio, and I figured it was even more of a disgrace, as if I'd forget what had happened without a constant reminder. But that wasn't it either. I'm going to stay with you, regardless."

Tessa raised her eyebrows. "So I'm the best-protected human being in Massachusetts?"

"In about an hour," Martin replied with a smirk, "you'll be the best-protected human being in Maine."

She snickered. Eric glanced at her, but then went back to his play set.

"I can't believe you never mentioned that." She rolled her eyes. "That would have been kind of an important thing to disclose."

Martin still sounded mystified. "I said I chose you for a reason."

She side-eyed Martin. "I couldn't figure out what on earth you meant by that. Maybe there was some kind of mystical thing that you couldn't reveal."

"But you knew you had a guardian." Martin said, "Who'd you think was guarding you?"

Tessa choked out, "Some really quiet angel who owed you a big favor...?"

Martin laughed out loud. "No favor would possibly be that big. You have no idea how long it took me to convince *myself*!"

Tessa glanced out the window. "But now it makes sense why you got upset when I said my guardian angel wouldn't have put me into a dangerous situation. You thought I was criticizing you. I wasn't."

"No, I see that. I'm sorry." Martin frowned. "I'll have to reevaluate some of our interactions. I thought you knew from the start because you were asking for help with mundane tasks, and why would you ask an angel who wasn't your guardian?"

"Back up a bit," Tessa said. "You said if the relic goes home, they'll rebuild the church, so the church will need a guardian again. You can't be in two places at the same time. I'm not moving to Barlassina."

"The church will go to someone else." Martin's wings raised, as if he were settling back into the seat. He'd gotten really good at managing the image. "Some other angel will get to deal with the next thousand offenses of the DiOrios and Monterosas. I'll be with you."

Tessa bit her lip. "That's not fair. You love Holy Cross. You've worked this hard to get it restored."

"We haven't restored it yet," Martin said. "You're ahead of yourself. For all I know, we'll get to Maine and I'll have to protect you from a shotgun blast."

All seriousness, Tessa leaned forward. "If he pulls a gun, you protect *Eric*, not me."

"Eric's got his own guardian."

"That's nice. You protect Eric."

Martin didn't fight, but it also didn't look like he agreed with her. Some things never changed.

"I'm serious. If someone pulls a shotgun, I'm putting myself in between him and my kid, so you might as well just skip a step and protect the kid."

"That's your job," said Martin. "And the same way you'd sacrifice everything to protect the child in your charge, I'd sacrifice everything to protect the one in mine. This is a nonproductive line of discussion, though. Wait." The world contorted, and she felt Martin reach out with his soul. With everything around her still spinning, Tessa shrank into the black coat, but then the feeling subsided and Martin looked brighter. "There isn't going to be a shotgun. Nor any kind of weapon."

She tried to regain her equilibrium. "Thank you for making sure."

He smiled at her.

"Now that I know when you are, I can say this: you've improved at managing your body language."

His laugh sounded self-conscious. "When you pointed that out to me, I asked for some tips. Apparently the trick is to access the human's unconscious perception of what body language she expects to correspond with whatever emotion the angel is projecting. So actually," and he glanced away from her, "you're the one doing the work. I'm setting the scene and plugging in the emotional subtext, after which you're creating the body language."

She snickered. "Really?"

"I didn't like the idea of you pinning me into a timeline based on my mistakes." His nose wrinkled. "But God has a sense of humor, so until we enter the next time pocket, you've got a perfect grasp of my timeline anyhow."

His fingers drummed against his leg. It flashed across Tessa's thoughts that maybe he might want to hide some emotions, but she let that go. Not her decision to make. He knew what he was doing.

She said, "You were singing before, in the car. Does that help you relax? I could turn on a playlist for you."

He shook his head. "I'll be fine. We'll be there in three hours, even if I can't skip the boring parts. At least we can be bored together."

The train snaked up the coast, stopping at too many places Tessa had never thought about. Eric ate his snacks, but Tessa's clenched stomach recoiled from any food whatsoever.

The relic might go home. And Martin was going to stay.

She kept reviewing their interactions and thinking, "No wonder." No wonder he'd said that, done that, assumed that other thing. No wonder he'd assumed he could call her Terry. No wonder. All along, she'd been assembling a puzzle but had been missing a piece that would make all the others fit together.

Old Orchard Beach. Portland. Freeport. And finally Brunswick. Tessa took Eric off the train, then gave Pryce's address to a waiting cab. Martin followed, silent. But the whole ride there, she could feel his anticipation building.

Twenty-Three

At Pryce's house, Tessa inhaled the woodstove scent. Back in Delaware, no one ever heated with wood, but here it wasn't unusual to see the chimneys in action, wood stacked alongside the houses or just dumped in a cord-sized pile on someone's driveway.

Ellen Ashland met them at the door with a caution similar to last time, but minus the hostility. "Come in." Her voice was low. "He's dozing, and when he wakes up, sometimes he's not clear for a little while. I don't know if this will have been a wasted trip, but he was so insistent."

Ellen went around the side of the house to the woodpile, where she gathered logs into her arms. Tessa loaded up as well, and Eric took one.

"I want you to promise to be gentle with him." Ellen wasn't wearing a coat, just her jeans, boots, and a sweatshirt over a turtleneck. "He's old, but I have to trust you on this. Your husband wrote all those articles, and he sounds nice enough. He could have named my father or even hinted at who he was, but he didn't. Everyone talks about mercy and being gentle, but then they go for the throat. I just don't want anyone to hurt him."

"No one's going to hurt your father." Tessa kept her voice even. "You have no idea how many people have spoken to my husband on condition of secrecy, and I need you to believe I know how to keep secrets too. I'm a midwife. I have to comply with HIPAA," Tessa added. "I cannot divulge information about my clients, legally or ethically. If Gary writes about it again, no one will ever figure out where the relic spent its last thirty-five years."

Ellen straightened. "But—"

"We traced it to Brent Fagan in Brooklyn, New York," Tessa said, noting how Ellen's eyes flared. "We narrowed it down to three men who could possibly have bought it from Fagan, but none of the articles hinted at this. You know the participants, and even you were surprised just now."

Ellen looked down. "You'd have found it regardless."

"No one's going to prosecute."

Ellen sighed. "Well, it's a little late for all that now."

They stamped the snow off their feet in the foyer, then went into the kitchen. Ellen said, "You can put that by the woodstove. Wait here. I'll go in and see if he's awake."

Tessa put down the logs, dusting splintery bits off her gloves and the front of her new coat. She shivered as the snowflakes in her hair yielded to the heat, losing their crystalline forms and running down the strands as drops. Eric set his log by the others, then turned to the dog. The dog padded across the kitchen floor, his tail giving a lazy wave, and Tessa watched to make sure the interaction would be friendly.

She shivered. She ought to go stand by the fire, but then she wouldn't hear their conversation, so instead she stayed in her coat.

From the living room came a clank as Ellen opened the other woodstove. "Dad? Dad, you have a visitor."

Tessa edged toward the wall so she could see. It was just a sliver, but Richard Pryce sat in a recliner. He struggled to work it upright, and Ellen helped him click it into place. The house smelled of woodsmoke and medication.

Martin flared into life inside her. It was here, it was here, it was here!

Tessa couldn't contain the smile that came from him. *I need you to back off,* she thought urgently. *I'm going to need my wits about me when I talk to him.*

She knew what she'd have to say to Pryce. She'd have to tell him it was all right, and that no one was angry at him. She'd dealt with dementia before, and so many people responded in different ways. But when she'd been here last time, she'd been able to break through the fog by being soothing and calm. She'd use the same kind tone, the tone you adopted as a teacher trying to calm a child in hysterics.

"We're so glad you're going to send it back," she would say. "Everyone in the town will be so pleased to know you kept it safe so long." She could tell him what she'd speculated about with Gary: "The relic survived because you took it out of the church." She'd keep him focused on the good he was doing now, rather than any wrong that had happened during the war.

Behind her, Eric laughed as he petted the dog, and the dog wagged harder.

Pryce said something to Ellen, who moved a few things so he'd be able to get up. More shuffling sounds. Then Ellen stepped away, and Tessa could see past her to an end table with a gold-toned object on it, small enough to fit into a pocket. It glinted.

Martin, that's it!

He felt electrified. He wanted her to go in there, but Ellen had said to wait.

"You wanted to give it to her, remember?" Ellen was saying. "She's here, and she's ready for it."

"I remember." Pryce sounded subdued. "I remember. I want to hold it again."

Ellen handed it to him. He gazed at it, then shuddered. "So much trouble." He shook his head. "So much trouble over something so small."

"You can give it back now, though. Someone's here to take it back."

"I don't want them to know." He sounded confused, urgent. "This shouldn't be here. I didn't take it."

"Dad, it's okay. It's going back where it belongs. Are you ready to give it to her? She's waiting in the kitchen."

She helped him to stand, a long process. He had the reliquary in one hand, and Ellen handed him his cane for the other.

"For a guest, you put more wood. Put more wood on the fire," Pryce said, wobbling uncertainly.

"Of course, Dad. I'm doing it now." Ellen vanished from view, and Pryce took a step toward the door.

Hearing his master, the dog raised its head, then trotted into the living room. Eric took off after the dog.

"No, sweetie!" Tessa called, and she took two steps after him, rounding the corner. She didn't grab him until he'd gotten into the living room, but then she grabbed him and hauled him up onto her hip. "Eric, no!"

Pryce looked at her and gasped. Eyes wide, he shouted, "No!"

Tessa took a step back, pivoting Eric away from him.

Pryce clutched the relic against his chest. "I didn't!" he exclaimed, "I didn't mean to!" and he lurched with the relic toward Ellen, where she'd just added a log. The fire flared.

She turned. "Dad, what are you doing?"

Pryce pushed her aside, cane in one hand and the relic clutched in his other. And then, with a lurch, he flung it into the flames.

Tessa dropped Eric and rushed to the cast-iron stove. She rushed past Ellen, steadying her father so he wouldn't topple onto the hot metal, and Tessa stared down into the stove. The relic was there, in the fire, flames shooting up all around it and licking at that little exposed bit of linen.

Another few seconds and it would be gone. Tessa lunged for it, hand extended.

Something hit her in the chest, slamming her backward.

The force knocked the breath from her. "Martin, no," she choked.

"It wasn't my fault! No!" Pryce kept shouting as Ellen guided him back to his chair. "I didn't want that!"

Tessa tried again to get to the stove but instead found herself looking right into the face of Martin. Martin, who had pushed her back from the fire before she could reach into it.

He wouldn't let her move forward. Her limbs wouldn't budge.

Instead she took a step back and found the fire tongs, then started shifting logs to get a clear shot at the reliquary.

Ellen looked horrified. "Dad, what's going on?" Then she turned to Tessa. "Is it—did it burn?"

Tessa didn't have gloves to handle the reliquary, so she spent an awkward minute maneuvering it out. The skin on her hands and forearms protested from the heat, but finally she set the reliquary on the stone hearth so it could cool. Even so, she didn't need to handle it to see the damage.

She was too late. The bit of linen cloth, the part with St. Peter of Verona's blood, had burnt. The relic of his heart was destroyed.

This was it, then. The end of the search.

Pryce stared at her with tears streaming down his face.

"Alicia," he whispered. "Alicia. I've never forgotten your name. Alicia."

Then it was him.

He'd shot her great-aunt. Tessa had rushed in here, in a black coat and a bun, chasing a small child. She'd come around the corner and surprised him. Seventy years ago, under the same circumstances, he'd shot another woman.

Tessa dropped to her knees in front of his chair. "Mr. Pryce," she choked out, "Mr. Pryce, you don't have to carry this anymore. You made a mistake."

"Every day." His voice broke with the tears. "I knew every day what I'd done. I don't deserve this. What I did. What I did."

She wrapped her hands around his bony fingers, and she looked him in the eye. "Mr. Pryce, I forgive you."

He shook his head.

"I forgive you," she repeated. It was too much, all the feelings erupting around her and inside her. Pryce was consumed by guilt. Martin was torn in two. Surrounded by them both, she couldn't begin to know what she was feeling, only the physical sensation of tears on her face. "You're forgiven. All this guilt you've carried, let it go in the fire. I hold nothing against you. You're free."

He touched her cheek. He whispered, "I know you."

"Alicia DiOrio," Tessa whispered. In all this time, through all this search, it had never once occurred to her that the men who stole the relic were also the men who stole her relatives' lives. She'd viewed them as thieves, not murderers. Soldiers, not killers. But this man who'd lived through it saw just the opposite. "You've carried that burden too long. Alicia forgives you too. In her name, I forgive you. For always and always and always."

He put his other hand on her other cheek, and he leaned forward to kiss her on the forehead. Then, with her head still in his hands, he sobbed again, but this time it was a cry of relief and a cry of release.

Ellen sat with Tessa at her father's side, each of them with a cold cup of tea.

The Downeaster would head back to Boston in an hour. Tessa didn't want to leave.

Pryce had talked himself out of the past and back into the present, then drifted into a different past. He knew Ellen, but he no longer knew Tessa. She hoped it would stay that way. Pryce wasn't really with them right now, and she stroked the thin skin of his hand.

"I'm so sorry about the relic," Ellen said again. "I had no idea he'd do that."

"We surprised him. I'm so sorry we brought that memory back."

"He talked about it, from time to time, but I didn't understand what he meant. He said she came around the corner. He reacted without thinking."

Today or back during the war, it didn't matter when. He'd reacted without thinking. He'd tried to run from his shame, and when it came to him, he couldn't handle it. He'd wanted to give back the relic to make things right, but in the moment, the shame had won.

Ellen traced a finger over the reliquary. The metal was cold now, soot-smudged but otherwise unharmed. The center sat empty. She'd let the fire die and poked through the embers, but to no avail. Tessa had dug out the three-quarter moon of glass from the front of the frame, but the linen had burnt.

Ellen produced the cardboard box that had been the reliquary's house for the past thirty years, declaring its contents to be a very modern two-slice toaster. She nestled the reliquary into the tissue paper, then closed it tight. Tessa tucked the box into her bag, then told Eric to get his things. Eric didn't want to leave the dog. Tessa didn't know what she wanted.

Half an hour later, they stood at the train station, ready to head back. Tessa checked her phone to find Gary had texted her. "Any updates? Wild success?"

How was she to reply to that? "Abject failure"?

Instead she texted, "Coming home now."

Before getting on the train, they bought food for the trip. Eric got set up with more toys, but it was already starting to get dark. Gary would have to pick her up at North Station when they arrived, or maybe she should take the T to Wellesley. She'd figure it out en route.

Gary's reply, when it came, said, "It didn't work out, did it? Talk to me. Are you okay?"

He knew. He always knew. He could read her mind even across two states, and she loved him for it. But at the same time, texting the words would make her failure all the more real.

Failure. Martin was devastated. He thought he'd failed before, and now it was permanent. She'd felt it at the same time he'd chosen her over the relic.

So she texted Gary with, "I'm fine, and Eric is fine. I'll talk to you tonight."

Gary let it go after that, although he figured out her schedule and said he'd meet her at the station. Then she just slumped for in her seat, looking out the window as they danced southward along the coast.

So many horrible things today. That horrible woman. That man's horrible guilt. And now wherever she looked, heartbreak. They were going to lose the vote on H.8937, and they'd lost the chance to save Barlassina.

Eric yawned. He climbed into the seat at her side and form-fitted against her, head to her heart. "I love you," he whispered.

Love. She'd failed, but he loved her. Tessa squeezed him tight and closed her eyes.

TWENTY-FOUR

Tessa folded laundry after Gary went to bed.

She needed sleep. She should have been prone in the dark in the softest clothing she owned and comforters piled over her, but more than sleep she needed solitude. Her brain kept firing off in every direction, and always back to that moment when she tried to reach into the mouth of the inferno to retrieve the one thing they'd struggled so long to save.

A continuous keening thrummed through her heart. It had for hours now. It had blended into the rhythm of the train and then merged into the rumble of Gary's engine. It didn't intensify when she'd disclosed everything to him in subdued tones while they coursed along I-90 back to the MetroWest area, and it didn't waver when she told Gary that she needed to stay up and do some thinking.

Thinking and laundry. They'd always gone together.

As she folded a white undershirt, she whispered, "Martin?"

The keening in her heart changed in tone. That was her answer.

"Can I see you?"

Her voice was low like a ticking clock, but he heard her. When she looked at the couch, he was there.

The look on his face had also been on Amanda's in the birth center, when Tessa let her see the ultrasound screen. It had been on her own face in the washroom at the state house. Martin should never have to wear that face. Not him, not an angel, not someone who by his own admission was powerful enough to guard the entire population of a country if God commanded him to do it. It wasn't helplessness or grief or any single emotion as much as the cocktail of disbelief and horror as he kept grappling with the same loss over and over.

He'd tucked up against the corner of the couch, looking beyond her as if she were the illusion rather than him. His wings had no color and neither did anything else. In fact, she could see through him. He'd made it sound easy that he projected what he wanted into her mind, but he couldn't do it now. He was struggling for her to see even this much.

Her voice was thin. "I'm so sorry."

Martin shook his head. This wasn't her fault. He didn't even want to say he didn't blame her because she'd twist that into thinking he *should* be blaming her. No, this simply wasn't hers to bear.

Unable to muster the energy for a rejoinder, Tessa folded another undershirt. Gary had done the white laundry today, so by the time she finished, she would have seven stacks smelling faintly of bleach.

Finally she said, "I'm sorry you're sad."

It was too encompassing, too shocking. He didn't know what to do. It couldn't be fair. He'd seen a clear path to making it all right and closing out his affairs with honor, and now this, now this, now this...

Tessa blinked hard.

She felt him apologize, and she turned. He was fading, looking nauseated. He apologized again and then a third time, so she crouched in front of him.

Without thinking, she extended her hand toward his on the arm of the sofa, but her fingertips passed right through. Of course. She tried to force a smile, but his heart gushed regret and failure, and then, with a jolt like an electric shock, fury at himself. The emotions whirled too fast to follow, like trying to track one ice cube in a blender. But there it came again, the sense of failure and the sense that he was just not enough, had never been enough, couldn't be enough.

He closed his hand through hers, and it tingled. "Hey," she whispered. "Since you've been around all this time, it's okay if you call me Terry."

He didn't react.

"I didn't mean to be rude when I told you not to. Only two people were allowed to call me Terry, but you can be the third."

Although she offered him a smile, he just stared through her.

"I feel like this is my fault," she said. "I didn't treat you with respect at the start. I got information from you that you didn't want to give me. I used it against you. Maybe if we'd been working together the whole time, rather than against each other, it would have succeeded." She blinked hard. "I don't know. I don't know what to say."

She expected either a negation from him or some kind of acceptance. *I forgive you,* he'd said that one time, but maybe forgiveness had to come from a place of strength. He couldn't give her what he didn't have even for himself. Instead he remained in shock, like a patient who'd lost a third of her blood volume.

A prickle in her mind warned her that he was gathering himself. Finally he said, "I'm compromised. I can't guard you right now. I called in a friend. He'll do it."

She leaned in. "I want you."

"I'm sorry. It's just until…" He projected again that he'd let her down. "I can't right now." The helplessness took him again, and he stopped speaking.

Tessa unfolded the blanket from the back of the couch and draped it over him. She had to make it kind of a tent, because of course he wasn't there to really tuck in. The ridiculous gesture was the best she could do, but even that left her with a residual feeling from him, that she was being maternal to him when that upended the whole job of guardianship.

"Don't think that," she said. "It's okay to get a breather. It's okay to rely on your friends. It's okay to hurt when you're hurting."

He faded further.

She sat a long time by his side, then rested her head on the couch. It wasn't until later that she jerked awake, no longer able to see him but feeling pushed that she should go upstairs. Go to sleep. She shouldn't hurt herself trying to help him, not when help was impossible.

The only good thing about Suzanne's venom-filled tirade was that Tessa knew where and when they'd be holding Benedict's funeral.

It turned out she could also tell the where and the when because as she drove near the church, she found five news vans, plus photographers and camera crews. And at that moment she had a decision to make.

She drove another two blocks, then pulled in at a McDonalds. Well then. Suzanne had gone for broke, had she? First Tessa would text Karen. It would be something along the lines of, "There's a media circus at baby Benedict's funeral. I'm not going in."

But when she pulled out her phone, what she found was a series of texts from Amanda.

"Tessa, I am losing my mind here. This is insane, and I'm telling the pastor to make them leave."

"I'm so so so so sorry about this. I hate that woman."

She'd blown up Tessa's phone during the drive, but the gist was: Amanda was beside herself with rage and distress at a time when she most needed the support of everyone around her.

"She says she didn't make them come. I don't believe her."

And then, woven through this, "If you come inside, I will hug you and seat you right at the front. This is insane."

With shaking hands, Tessa struggled to text, then gave up and resorted to dictation. "Today is not about me." Even her voice wobbled, but the phone deciphered her words. "I'm two blocks away, but I'm going home. I'll see you another time, and I'll hug you then."

The text got sent, got marked, "Delivered," then got marked, "Read," and then her phone rang.

Amanda was sobbing. "I'm going to call the cops and make them haul her out of here."

"No. Amanda, listen to me. You are not going to do that."

"I don't even want her here! She's smug and self-satisfied and my husband gave in and he let her do *everything* she wanted to do—and I've had it!"

"Amanda!" Tessa's voice picked up that no-nonsense quality that always cut through panic. "Listen to me. No drama. Not now. Now is all about your baby."

"Now is all about *her!*"

Tessa urged, "Let it roll off you. I'm not giving her a photo op by showing up. Don't talk to the cameras. Don't say anything. Don't do anything. Have the pastor tell them they need to leave their cameras outside or he won't start the funeral, but other than that, don't do anything. Drama is what she wants."

"I got out of the car and they had microphones in my face. 'How do you feel now that you killed your baby?' I didn't kill my baby! She went in front of everyone and told the whole world I'm an unfit mother!"

No. No, no, no, no. That witch. Of course that's how Amanda heard the accusation. She didn't hear, "The midwife ensorcelled my daughter-in-law with her herby ways." No, Amanda heard the other undercurrent, the one Tessa had completely missed because she'd been so focused on herself. Amanda had heard, first and foremost, and most importantly, "My ignorant and stubborn daughter-in-law murdered my grandson."

Tessa closed her eyes.

Amanda exclaimed, "So how can she show up and pretend to be supportive now? When she's turned the whole thing into a freak show?"

Tessa lowered the pitch of her voice. "Have the pastor put everyone out, then. Have a private funeral. Just you and Jeffrey. No one in the building. Kick out everybody."

"I can't do that." Amanda was sobbing. "I can't."

Tessa bit her lip. "I'm so sorry. I wish I were there to hug you. I'm so, so sorry."

"I'm sorry about what she did to you. I hope she dies."

The mother in Tessa wanted to say no, you never hope for that. You don't wish evil on people. But the other mother in Tessa wanted to swoop in and protect Amanda from the agony. She couldn't give back Benedict. She couldn't give Amanda the quiet and dignified funeral she craved, along with all the consolation of the rituals she needed.

So instead Tessa said, softly, "Are you going to be all right?"

"No." Amanda's voice was a hush. "I'm never going to be all right again. No one's here for me. My baby died, and no one is here for me."

Tessa said, "I'll come and be there for you. Is there a back door? Can you sneak me in?"

Amanda choked out a laugh. "Maybe you can hide in the broom closet?"

"The janitor can smuggle me in with a delivery of cleaning supplies."

"Maybe I can hide you in one of the big flower arrangements." Amanda's voice was still wobbly, but she'd picked up some tone again. "If she comes close, you can leap out and scream at her. Then she can have a heart attack and they'll cart her away."

"Will it help you to know Karen's talking to the birth center's attorney about suing her for slander?"

Amanda gasped. "Really? That would make my day."

"The attorney also wants me to talk to the police about battery charges, since there were several witnesses."

"Go for it. I'll testify. I'll even perjure myself and say she had a horse whip."

Tessa glanced at the clock. "Where are you? Are people looking for you?"

"I locked myself in the ladies' room in the basement. I don't want to go back up there and deal with everyone."

Tessa steeled herself. She didn't know this church, didn't know if they had a back door, didn't know anything about how she could make this work. "I'll face the cameras if you need an ally."

Amanda went silent, and then, "No. I know what I'm going to do. You stay where you are. I appreciate that you came out here for us." She sounded stronger now. "I'll do what you said. She isn't dignified, but I'll be. I'll have the pastor kick them out. He'll speak up for me. He's good that way. But don't you come because I don't want them to involve you."

Tessa said, "You have an appointment for Monday, and I want to see you then."

"I'll be there. Thank you for talking me down."

She said goodbye, and Tessa found herself holding a silent phone.

Well, then. That was one thing she didn't have to do.

Her next stop was less exciting. She drove to the Hopkinton Post Office and went inside with a box. "I need a customs form," she said at the desk. Monotoned it. She could have been mailing anything at all. The clerk handed her a long form and then watched as a sheet-white woman all in black filled out all the boxes (press hard for three copies) to send a box to Italy.

Tessa had no idea what to check, what value to estimate, or how to describe it. Was it a gift? A product? How much do you insure a thing like that for, to get it there? And then at the desk she paid extra to send it overseas all the faster.

Who to send it to, though? At first it had seemed obvious she should deliver it to her cousins, but Gary thought maybe Maria Contessa had a claim to it. They could send one the reliquary and the other the third-class handkerchief, but that didn't seem fair. Eventually they'd agreed she should send both to the abbot of the monastery in Barlassina. "At least this way," Tessa said, "the DiOrios will be angry at me rather than having the Monterosas angry at you."

She'd asked Martin for input, but none had come. He hadn't spoken to her since last night. Another angel was covering for him right now, but she hadn't thought that meant Martin was going away. Regardless, she hadn't had any communication from the substitute angel. Her world felt about the same, except that whenever she thought about Martin or the relic or that last meeting with Pryce, everything contorted inside her heart. It shouldn't have ended this way.

How was this fair?

Asking herself that question would never net any answers. She'd been living with specific unfairnesses all her life. The unfairness of a woman like Amanda losing her baby, or a woman who'd make just as good a mother never being able to conceive, while at the same time evil women like Suzanne reproduced and never valued their children as more than things to control.

Martin had a boss. She went over Martin's head.

Well? she prayed. *How is this fair? Martin did good work for You. Martin did everything he could, and he's been paying the price for one lousy mistake for the last seventy years. How could You let it work out this way?*

She'd never prayed before. It had never made sense that God would exist, but she'd trust Martin. Martin had never been anything but up-front about what he wanted: he wanted to do a good job at his assignment as an act of service to God.

You let that happen. It would have been easy to let it work out any other way, so I have to believe You wanted it this way, and now I'm angry. That wasn't right. When someone's working for you and working hard, a good boss doesn't snatch away the only thing they ever wanted. He'd have done it. You know he'd have been able to do it. Look how far he got before You sabotaged him.

Tessa glared at the paperwork in front of her with enough intensity to set it on fire. *If You really know everything, then You know he's going to blame himself for this forever, and I'm not happy about that. They say You love us, but really? Martin deserved better. If anyone deserved to succeed at an impossible quest, it was him.*

She finished filling out the form, pressing hard enough that she could have made ten thousand copies. Contents? An angel's broken heart. Value? Probably more than any of us will ever see in our lifetimes. Fragile, liquid, or perishable? Yes to all three. Unexpectedly so.

The clerk handed her a receipt with the tracking number circled in highlighter yellow, and Tessa went back to the parking lot. As she got back into her car, a silver-black minivan with a funeral home logo passed her, headed toward the church. She sat in the parking space for several minutes, eyes closed, wondering if she could feel an angel cry.

Twenty-Five

Voting day for H.8937. Karen and Tessa went back to the state house.

"You really don't want me here," Tessa said as Karen took them up the Mass Pike toward Boston.

"You keep saying that; I keep saying I really do. If they recognize you at all, and that's a big if, you'll get a chance to speak to the cameras. That's what matters."

Gary had, bless him, prepared statements for her on index cards. "Do not go off script," he said. "I know how these guys work. You need to do their job for them by giving them sound bites. The video editor won't include their questions but will cut your nice little sound bites into chunks they can run on the news. You'll be fine."

She'd memorized all three statements and practiced them in front of the mirrors, practiced in the shower, practiced while folding laundry. Gary would stick a spatula in front of her and bark out a question like a reporter, and she would click into one of the three statements.

"You don't even have to answer the question," Gary said dismissively. "Politicians never answer the question.

Neither do lobbyists. They give a vague response praising people for asking the question in the first place, give their sound bite, and then make a vague assertion that smart people will ask the question they just answered, as though that were the question in the first place."

It didn't feel like she was well armed to handle the press. It felt more like she was walking into the middle of a firefight with armor constructed of exactly three index cards, and she couldn't even hold them in front of her.

Karen played music as she drove. Martin didn't sing. Neither did Tessa.

They parked and carried their signs. The Milliston contingent was meeting at a specific place, and Tessa found herself hugged by any number of women, many of whom were livid. "I know you'd never do any of what that woman accused you of," said a mom with her three-month-old in a sling. "I called every representative every day for the past three days and told them that."

Their group joined up with patrons of another midwifery practice from north of Boston, and they started chanting and waving their signs. Every time a news camera pointed in their direction, Tessa tensed up, but no one spoke to her.

She scanned the crowd. *Martin? Can you tell if Suzanne is here?*

She wasn't sure what she'd do if the answer were yes. Avoid her? Seek her out and kick her in the shins? Would it be more advantageous for their side if Suzanne attacked her? Now there was an idea. Martin hadn't liked it when Tessa put herself in danger to provoke Suzanne into assaulting her, but it probably wouldn't be too terrible an outcome with this many police officers and witnesses to step in. Violence was always hard to predict though.

It also didn't matter. If Martin answered her, he wasn't loud enough to detect.

The rally continued until it was time to go inside to the spectator balcony. Tessa stuck close to Karen.

There were preliminaries, and Tessa grew more tense the longer they went on. But finally, the speaker seemed ready to call them to action. "But before we begin," he said, as though they hadn't already begun for half an hour, "we have one more speaker who wanted to address everyone on Thursday but was unable to be here. I would like to introduce Amanda Erickson."

Karen gasped, and Tessa's heart skittered.

A staffer escorted Amanda to the podium. She looked pale, and she seemed terrified. The speaker stepped back so she could have the microphone, and she swallowed hard.

"My name is Amanda Erickson," she said in a wavering voice, "and on Thursday, my mother-in-law lied to everyone in this hall."

Tessa's eyes watered. Sound went distant and her vision filmy. Was that the kind of thing you felt right before you fainted?

"When Suzanne asked for a photo of my baby, Benedict, I thought she wanted a memento, something to treasure from her grandson's brief life. I didn't know she planned to degrade his existence by using him as a cudgel against the very people who helped get me through his loss."

Amanda was just reading her speech right now. The poor thing looked exhausted. She should have been in bed, not standing here with her breasts engorged with milk and her body still bleeding. Her hormones had to be going crazy, and at every moment she'd be aching to hold the baby she should still have been pregnant with.

Amanda said, "My mother-in-law blamed Teresa Testerman and the profession of midwifery for Benedict's death. She didn't tell you that she'd harassed me until, in the third month, I started seeing an obstetrician in between my visits to Milliston Common Birth Center. She didn't tell you that I'd had an ultrasound at the obstetrician's office only two days before Benedict died. She failed to tell you that before I called Tessa that night, I'd called the obstetrician's office and been told everything was probably just fine."

She reached for her bottle of water. "I'm sorry," she choked out. "I'm not really up to this. In my day job, I'm a bank teller. We speak to one person at a time."

Light laughter and some applause came from the legislators.

She went back to her printed speech. "My mother-in-law stood up here and blamed my baby's death on substandard care, knowing full well that I'd received exactly the care I would have gotten from an obstetrician because I was also seeing one." She looked out at the audience. "But I'll go one step further, because the care I received from Tessa was superior to the obstetrician's office. She counseled me about nutrition. She gave me advice about my sciatic nerve when Benedict was pressing on it. She even gave me an extra appointment so I could bring Suzanne, my mother-in-law, to visit the birth center and see that they have all the safety equipment you'd find in a hospital room."

Amanda wavered. Tessa wanted to run down and take her off the stage. She was weak. She was grieving. Tessa's job all along had been to help Amanda, not to invert the whole thing.

Amanda said, "I have something else to say. I know Suzanne blamed me for Benedict's death. She thinks I wasted a year of my life being pregnant with a baby I didn't get to bring home. She says I failed and that Tessa failed. But…" She swiped away a tear. She was totally off her notes right now. "I had a baby because I wanted to love him. I lost Benedict, but that doesn't mean I failed. I am still Benedict's mother, even though he's not with me." She shouldn't have bothered with that first tear; dozens more were streaming down her cheeks, visible on the screen that showed her face to either side of the podium. "I loved him for every day of his life. That's a success, and I will not regard my pregnancy as a waste of time. The act of loving is a victory of its own. I love Benedict, and you have to believe me about this: so did Teresa Testerman. She took care of my medical needs, but she loved me too. She cared for me. We weren't just clients shoehorned into seven-minute office visits. She knew my name and asked about my job at the bank and was interested in my life. And when Benedict died, she hugged me and cried with me, and she stayed with me at the hospital for twenty-four hours straight until he was born."

She pulled out her notes and looked at them. "I'm sorry. I went off script, and I'm not very good at this." She scanned over the page. "Okay. In conclusion, I want you to vote for women to have the right to visit certified professional midwives. Please disregard my mother-in-law's nasty and well-rehearsed lies. Please cast your vote for the thing that makes Massachusetts strongest: our commitment to allowing people the freedom to make their own decisions." She braced herself, then said, "Next year, I hope to have another baby. And when I do, I want to have Teresa Testerman there to deliver him, and I want it to be here, in our great state of Massachusetts. Thank you."

Everyone applauded. Everyone except Tessa, who sat stunned.

Flustered, Amanda looked for the staffer who'd brought her to the podium, then followed him back down.

Tessa collapsed, face in her hands. Amanda shouldn't have done that. She shouldn't have done that. She'd just ended her marriage right there, on television. Her mother-in-law would force Jeffrey to take sides, and Jeffrey had proven he'd always choose his mother. The war would never end. Amanda would lose.

But then Tessa realized, Amanda knew that. Amanda had made her decision with open eyes, and she'd chosen to stand up for herself anyhow.

The applause died down, and the speaker said, "I thought it necessary to correct the record. Thank you for hearing her speech, and now we'll begin the voting."

The votes began coming, but Tessa's mind stayed on Amanda. Amanda, crying at the podium. Amanda. Amanda who hadn't failed.

Martin? Martin, I need you to talk to me.

Karen was rubbing her shoulders, but Tessa didn't raise her head. *Martin, I'm going to ask you to do something. I need you to do it for me. As your human charge, I'm asking my guardian angel for a favor.*

She felt him pop into her thoughts.

Just listen to me, she thought. *What Amanda said is true. She didn't fail. Her victory was in her constancy and her love. And you didn't fail either. Don't protest,* she thought harshly because he'd already protested. *You didn't fail. I am going to ask you to do the thing you said you couldn't do until you returned the relic. I'm asking you to go present yourself before God and close out that last assignment.*

Inside her whirled up any number of protests, and then anger, and that bitter taste of shame, and then something else: dread.

That was a thing Tessa had never considered, that maybe presenting yourself before God was kind of scary. Wasn't the whole thing about God that God was everywhere and God knew everything? Why was this different?

Martin's negation came again: No. Absolutely no. He couldn't go back and report this, own up to this multiplied failure. He could figure this out. There had to be a way.

Tessa sat up. "I need to find Amanda," she whispered to Karen. She slipped out of the row, then up to the back and into the hallway.

She texted Amanda. "Where are you? I'm in the building."

The text that came back was riddled with typos, but it said in effect that there was a suite and she was sitting in a waiting room.

Tessa retraced her steps from her last visit to the state house. A guard tried to stop her, and she started explaining why she needed to get in. It didn't work until she texted Amanda, who had a staffer escort her in.

The voting had been going on for ten minutes at this point. Amanda was white as a ghost. "You need to be resting!" Tessa exclaimed, rushing past the staffer. "What do you think you're doing?"

"I'm fixing what my mother-in-law did." She let Tessa guide her to a seat. "You're right. You've been right about everything all along."

"Sweetie, you need to rest. How did you get here? You didn't drive yourself, did you?"

"I did. I made Jeffrey go to work today, and then I took the car." She gave a wry chuckle. "I'll probably be okay to drive back, right?"

Tessa sighed. "How about I drive you?"

"If I wait long enough, Suzanne will come in here and start yelling at me."

"I hope she does." Tessa sighed. "She'll leap across the table to strangle me, and I bet there are cameras all around, not to mention the security guards."

"Well, Christmas should be fun, at least." Amanda put her head in her hands and massaged her temples. "I already decided to cancel Christmas. How am I supposed to celebrate when..."

She put her head on her folded arms and cried onto the super-shiny tabletop. Tessa rested her arm over her, and they stayed that way for a little while, Amanda slack and Tessa just holding her.

Inside, she felt Martin send her a disgusted message: she needed to stay out of his decision-making processes.

Tessa thought, *Do we really need to do this now?*

His response was a decided no. No, they didn't need to do this ever again as long as she didn't try to meddle in the way he conducted his affairs with God, a subject in which she had no expertise whatsoever.

Tessa didn't respond, only stayed present to Amanda. But at least Martin was angry. Martin angry was Martin recovering. She could deal with that.

"Don't worry about Christmas right now." Tessa squeezed her. "Could you guys go out of town and maybe go somewhere that you won't have to deal with trees and lights and Madonna-and-child cards? Maybe a cruise?"

"I hadn't even thought about Christmas cards." She shuddered. "I should just throw them all away unopened. Everyone knew. There was something I loved more than anything in the world, and they all knew about it. And now they know I lost him, so they know I'm hurting."

"There's nothing wrong with being vulnerable." Tessa squeezed her. "But there's also nothing wrong with finding a rental cabin up in the mountains and not talking to anyone until New Year's Day."

"I meant what I said about you delivering my next baby. I don't know if I'll ever have another baby, but if we do." Amanda rubbed her temples. "They did a genetic test. We'll find that out sometime. But even then. I don't know. I don't know if I could. I mean..."

"There's no need to decide now. Take your time."

Amanda leaned forward again on the table, temples in her fingertips.

And then for a few minutes it was quiet. Martin was quiet. Amanda was quiet. Tessa sat in quiet too, wondering about the voting and about Martin and about whether Suzanne was sharpening her fangs somewhere in the building. She wondered how Amanda's husband would handle the war that was soon to result, and then she wondered if Karen really would sue for slander. Maybe they could let it all go. Maybe prolonging the anger offered nothing to be gained.

And yeah, she wouldn't push the issue again with Martin. He'd heard her out. He was right that the decision was his, even if she thought it absolutely the wrong decision. She'd just let him figure out her concession for himself when she never mentioned it again.

Her phone chimed with an incoming text from Karen. "WE DID IT!"

Tessa laughed, and she said, "Apparently you turned the vote around."

Amanda sat up. "Really? Really, that worked?" She hugged Tessa, then buried her face in Tessa's shoulder. "I'm so glad for you. I'm just so glad I didn't ruin everything for you too."

Tessa squeezed her. "It wasn't you. It wouldn't have been your fault." She glanced at her phone as more messages flooded, but she didn't read them. "But I'm so glad you didn't give up."

TWENTY-SIX

And then everyone went back to work.

Tessa attended three consecutive births around the new moon, two of them in the birth center and one at a client's home. Around those she fit any number of office visits.

Gary wrote his monthly columns and produced an article for the New York City diocesan newspaper about the underground trade in relics, plus had contacts from two national magazines intrigued by his skill in long-unsolved war crimes.

Martin returned to full-time guardianship over Tessa, although he hadn't yet left the tunnel of linear time.

"Why is it taking so long?" Tessa said in her office between clients. "You said a week is the longest you've ever been. Is there something we need to do so you can enter the next time pocket?"

Martin sat crosswise on her rocking chair, wings up and legs thrown over the armrest. "It's not something we influence. For some reason, God wants me linear right now."

"So it's not like a quest? Or like sending Alex to his room until he's ready to go mow the lawn like his dad told him to?"

"It's not a punishment." Martin shrugged. "If God asks me to mow your lawn, I'll get right on that."

The lawn was currently under two inches of snow, so Tessa said, "How about shoveling the driveway instead?" and Martin only smirked at her as he shot back, "I'll keep you advised."

From time to time she still picked up his sadness, although not the gutted sensation she'd felt the first night. The confusion and lostness had ebbed, and now when it came, it felt more like defeat. While driving, she'd feel the gears of his mind turning, one into the next, as he tried to devise a plan to sort it out. Nothing ever caught. Although she anticipated an *aha!* moment, one never came. And then once more she'd pick up the defeat. But never surrender.

Amanda's car pulled into the lot, and Tessa went out into the waiting room to meet her at the door. "Hey!" she said as Amanda entered, and then had a surprise when Jeffrey followed her.

Tessa brought them right in to her exam room. *You didn't tell me Jeffrey was coming too.*

How could I? I found out the same time you did.

I just figured you knew these things. Tessa had them sit and then closed the door. "How are you guys holding up?"

Amanda shook her head. "It's awful. Everything's a reminder, and I hate everything sometimes."

That was actually the best thing Amanda could have said. The moms who led off with, "Doing really well actually," were the ones who needed a lot more encouragement to grieve so they didn't crash in six months.

Tessa modulated her voice down. "Everyone's back in their regular routines now?"

"Someone actually told me I should be over it. I mean it's been what, ten days?" Amanda reached for the tissue box and grabbed five. "Sorry, I'm going to need a bunch of these. But yeah, apparently I'm young and can have more, so I should just get over it, and I should be glad because there was probably something wrong with Benedict. Oh, and God needed another angel."

Tessa frowned. "I think that's really bad theology."

Martin put into her head, *I know that's really bad theology.*

Amanda pointed to Jeffrey. "He's got it even worse because apparently fathers aren't supposed to feel even a little bit sad when these things happen. He's supposed to be strong for me and never let me see him feeling so much as slightly wistful that his son died."

Tessa glanced at Jeffrey, saying, "The same people who think God forgot to carry the two when He made the heavenly host?"

Jeffrey had his hands clasped between his knees. "I had no idea it would be like this."

Tessa had booked their appointment for a full hour in the last slot of the day, with the idea that not only would they need a lot of time, but they might need more than a lot. This way she could stay as late as they needed.

So they talked for a while about what to expect from grieving. She gave them a book she'd found very helpful for bereaved parents, and then she did a physical exam.

"Everything's going back into place the way it should, but if you see anything that worries you, I want you to call me right away."

Tessa handed Jeffrey a postpartum checklist for grieving moms, a list that made no mention of problems to watch for in the baby, plus pamphlets for infant loss groups at two local hospitals. By now he'd amassed a stack of reading material.

She sat back down with them, and Amanda said, "His mother is furious at me."

Tessa said, "I thought she might be."

"She's been awful. She came right out and told me I killed Benedict, so I hung up on her."

Jeffrey said, "I called her back, and she told me she never said that."

Tessa waited. That could go either way.

Jeffrey glanced at Amanda. "So I told her that until she apologized for being so rude to my wife, I wasn't going to talk to her."

Tessa's eyes widened. "You did?"

Jeffrey couldn't meet her eyes. "She told me she had no need to apologize, so...yeah."

"We changed her ringtone to silent so he can get her voicemails later on and see what's happening," said Amanda. "It's not fair that we have all this nonsense to do now. She told everyone in the family that I lost my mind because of grief, so she has other relatives calling us now to harass us. I'm keeping my phone turned off all the time, and it's not fair. When my friends call, I don't know until later. But that's how it is. And we took your advice to book an adults-only cruise for Christmas."

Tessa chuckled. "That's good. You guys need a break."

"I'm worried, but yeah. I'm supposed to go back to work next week, so that will distract me."

"Do you feel up to it?" Tessa asked. "I can write to HR if you need more time off."

She shook her head. "I'd rather work through it. It'll give me something to do rather than just sitting at home and feeling like garbage. I'd have been home with Benedict." She stared at her lap. "I don't want to be at home now without him. If I had to lose everything I ever wanted, at least I should be keeping busy with some kind of job."

On the drive home, Tessa said, "I'm sorry you had to hear that."

Invisible, Martin replied with a sense of puzzlement.

"About the replacement job. I'm that for you, aren't I? A job to keep you busy?"

Again she felt him in her head: he'd already been doing the job of guarding her for four and a half decades. She wasn't his consolation prize.

Tessa said, "You said I was a downgrade. That you felt disgraced by being assigned—"

"That's not what I said!" Looking urgent, Martin became visible in the passenger seat. "I said because you were a DiOrio, it felt as if God was reminding me how I'd failed to look out for the whole clan, so now I got to look out for one individual."

"You never forgot Holy Cross for even a minute, so I don't buy that. You said you felt insulted by the assignment because archangels don't guard people. They guard institutions and classes."

"I'm sorry you got that impression, but that wasn't the case. It did feel like the most public no-confidence vote from God in the history of angelkind." His eyes darkened, and some of the fire eased off. "Now, though? I don't think that was it. Guardians are assigned to individuals for a reason, and several years ago I figured out why you needed a more powerful guardian than average."

Tessa chuckled. "Because I cause more trouble than average?"

"Because you have other human beings' lives in your literal hands." Martin straightened as he spoke faster. "You're standing in the pinch-point of a lot of vulnerable people. They're pushed out of one life through a narrow passage, and then out into a bigger life they never imagined, but you're standing at the gateway between them."

"They're not very happy about that," Tessa pointed out.

"But it's a very important moment, and you're positioned right there to help." Martin sounded pleased. "A church is like that too. At the pivotal moments, or the pinch-points, where do people go? They go to their church after birth, when they marry, when they die. When they're grieving, where do they go? When they're celebrating? When they were looking for reassurance or direction, they came into the church, and the church became their gateway. I was there. I saw it. And then I saw you delivering babies and realized it was the same flavor of work."

Tessa smiled. "So I'm kind of like you?"

"Maybe a bit." He grinned at her. "A little. Don't let that go to your head."

She laughed. He seemed more relaxed today than he'd been in a while. There hadn't been any joking at all after Pryce destroyed the relic, so the bright eyes, raised wings, and shared laughter felt like the resolution of a troublesome symptom. Midwifery always meant treating the whole person, and finally he sounded more whole. The wound was there—she could hear it—but it wasn't dominating his world.

"At any rate, this is my job." He stopped abruptly, and then when he resumed, his voice was very soft. "I'm sorry. I owe you an apology, but last night I give up on everything else."

Tessa glanced at him. "You don't need to apo—"

"Stop. You're quick to tell me to shut up and listen, so do the same for me. I'm sorry I put you through all that for a cause that was ultimately futile. There's a huge sunk cost. But I can't continue our side quest." He looked filmier. "There's no way to fix Holy Cross or repair what I did to Barlassina. I tried everything possible, and you helped me in every way you could, never holding back at all. I disrupted your family life, but you didn't complain."

"Didn't complain *much*," said Tessa. "This sounds like revisionist history. I recall being pretty stubborn."

"You were fine." Martin stared at his lap. "But after all that, last night after an honest assessment, I had to concede. It's over. Eventually they'll tear down the remnants of the church, and the town will disintegrate. Like you said, everything ends."

"I'm sorry." Tessa swallowed hard. "I didn't mean you should give up."

He didn't reply. No, he'd have thought this through a long time before admitting defeat.

The snow crunched under her tires as she pulled into her driveway. Before she even had the engine off, Gary was on the front steps. "Terry! You've got to see this!"

She flew out of the car. "What's going on?" She hadn't seen Gary this excited in ages, but right now he looked like a kid who'd found a puppy under the Christmas tree.

Inside the house, as she struggled out of her coat, he dragged her in front of his laptop. "Have Martin read this. I've been limping along with Google Translate, but I think it's the news you wanted."

Silent, Martin stared at the screen. The awaited translation never came.

Gary said, "He's with you, right? Can he still translate?"

A sense of wonder bloomed inside Tessa, and as she pulled off her hat, a warmth like a hearth bubbled up in her. On the screen she found an email full of words she shouldn't be able to understand. Only all of a sudden, with joy, she could.

"Dear Mr. Testerman," she read aloud. This was different from the way Martin had translated before, so maybe he'd changed things up the same way he'd finessed his body language projections. This translation felt more as if she were understanding directly, thinking in Italian and English at the same time. "All of Barlassina is celebrating because of you, and we want to make sure you know how thankful we are for your help."

She glanced at the name at the top. Maria Contessa Monterosa.

Gary said, "Whatever happened, three emails from Italy all came in at the same time, two Monterosas and one DiOrio, and at least one seemed to indicate they were emailing you too."

"I didn't even check." Tessa pulled out her phone. It had filled up with texts since she'd turned it off for the drive from the office.

She returned to the email, and once again she simply understood it. "The abbot of Holy Cross called in the heads of all the Barlassina families this afternoon. We didn't know why, but when we got there, he showed us the reliquary."

Martin trembled.

"We are so grateful for all your work, for everything you've done to return this treasure to us. The abbot told us how it had gotten broken, how it had passed from hand to hand, and how the relic itself was burnt by one of the soldiers. But now here it is, back in our home: the finest artwork ever produced by either the DiOrio family or the Monterosa family."

Gary said, "Oh. Oh wow. So even without the relic in it..."

"The abbot asked us all to sit with him and talk," Tessa continued, "and we stayed at the abbey through lunch and almost until dinner, but we finally hammered it out. The permits for the church will be issued to rebuild. The different families have settled out how much money each will contribute, and all the money will be held in common by the abbey until repairs are completed. We will set a square of the third-class relic into the reliquary, and after that, the reliquary will be on display at the church for half the year. For the remaining time, we will loan it out to museums. The abbot already has one museum interested in paying for the right to display it for six months. Those fees also will go toward rcpairing Holy Cross."

Tessa's voice broke as she finished the last paragraph. Martin had crumbled.

"The abbot reminded us that the reliquary always stood as a symbol of hope. It was a sign of the beauty that our families could create when they worked together rather than at odds. Although the relic itself was destroyed, the spirit of Peter the Martyr has not been. It has helped bring us to peace at last."

She signed it with love, much love, Maria Contessa Monterosa.

Gary sat, wide-eyed. "That's...not what I expected at all."

Tessa's cousins had texted her. "They did it! We've got the permits!" and, "They've got the funding!" and lots of excitement sent line by line from overseas.

The other two emails were the same: there was peace, there was gratitude, there was a resolution to rebuild.

Today was, in effect, armistice day for Barlassina. Their war prisoner had come home. World War II could finally end.

Martin? Are you okay?

Martin was dampening his emotions so as not to overwhelm her. Which might mean he felt too overwhelmed even to answer. He'd wanted this for decades.

You did it, she thought to him. *You did it!*

Silence.

Tessa texted back everyone, then wrote replies to all Gary's emails in fluent Italian, wondering if maybe Martin had called in another friend, and the friend was doing the translating.

And then, because the world hadn't stopped, she had to prepare dinner (frittatas) and make sure all the boys had done their homework. Her mother was thrilled. Her cousins were ecstatic. Both the Monterosas and the DiOrios thought they'd won. The abbot had sent a letter in painstaking English to thank them for their help, so Gary replied to that one in English. And while Brian was ciphering out his multiplication, Tessa sent a letter to Ellen Ashland, letting her know that because her father had returned the reliquary, all these good things had happened across the ocean. She thanked Ellen, and she said all the people in Barlassina were praying for him and thanking God that he'd sent their treasure home.

Ellen replied, subdued but very glad. Her father had been remembering Barlassina all day. "I'll tell him. I hope he'll be at peace with it now."

After the boys were in bed, Tessa couldn't toast the evening with champagne because she was on call, so instead she folded laundry while Gary worked on an article about veterans and healthcare policy.

Martin? Talk to me. I'm worried about you.

He didn't appear. It felt like he was all around her, though, as if he were giving her a hug.

You did it, she thought to him.

He rejected her assertion. He hadn't done this. He'd had a specific outcome in mind, and he'd failed. This wasn't his doing.

Tessa thought, *But it's done.*

He kept silence, but she knew now to keep a silence of her own, the same way she'd sit with a laboring woman and let dilation progress on its own. He was birthing a conclusion, and like any good midwife, she'd watch the delivery roll through at its own pace, at the speed it had to. You don't need to rush a process that's moving along. Forcing it to happen on her schedule, because it was something she thought should occur, would shut down the whole process in a way she desperately didn't want.

Hadn't she told Martin that this might happen? Not this way, because she hadn't anticipated this way, but hadn't she said reality might not follow the script? Treating wasn't healing. And shame didn't get fixed just because the shameful situation was resolved. Wasn't Pryce's continuing guilt a testimony to that?

When Martin had been quiet too long, she thought, *That wasn't you translating for me, was it?*

No, that was the Holy Spirit.

She froze. *Really?*

Inside, she felt him shocked: he wouldn't joke about an act of God.

Sorry.

He apologized too for being short with her.

Are you still in linear time?

He agreed: he hadn't had any clue this was coming down the pike.

She finished the laundry, each in its proper pile, and went upstairs for bed. Pajamas. Teeth. Thermostat adjusted. She bundled under the covers and turned off the light.

Martin felt really close to her right now.

Is something wrong?

No, I just... He sounded hesitant. *I'm going to go now. To present myself.*

She tensed. *It'll be okay.*

He disagreed.

Wake me up when you get back, okay?

He didn't agree to that either.

You'll come back, she thought. *God won't take this assignment away from you.*

You can't be sure. His heart was full of what-ifs, and Tessa instinctively reached forward as if to touch him. *My work was important. My work with you is important too. I didn't do the first one the way I should, but I've been given so much. How can you make a return on all God's gifts except by doing a good job to show Him how much you appreciate it all? But I didn't. I couldn't fix it.*

Tessa thought, *You did fix it. There's peace, and the church is being rebuilt.*

No, Martin said for the second time that night. *That was the Holy Spirit.*

Impressions tumbled through Tessa's mind: That was God's action, making good out of evil. But in possession of infinite time, God had waited it out. He'd let Martin have the chance he craved to set everything right. Only it was too big. The mess was too vast, and Martin couldn't. So now it wasn't just one failure. It was two.

Tessa thought, *You're smart and funny and hard-working and amazing. You're determined, and you have high standards. Won't God see all that in you too?*

She got the sense that all Martin could see was failure.

You tell me God is bigger than this and understands things we don't. But then you assume God sees this situation exactly as you do. Maybe there's something you're missing. Maybe when you visit Him, He'll tell you that.

No, she felt. This wasn't a visit. God wasn't going to greet him at the front door and take his coat and put on the tea kettle.

She wasn't going to convince Martin otherwise. He'd just have to go through with it. *Go,* she thought. *Do what you have to do. I'll be waiting when you get back.*

Don't stay awake. Martin shivered inside her. *I'll talk to you in the morning.* He hesitated, and then, *I love you, Terry.*

I love you too. She tightened her eyes. *Go. And be at peace.*

Suddenly the world felt empty.

She couldn't relax enough to sleep. Gary joined her eventually, and after she snuggled up to him, she did manage to drift off. Every so often she'd wake up and listen to the silence, both in sound and inside herself. At about two o'clock she thought, *Martin?* but got no response. How long did it take to present oneself to God?

How long were God's office visits? Her primary care physician scheduled appointments ten minutes apart. Tessa slotted clients for forty five minutes, but longer when they needed longer. How long did Martin need? What was God's equivalent of measuring fundal height and palpating position and getting a good heartbeat? And when God had the spiritual equivalent of a blood pressure cuff on Martin's arm, instead of asking about nutrition, would God say something like, "Let's talk about how you see yourself, and how you define success"?

Artists always envisioned a Throne of Glory atop a long staircase, surrounded by choirs and beams of light. Maybe instead God would meet Martin in a small room looking out at a parking lot, equipped with a desk and a bed and a rocking chair. He'd relax in the rocking chair while Martin clenched up at the edge of the bed, hands between his knees. Maybe God would look at the chart, then toss the chart onto the desk and say, "You know what? Just talk to me. I want to hear in your own words what you think is going on."

How many times had Tessa gotten the real story that way? How many times had a frightened mother learned that her anxieties weren't as vivid a concern as she'd blown them up to be in her mind?

At five o'clock in the morning, Tessa checked the clock and felt Martin tentative in her mind.

"You're back?" she whispered.

Relief flooded through her. Like trying to make sense of the shapes in a kaleidoscope, Tessa struggled to decode the multilayered feelings and images streaming from Martin. Thoughts flashed through her head: geysers of light, prayers rising like incense, fellow souls clustered in close, and then the terrifying reality of being face-to-Face with God. Martin was more energetic than she'd ever felt, and at the same time, relieved.

"I'm glad." Her words were just a breath in the dark. Martin felt as close as her own skin. "Did God...?"

She stopped herself. Martin had said not to get into their relationship.

Martin's feelings coursed into her, and although she resisted momentarily, he wanted her to hear this. God hadn't reprimanded him for failing Holy Cross. Instead there'd been a different reprimand, or more like God had redirected him. She flinched, wondering if he'd been punished, but it seemed more like he'd been set straight.

She saw again the midwifery office where she'd imagined God meeting Martin. The thoughts flowed into her one after the next: God was a midwife too, and God didn't demand perfection from His angels or His people. God wanted their love and their service and their genuine concern for one another. That when God's creations took care of one another, that was a way of loving Him. It wasn't about checklists and achieving a perfect score. The perfection God wanted was in the love, not in the results.

Martin put into her mind that God had chided him for staying away.

You were chosen for a reason, Martin said to her. *I chose you to find the relic because you were my charge and you were already speaking to me. But He chose you for me because He wanted me to learn midwifery. I was being too obstetric.*

She grinned in the dark. *It's all about the charts and the numbers and statistics?*

I'd made it that way. But I should have been more about the watching and the waiting and the standing by. I'd done that for nine centuries with Holy Cross, but I'd abandoned that methodology in favor of outcomes. Instead it's about the guiding and the listening and expectant management.

She chuckled, then whispered, "Are you out of linear time?"

Not yet. Martin sounded pleased. *By the end of today, though. Time is getting wider.*

She nodded. *And you're staying?*

I'm definitely staying.

A stolen work of art had gone home. An old man had been relieved of guilt he'd carried for two generations. A destroyed church was being rebuilt, and a rift between families had at least a temporary bridge.

Amongst all of that, however, something else had been mended, something simultaneously stronger and more delicate than a gold reliquary or a stone church in the mountains. Eyes closed, Tessa basked in the harmonic sensations streaming from the angel. Relief. Acceptance. Completion. But underlying all that, thrumming with a persistence like the whoosh-whoosh of a heartbeat, was the certitude of being loved.

TWENTY-SEVEN

Aching all over, Tessa unfolded herself from the back seat of a van she'd been jammed into for the past two hours. She didn't have the chance to so much as stretch before five different people clamored over her and her mother, then over Gary. After a full day of travel, they'd arrived at Barlassina.

Tessa's heart went off like fireworks as Martin spread out and coursed through the familiar streets. He dragged her vision toward the church spire towering over the town's center. The tarps had come off the roof, and the outside was still covered in scaffolding, but the structure appeared whole.

Stained glass windows had been replaced. The roof shone with new tiles. The boards had come down off the doorways.

All around, DiOrios chattered at them, asking questions in English and waving off their attempts to speak Italian. "I want to practice," one of her cousins said. "Later on, you can practice."

After six months of reconstruction, the church was in much better shape than it had been for decades. They'd aimed their first attention toward structural issues: the roof and the windows, clearing the wildlife and feral plants off the structure, and securing all the safety issues. Then came the cleanup, and now they were tackling the beautification and the interior.

"We'll have a big dinner tonight at the abbey," one of her cousins said, "but that's with the Monterosas, so they'll insist on doing the food the wrong way. You'd better eat first with us."

Half a year after the reliquary's return, the town had another cause to celebrate: the local bishop had decided to recommission the Church of the Holy Cross. The DiOrios wanted Gary and Tessa there for the ceremony, and Mom had jumped at the chance to see where her mother was born. The reliquary had come back from the Vatican museum for this event, after which it would return to complete its tour.

The town felt simultaneously familiar and strange after the spate of emails, texts, and photos her relatives had sent. Thanks to Facebook, Tessa had heard all the family news and seen step-by-step pictures of the machinery coming through and the scaffolding going up. Every time pictures came in, Tessa would call Martin to look over her shoulder, but more often than not he'd be the one urging her to go check. "Giorgio just sent more photos," he'd prompt, and she'd bring them up on her phone or her laptop.

"You could just jump ahead in time and see it finished," she'd teased one day.

"That wouldn't be fair," he'd said, unexpectedly serious. "I want to see it again for the first time with you."

Today, finally at Barlassina, she asked if they could go see the church right away, before the recommissioning ceremony. So off they trooped down the bumpy cobblestone streets. Martin thrummed with excitement as he pointed out different locations. This was where the DiOrios had lived for so long. This had been the home of Ercole Monterosa.

She stopped when they turned a corner, Martin's information filling her. She closed her eyes.

Startled, Gary turned back.

"Alicia died right here," Tessa whispered. "Martin saw it."

They kept going, and then, around the next corner, she found herself facing the church.

Here, Martin was telling her. Here was the place Martin had first popped into Barlassina a thousand years ago on God's prompting. Martin hadn't known before arrival what he'd be doing. He'd looked up, much as she was doing now, and beheld the church. *This is yours,* God had said. *It's Mine, but I'm entrusting it to you for your protection.*

She could feel the newness, the excitement. His? His alone? First he'd examined every part of the church, then the priests in charge of it, then back around to inspect every little nook and stone and ornamentation in the building. Next came the people of the town, their joys and tragedies and everyday annoyances, every one of which he'd come in contact with one at a time across the centuries.

Inside, Tessa beamed as she tried to take in the cavernous interior. It overwhelmed her with its height, its colors, its layout. "We're making it modern," said her cousin. "We'll have sound and lights and fans, but still the same church."

But the rest of it looked old. The stone floor with cracks running through it, the dark wooden pews, the stained glass art towering thirty feet overhead and the gigantic rose window, the mosaics, the stations of the cross, and then two side chapels flanking the main altar and four little side altars lining the church's right side.

You had to look everywhere, and everywhere you looked was some new detail you'd never seen before. A baptismal font with a gold-leaf lid. A rack of books and free Bibles. A statue of some saint everyone but you probably recognized. A wooden box nailed to the wall collecting donations for the poor.

Flush with excitement, Martin kept yanking her attention from one thing to the next. The altar was the same. The crucifix was new. The tabernacle was the same. That statue was old but had been refurbished. Most of the stations of the cross were original, but the fifth and sixth had been remade, close to the style of the ones that had been destroyed. The seating was all new.

Martin drew her attention to a pair of angel statues in the sanctuary. Angels in robes, wearing sashes, and with angular features. *See?* he said. *You surprised me the first time you asked me to appear, and I needed a model. I'd never thought about what I'd look like, so that's what I used.*

She giggled. It really did look like Martin.

But there, that over there—and Tessa couldn't have torn her eyes from it if she'd tried—that side chapel to the left of the main altar had been the repository of the relic of Peter of Verona.

Gary went to the front, taking photos of the refurbished altar and sanctuary space. She walked to the left side chapel instead. *Can I touch it?*

It's just a marble altar. Martin sounded amused. *Touch it all you like.*

She stroked the smooth and cold stone with her fingertips, noting as she did the nautilus fossils gleaming in the polished marble. Above her hung a painting of Peter of Verona (*That's new*) with candles on both sides. In the center was a space where the reliquary would stand, and in front of that was a plaque written in Italian. Her ability to understand Italian had been, apparently, a single-use gift, so Martin read it to her. It told the story of the relic's theft, its slumber, its destruction, and the reliquary's return. The reliquary was vital as a symbol of unity and a remembrance of the desire to honor God with acts of beauty and selflessness.

And devotion, said Tessa. *You never gave up.*

Martin hugged her.

Then he burst with excitement. He started speaking to another angel in another language, far too rapid a conversation for her to understand. She pivoted instinctively to see who it was, but of course there was no one visible.

Martin appeared, followed by a second figure who seemed more than a little flustered. "Tessa, I'd like to introduce you to the guardian angel over Barlassina. We worked together all that time."

Tessa bowed her head. "A pleasure to meet you."

The guardian clearly hadn't been prepared to become visible. He said, "I'm glad to meet you too. Maritenael must be an excellent guardian to you."

"The best," she said, and Martin snickered.

Then both angels turned, and Tessa filled with a sense of wonder as a third angel showed. He looked around, glowing, wings spread and eyes wide. He projected a sense of disbelief and then a thrill. The thrill of being entrusted with a job: the job of guarding a church.

Martin's joy rushed through Tessa, and he turned to her. *It's the church's new guardian!* Then he turned back to the new angel, and whatever he said next evoked a stream of delight and laughter from the new arrival.

Gary called Tessa to the front, so she went with him to see the restoration work. The mosaic behind the altar, showing the scene of the crucifixion, was in process of being repaired as a great portion of it had collapsed. Then Gary went to photograph a pair of angel statues on either side of the altar. Tessa took a moment to kneel at the communion rail.

Thank you, she prayed. *Thank you after all this time for bringing Martin home.*

No, Martin corrected her. *This* was *my home. Now, you're my home.*

And thank you for giving me a pedantic guardian angel to correct my slightest mistakes, she added, smirking.

It's called accuracy, he shot back.

If you don't mind, I'm praying here.

He knelt beside her. Martin's prayer engulfed her with a sensation of the world stretching to Heaven, and Heaven reaching back with an enthusiasm and a brilliance that dwarfed anything Tessa could feel on her own. This was the world, and it was good. This was an angel, and he was good. And this was Tessa, presented toward God by the angel, so God could delight in her as well.

Thank you, Martin was praying. *Thank you for this all, for restoration and for healing. Thank you for this church that was my past. But here,* and he touched Tessa. *Thank you for this, my future.*

"You say you've failed! We never fail. You placed your confidence wholly in God. Nor did you neglect any human means. Convince yourself of this truth: your success—this time, in this—was to fail. Give thanks to our Lord…and try again!"
—The Way no. 404 by St. Josemaría Escrivá

THANK YOU!

Thank you first of all to my readers. Stories need to be shared, and it's a pleasure to share them with you.

For research, I leaned hard on James Holland's *Italy's Sorrow*, Stephen Ambrose's *Citizen Soldiers*, and Tom Brokaw's *The Greatest Generation*, which I won accidentally in a Yankee swap. (You're going to notice a thread running through this.) I read interviews with World War II veterans whenever I could, and I thank every one of them for their service.

Saint Peter of Verona actually is the awesome guy talked about in this story. How I found him? A Catholic website had a "saint of the year" generator where they match-make you with a saint for the coming year. I'd been toying with the idea for this story when I hit the randomizer and requested a saint. As soon as I researched him, I realized he was the one. Patron saint of midwives *and* inquisitors? And murdered right in the place I'd already planned to set the story? It's actually easier to believe in divine intervention than to credit coincidence.

Charlotte Volnek was working on the cover while I was still writing the first draft, and she nailed it. The angel statue in the background comes from a war memorial I found one day while driving to Ikea to buy a shelf. No, really. I had to pull over and photograph the statue, posted it on my blog, and asked for help identifying the war. Yes, that's a World War II soldier in the angel's lap. Again, this is not something I planned.

Thank you to my early readers: Bokerah Brumley, Lisa Karen Johnson, Amy Bartelloni, LS King, and Louise Thygesen. Thank you to my editor, Heather Turner. A special thank you to Madeline and Evan.

Please consider leaving a review wherever you obtained this book, as well as at Goodreads.

If you enjoyed reading about Tessa, I've got another midwife in my novel *Half Missing*. Amber Brickman is a fire marshal who's great at reverse-engineering crimes via the smallest details. One night she turns on the TV and sees a woman who looks and sounds just like herself, she's stunned — and her mother always swore there were twins, and the hospital handed over only one baby. Now she's got to decipher her own past and figure out what happened twenty-four years ago in that delivery room.

If you preferred reading about Martin, I've got a whole series about angels just like him. Come meet the Archangel Gabriel in *An Arrow in Flight*. We're deep in the Old Testament, the Northern Kingdom of Israel in exile and the Southern Kingdom of Judah is headed that way in a hurry. When Gabriel fails to carry out an order exactly as given, Jerusalem's destruction hangs in the balance— and Gabriel gets shut out from Heaven for a year. Gabriel wants to use the time to help humanity, but it may be that the one most in need of help is himself.

JANE LEBAK

WITH

TWO

EYES

INTO

GEHENNA

A rosary in one hand.
A dagger in the other.

Sister Magdalena never heard of the Catherinite nuns until the day she faced her own death sentence.

Rome, 1562. It's the era of the Index of Banned Books and the Roman Inquisition. Kings still burn heretics. The worst threats come from within the Church itself

Only seventeen, Magdalena killed a priest who tried to rape her within the walls of her convent. His powerful family will see her executed, and then they'll destroy her mother and young sister.

Instead, the pope makes an offer. To save her life and protect her family, Magdalena can disappear into a secret religious order, one with a demanding physical regimen to go along with the prayers. She'll pray the psalms and learn to climb walls. She'll sharpen her mind and fine-tune her body. Perfected, she'll infiltrate the Council of Trent.

Magdalena's order slips through cathedrals and palaces at the council, the Pope's silent operatives. They act as bodyguards for the cardinals They gather intelligence. If they find heresy, the penalty is death.

But when one of the pope's own men is named a heretic, Magdalena must decide how far she'll go to protect her church.